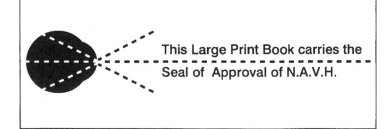

This Large Print Book carries the
Seal of Approval of N.A.V.H.

ANNETTE MEYERS

MURDER ME NOW

Thorndike Press • Thorndike, Maine

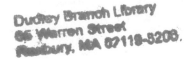

Copyright © 2001 by Annette Brafman Meyers

This book is a work of fiction. Names, characters, places, and incidents are the product of the author's imagination or are used fictitiously. Any resemblance to actual events, locales, or persons, living or dead, is coincidental.

Published in 2001 by arrangement with Warner Books, Inc.

Thorndike Press Large Print Mystery Series.

The tree indicium is a trademark of Thorndike Press.

The text of this Large Print edition is unabridged.
Other aspects of the book may vary from the original edition.

Set in 16 pt. Plantin.

Printed in the United States on permanent paper.

Library of Congress Cataloging-in-Publication Data

Meyers, Annette.
 Murder me now / Annette Meyers.
  p. cm.
 ISBN 0-7862-3079-7 (lg. print : hc : alk. paper)
 1. Women detectives — New York (State) — New York
— Fiction. 2. Greenwich Village (New York, N.Y.) —
Fiction. 3. Women poets — Fiction. 4. Large type books.
 I. Title.
 PS3563.E889 M93 2001b
 813'.54—dc21   00-051161

For Marty, first and last

Acknowledgments

My thanks to the caring professionals at Mysterious Press/Warner, who truly know how to nurture their authors, especially Sara Ann Freed, Bill Malloy, Susan Richman, Vicki Bott. To Honi Werner for another ravishing cover. To my stalwart agent, Stuart Krichevsky. And to my friend Sandra Scoppettone.

I am particularly indebted to Barbara Collins and Bob Randisi for including my short story "The Bedford Street Legacy" (Olivia's debut) in their first *Lethal Ladies* anthology.

My thanks as well to Mary Lou Vehn of the venerable Yale Club on Vanderbilt Avenue in New York City, and to Jim Parish for the silent film star Richard Barthelmess.

And special thanks to H. Terrence Samway, assistant director, Office of Government Liaison and Public Affairs, and Mike Sampson, archivist, both of the United States Secret Service, for their generous sharing of archival information.

O I have kissed your lady lips
And pledged to love with all my heart,
As you have kissed my lady lips
And sworn that we would never part.

But time is short for making hay:
Sun is frugal with her shine.
Thus pledges do I castaway;
Fealty in love's Divine.

"To Artemis"
Olivia Brown, 1920

Chapter One

Truth we call it, and it's a game. But there's truth and there's truth. And too much truth can be perilous.

The canvas of our lives was Greenwich Village. In the years after the Great War we created with broad strokes, with style, and, I must acknowledge, with brilliance. We had come here to be our true selves.

In this small enclave of narrow, crooked streets lined with old brownstones and small shops, tearooms, cabarets, and speakeasies, we created our art, and we played.

Oh, how we played.

Certain tragic events, barely in the past, had turned my life upside down, inside out, when friends were not friends, and lovers, past loving. I'd despaired going on, yet here I was, frivolous soul that I am, in love again. The object of my current affections was Paul Ewing, that tall young man of the broad shoulders and fair hair, whom I, to rid him of his saintly moniker, had dubbed Paulo.

We'd come, a grand group of us, to Croton, where Fordy and Kate Vaude lived the domestic life, and where some of our Greenwich Village friends had let houses all along Mt. Airy Road. Now and again, Fordy and Kate would throw a house party, and we'd all arrive by train or motorcar, if we were lucky, for a weekend of conversation, wit, booze, games, and the lure of making love in a rustic setting. Food was the least of attractions. It was the company we kept.

The last time we'd come to Fordy and Kate's, we'd played with a round-robin ghost story, making it up as we went along. Larry Langner, who's gone up-town on us and formed the Theatre Guild company, made a play of it, *The Haunting of M. Vaude*, and our own Jig Cook, the heart and soul of the Provincetown Players, took the play and mounted it for the Players. I played the ghost of a woman who takes revenge on the man who'd murdered her. One critic said, "The ravishing Olivia Brown, poet one moment, actress another, continues to dazzle us."

On this particular night, to the accompaniment of the voluble fire in the grand stone hearth, we'd settled round the big trestle table in the kitchen of the farmhouse in Croton, gin lavishly replenished.

"Drink up," Fordy said. "There's plenty more where that came from." Fordy had the moolah all right, thanks to some sort of Wall Street job by day, which also allowed him to keep a studio in the Village, where he pursued what he claimed was his true calling as an artist.

Amid hoots and whistles, Paulo said, "I'll have the name of your bootlegger." He gave my "ravishing Olivia Brown" thigh a loving fondle.

We'd been playing charades, but our play had gone dyspeptic, and in unspoken desperation, we'd turned to Truth.

It's deceptively simple. One of us is chosen. We then decide on the character, mannerism, even feature — it could be a nose — of the chosen one, and we each write a paragraph "biography" on a piece of paper concerning, let us say, the chosen's nose. Any approach may be taken, be it sensual, humorous, or serious.

We try to be literary, and clever, but we don't always succeed, and sometimes, as you can imagine, things get personal, even savage.

Folding our anonymous paragraphs, we deposited them in Dave Wolfe's soft felt trilby. As I did mine, our fingers grazed, and Dave winked a sultry eye at me as if we had a lover's secret. Dave, a Jew, dark and mysterious as a sheik, was writing a novel. He'd been encamped for the last few months at our friend Max's cottage across the way while Max was in Paris.

After a good shuffling, each paragraph was read aloud by a "reader," chosen by all of us, the "reader" never, of course, the subject for the round.

We'd even inveigled the Vaude nanny, a slim, severe girl named Adelle, to join us, as Harry had gone out for a walk, holding, he quipped, no brief for Truth. Harry is H. Melville, a private investigator with whom I work from time to time. I inherited him, along with my house on Bedford Street in Greenwich Village, from my great-aunt Evangeline Brown. Her will left the downstairs flat to Harry in perpetuity.

The Vaude farmhouse was a comfortable old place with low ceilings and wide floorboards. The hearth gave off enough heat to keep us from the chill outdoors. Gin did the rest. The faces of the Truth players at the table appeared to me through an undulating mist. Our hosts, Fordy and Kate. Dave Wolfe. My Paulo. Bunny Wilson, one of my editors at *Vanity Fair*, and his girl,

Daisy. And Adelle, the nanny.

We'd played several rounds as we worked our way through the hooch, and then the game slipped and took a bad turn.

In the days, the weeks, that followed, I would relive the strange intensity of each successive game we played that night and see it as foreshadowing the horror that was to come.

On the last round, Kate Vaude was "reader," and in her fanged presentation, each "biography" became spiteful and petty. And this last time, it was directed at poor Adelle, in particular, her heavy-lidded eyes, moistly myopic behind thick glasses. One of us, not I — as I do not write mediocre or mean verse — had written:

With Judas eyes does she betray
Thus will not live another day.

There was more, though perhaps not nearly so sinister. Adelle's reaction was bewilderment, and something else I couldn't quite fathom. She sat in stunned silence, listening to the cruel barrage.

"I love all my friends," I said, attempting to lighten the mood, "but not right now. See what a bad impression we're making on Adelle."

"Adelle knows it's a game," Fordy Vaude said in his condescending manner. "Don't you, my dear?" He took Adelle's "biographies" from Kate and tossed them into the fire.

Adelle responded with a small, stiff smile. The "something else" was fear. "You're quite right. I've played the game before." She excused herself and went upstairs.

What a nasty and competitive lot we can be when we drink too much. But still, we don't hold grudges. And we do not begrudge one another's achievements.

The unsettling atmosphere eased with Adelle's departure and our move from the kitchen to the parlor. Harry rejoined us, and we sat around the fire, drinking, smoking, and talking well into the night.

Later, Jack Reed — writer, editor, poet, journalist . . . lover — came and sat with us, in spirit only, for he was newly dead in Moscow. Already revered among the writers and artists who lived in the Village, he'd gone to Russia and reported on the Revolution, achieving international renown by writing its story: *Ten Days That Shook the World*.

Alas, my arrival in Greenwich Village coincided with Reed's return to Russia, so we had never had a chance to meet, but I'd read his stories and poetry, his plays. I'd seen in his photograph a man of some size, whose wild hair, burning dark eyes, broad intelligent forehead, all spoke to me of adventure and romance. I felt his magnetic force. Who could not?

As tales of Reed rose Bunyonesque, laughter filled the room, and I felt his presence linger like that of some departed lover. *Just one last cigarette and I'll be gone.*

Eventually we wore the night away, and all our talk and wine turned to making love.

What woke me was my brain, aswirl with quatrains and couplets. Or so I thought at first. But, no. What had interrupted my sleep was the curious swerve in the course of our game. I needed to know the author of the most sinister of Adelle's "biographies."

Detaching myself from the arms of my sleeping lover, I left our bed and glided down the stairs. The farmhouse was more than cold, the fires having gone out, our attentions elsewhere. Passion, with a jug of wine, could keep us warm.

As I passed through the parlor, stepping round cleaving bodies on makeshift pallets, a girl I didn't know peered bleary-eyed at me over the bolster of the sofa and then sank back into Dave's arms. I knew it was Dave from the brown corduroy shirt, which only he wore. I wondered briefly why he hadn't gone back to his own house just across the road.

The kitchen was dark save for the flicker of a candle near the hearth. I stood silent in the doorway. Someone had had the same thought as I. Someone, on her knees, was pawing through the ashes in the cold hearth. She turned her face into the light for a moment. Adelle.

I ducked into the hallway and listened to her soft tread upon the stairs, the even softer closing of a door.

Chapter Two

The candlelight made architectural shadows of the stacks of dirty dishes that covered the wide planked table and filled the sink. Worldly things could wait. Well, almost all. I opened the glass-faced cabinets one at a time until I found a tin of cigarettes, two left. Now one. Leaning against the icebox, I let the tobacco work its snaky wiles, until the tingle reached my bare feet.

I crouched at the hearth. Paper ashes, soft as cream, covered the burnt-out log. Nothing to read, nothing to trace. Perhaps it was better this way.

The farmhouse floated in dense, unearthly quiet, as on a becalmed sea. I hesitated only for a breath, then opened the back door and ran out into the yard.

Gusts caught me up, spun me round and round, a spontaneous cordon of snow. Yet not a prison at all. This was the first snow of the season, and I was in love. I stood in my nightdress, lifted my face, my arms, and howled at the bloated, blue-faced moon.

The moon yelled back at me, "Bloody hell!"

It was enough to make me stop swirling. Not the moon, but Harry Melville. "Killjoy," I responded.

"Ewing, she's your charge. Do your duty, man." A window slammed shut.

And Paulo of the broad shoulders and sad gray eyes came and gathered me up in his arms and carried me back to bed, where he kissed the blue cold from my poor feet.

When I awoke again, I was alone. Paulo was gone, but his scent remained in the pillow, the bedclothes. On me. Stretching across the small bed, I let the pleasure work its magic. But then I remembered; everything had changed. I lit a cigarette and had a lazy smoke as the house stirred round me.

Paulo had proposed marriage.

I'd protested, "But why should we change something lovely?"

"When I love a girl, I want her to be mine forever," said he.

Oh, drat, I thought. Drat. "I am my own person. I could never belong to anyone forever."

"You mustn't say no, Oliver."

So Oliver, as my friends call me, said she would think about it.

There was nothing to think about. My work, my poetry, was the most important thing in my life. Love was transient. Much as I loved Paulo, oftentimes he embraced a shifting melancholy, as did many of the boys who'd been in the War. It made me uneasy.

I stubbed out my cigarette, plucked my nightdress from the floor, and pulled it over my head. In the hall I met Adelle, coming out of the bathroom with Lucy and John, the darling two-year-old Vaude twins. Scrubbed and dressed, they tugged my hands. "Story," they demanded.

"Sorry about last night," I said. Had she found more in the hearth, I wondered, than I?

Adelle pursed her lips. Too young to purse lips. "It really doesn't matter." I might have said the same were I among strangers.

She was quite tall, though everyone is tall by my comparison. Her dark hair was pulled back in a tight bun, and she wore shapeless clothing and thick-lensed, metal-framed eyeglasses. Yet under all this tight control was a nervous current, almost panic. "No, children, we mustn't bother

Miss Brown." Her eyes behind their oval windows veered away from mine. "Breakfast comes first. Perhaps Miss Brown can read a story later?"

"Perhaps," I said. But Miss Brown had had too much gin the night before and was feeling the aftermath.

Adelle herded the children to the stairs, calling back to me, "There's —" She stopped in midspeech.

The girl I didn't know, the one I'd seen sleeping with Dave, stood at the foot of the staircase, looking up, shading her eyes. Adelle didn't move. I felt a certain tautness in the air between them that even the children must have felt, for they were uncharacteristically silent.

"Adelle?" I broke the spell. Adelle turned to me, her face a mask. The girl below slipped away.

"There's no hot water," Adelle said.

So I had a quick cold wash and dried my slender, shivering body with the damp towel Adelle had used for the children, puzzling over the scene I'd interrupted. By the time I finished I was wide awake and my headache had eased.

In the bedroom I dressed, rolling on a pair of lisle stockings Kate had loaned me. With the side of my fist, I cleared a porthole in the frozen mist on the window. The snow had stopped and sunlight sparkled off a thin, white blanket. I felt an urgent need to be outdoors, to mark my footprints in the pristine picture, and paused to jot those very words on a scrap of paper.

As I made my way downstairs, Adelle, in a black cloak and brimmed hat, was rushing the twins, fat bundles in woolly red caps and mittens, out. The door shut with a smart slam.

I peered through the ice-etched window, eager to trek out myself. On the veranda I saw Adelle challenged by a girl in a fox fur — Daisy, Bunny Wilson's girl — who took her arm and tried to engage her in earnest conversation. But the heretofore passive Adelle spat angry words, wrenched her arm away, and pushed Daisy aside with what seemed to be unwarranted force.

Chapter Three

I repaired to the kitchen, where someone had cleaned up the mess so that little remained of the previous evening's bacchanal.

A grim-faced Kate stood, back to the sink, gesturing with her cigarette as she spoke to Paulo, who sat smoking, ashes flecking a syrup-glazed plate.

". . . right under my nose —" she said, then she saw me and stopped in mid-sentence.

Paulo looked down at his plate. I was decidedly *de trop*.

"Don't mind me, my dears," I said. "I need but a cup of coffee and then I'll be on my way for a tramp in the snow."

"We've run out of coffee," Kate said flatly.

"Then I'll walk into town and bring some back."

Kate hesitated. "It's Sunday. Nothing will be open. It's not Greenwich Village, you know."

Paulo pushed his plate away. "I'll go with you." But he didn't stand.

I marked that, along with Kate's tart

comment, so my "no" was more curt than I'd intended. "I'm working on a poem, you see." I wasn't. I had nothing at all in my head now except my puckish curiosity.

"You'll find galoshes in the hall closet," Kate called.

As I passed the front parlor, I heard sounds of ill humor, a whispered quarrel, female versus male. Well, we'd all had too much to drink last night. Tempers might well be short today. I longed to be home in my cozy little house on Bedford Street, which was always full of grace, thanks to Mattie, my friend and housekeeper.

I slipped into my tatty old raccoon coat and cloche hat, then rummaged in the bottom of the hall closet, looking for a pair of galoshes, which I found. Lumpy rubber ones, miles too big, but what did it matter?

The bright cold dazzled diamonds in my eyes. I danced off the porch a bit clumsily in my rubbers and made giant footsteps across the front lawn. Laden tree branches leaned a welcome to me, glittering in the sunlight, coated a white radiance.

I thought I'd be the first, but there were other footprints, many, in fact, and on the road, even the distinctive tracks of an automobile.

With winter birdsong for accompaniment, I tramped out onto Mt. Airy Road. It was perhaps a mile to the town of Croton, where I was greeted by church bells, and as Kate had predicted, all the stores were closed. I passed a grocer, a chemist's shop, and a small dry goods emporium, then paused in front of the next shop. A green-and-white gingham curtain was drawn across the lower portion of the window, and above it was the sign: CROTON BOOKSHOP. And below it: ORDERS WELCOME. ALL LANGUAGES ACCOMMODATED.

Closing my eyes, I wished the charming shop open, to no avail. I continued the length of the little village street, past a red-brick school, a whitewashed, tall steepled church. We could have been in any small town, yet how many other small towns would have welcomed us bohemians? There seemed here in Croton a kind of live-and-let-live atmosphere.

I don't know when I realized I was being followed. Perhaps when I turned in front of the funeral home to survey the picture-postcard scene. My Nimrod was but five feet from me and looked every bit the scared rabbit, a very tall one at that.

I confronted him. "Well, what do we have here?"

The young man's face, under a tweed deerstalker hat, was covered with freckles, which became, as I watched him, even more pronounced. "Oh, miss — sorry, miss — didn't mean to startle — you are Olivia Brown, the poet?"

"I was when I awoke this morning."

He wore no overcoat and didn't seem to mind the cold. "And you're staying at the Vaude place?"

"You seem to know a lot about me, young man," I said, though I was hardly older than he.

"I heard you read your poems last week at the Murray Hill Readers Society. You were wonderful."

"Thank you. You wouldn't know where I can get a cup of coffee, would you, Mr. . . . ?"

"Oh, excuse me. My name is Carl Danenberg. We have a little shop not far from here."

"All the shops are closed."

"We live behind the shop. My mother will be delighted to meet you. She makes wonderful strudel."

He offered his arm and I took it. "I would be delighted, Mr. Danenberg."

Of course there were other reasons I accepted this nice young man's invitation to meet his mother. I had, finally, some need for sustenance. And given the contentious atmosphere at the Vaude house, I was in no hurry to return.

Chapter Four

Carl Danenberg's shop proved to be the very bookshop I had willed to open. I stood on the doorstep, delighted.

"We must go around the back," he said.

"Oh, but I would love to see the shop." I dusted the snow from my galoshes and, leaning on Carl's arm, pulled them off.

After a moment's hesitation, he opened the door. I stepped inside. He picked up my overshoes and followed. I noted in his demeanor a sudden edge of caution, then chastised myself for allowing the atmosphere of the Vaude house to color my common sense.

Heavy cartons of books were stacked in a corner, as if they'd just arrived. Shelves lined every wall, the shelves well stocked with books, many leather bound, all looking quite undisturbed, like trompe l'oeil.

I would have dallied, but Carl Danenberg, still carrying my rubbers, drew me quickly away from the shelves to the small flat behind the shop.

Mama Danenberg, thin, dark hair in a fat knot on top of her head, broad hipped and full bosomed, wore men's tweed trousers. "For comfort," she said. "I am up and down the stepladder all day while Carl goes to college and Papa is away buying books." She sat me down at the kitchen table, placed a fragile cup and saucer in front of me, and filled it with the blackest brew.

"College?" I asked.

"Columbia," he said. He settled my galoshes near the back door and took off his deerstalker cap, revealing hair the color of red gold. Hence the winter freckles.

We were *comme deux gouttes d'eau* — like two drops of water — for I have summer freckles, though the color of my hair is closer to brick.

"May I offer you some strudel, Miss Brown?" Mama Danenberg's knife poised over the sugar-dusted mound.

"The very reason for my visit, Mrs. Danenberg."

"You have known the Vaudes for long?" She gave me a searching look, a judgmental crease between her brows.

"Only a short time. We became acquainted through mutual friends." The strudel was sweet and tender, and the coffee was bittersweet in my mouth. "They must be good customers, as we are all book people."

Her assent was most peculiar: barely a tilt of the head.

Carl Danenberg asked, "When will we have a book of your poems, Miss Brown?"

"I am working toward that goal, Mr. Danenberg. Harper and Brothers has asked me for one."

"My Carl is a writer, too."

"Mama! Not like you, Miss Brown. I'm a journalist. I have a small job at the *New York Times* while I'm going to school."

When I was ready to take my leave, Mama went into the shop and, returning, pressed a leather-bound volume of John Donne's poems in my hand, saying, "It's been an honor, Miss Brown." Whereupon she hustled me to the back door and stood over me as I slipped on the galoshes. "Carl, we have the accounts —"

"I won't be long, *Mutti*."

Carl walked with me until we caught sight of the Vaude farmhouse, when he stopped. "I must leave you here, Miss Brown." He shook my hand, bowed, and made a hasty retreat as if . . . he, too, had the feeling that the Vaude house might be contaminated.

Slowing my pace, I trudged toward the house. Children's voices shrieked, and Lucy and John came slipping and sliding down the road toward me. Each fought for my free hand — the other held John Donne. They settled both for one, and I pretended to be pulled forward.

"Where's Adelle, urchins?" I asked, breaking into their wild laughter. Little John took a tumble. As I brushed off the little snow boy, a whooping whistle surrounded us and I saw Harry come out of Dave's cottage across the road and approach us. The children screamed and raced into the wood surrounding the property.

Harry's cigar was pungent. He contemplated me for a moment, then wet his index finger and raised it to the air. "Weather change, Oliver?"

"I'm sure I don't know what you're implying, Harry Melville," I said. But I did know. He'd come to know me, I think, better than I know myself. He'd sensed that my passion for Paulo had cooled.

He grinned. "Sure. How about we catch the four o'clock?"

"Fine." I turned my back on him and, with as much dignity as I could muster in my clumsy galoshes, shuffled up to the front porch. Another pair of snowy over-shoes sat on the entrance mat. I leaned against the door and pulled mine off, drop-ping them next to the others. When I looked back for Harry, he'd become a pen-umbra on the porch of Dave's cottage.

It was an odd relationship Harry and I had. Although there was at least twenty years' difference in age between us, he was my friend, the kind of friend who might not approve of everything you did, but whose friendship was unwavering. We had never been lovers, as some people assumed. Each of us would find the thought ludicrous. Besides, I knew Harry had a lover, for I'd once caught a glimpse of her, an uptown, mature woman, prob-ably the bored wife of a banker, which was why we never saw her at these house par-ties.

"Have you seen Adelle and the chil-dren?" Kate held the door for me. "Just leave the wet overshoes out here. Oh, I see you've borrowed Reed's."

Unaccountably my heart took a strange leap. "Reed? Jack Reed?"

"Yes. Well, he won't be needing them anymore, will he? He wouldn't have minded anyway. He would have liked you, Oliver."

Liked, I thought. Liked?

Quite cheery now, Kate came out and stood on the veranda, hugging herself, and called, "AdelleLucyJohn," running the names all together.

"The children were playing here a few minutes ago, but I didn't see Adelle. They ran into the wood."

"LucyJohn! They know not to go there. LucyJohn! I've told Fordy a thousand times that Adelle is irresponsible —"

We heard them before we saw them. They crept out, giggling, from the side of the house and yelled, "Mama!"

"In the house, right now," Kate ordered. "Where is Adelle?"

They looked at each other and giggled. "Monkey," Lucy said.

"Come on, off with those galoshes," Kate said. She took John and I took Lucy. We bustled them into the house. "If I didn't know better," she told me, "I'd think they've locked Adelle away somewhere."

I hung up my coat and hat and left Kate to her brood. In the parlor, Bunny Wilson and his girl, Daisy, pretty enough but terribly earnest, were snapping at each other over cold ham sandwiches.

"Oliver!" Bunny exclaimed, distinctly relieved to see me. "Come join us." He offered me half of his sandwich, while Daisy sat perfectly still, oozing gloom.

I was unwilling to set myself into the middle of a spat and declined. What I wanted was wine. There was none left. I settled for gin and went upstairs. "To write," I said. For we all understood our eccentricities and respected the Muse. I propped up the pillows and lay down with my notepad and pencil, a glass of gin on the floor next to the bed.

Peaceful is the pastorale to the obtuse eye,
But underneath the perfect scene the narrative's a lie.

The lines came quickly. A good beginning, but try as I might, I couldn't go on from there. I lit a cigarette and thought about it. Had a sip of gin, opened my new book to Mr. Donne's love sonnets.

Yet I couldn't shake off the sensation that somehow I'd been assigned a role that must be played out. This place, this house, the squabbling, backbiting, the undercurrents of emotion: elements of a subplot I didn't understand, didn't want to understand.

Chapter Five

The argument had been going on for a while, for I had joined it in my dreams, thrashing among the bedclothes. I sat up, wide awake. No Paulo. The anxious murmurs of the Vaude children reached me through the wall that separated our rooms. I pulled the blanket from the bed and wrapped myself in it. My book fell to the floor next to my empty glass. It was deadly cold.

I found Lucy and John huddled in their parents' bed. When they saw it was I, they reached their little hands out to me. I sat on the bed and they crawled into my lap, as well as they could since I am not much bigger than they.

"Where is Adelle? Don't tell me she hasn't come back?"

Lucy shook her head. "Play monkey in tree." Giggling, she pointed to her brother, who began to swing from the bedpost sticking out his tongue.

The argument below, louder now, pierced through the closed door. Fordy's voice. "Fury" is a word I'd never have considered in the same context as Fordy Vaude. He appeared to be a civilized man, always in a suit and tie no matter the occasion. He was in insurance or finance, or something equally dull, a family business, though there was a regretful air about him and the implication that he'd rather be a painter and live the bohemian life of his friends.

Easing the children off my lap, I tucked them under the covers and kissed their moist foreheads. "It's all in fun, my dears. Nothing to worry about. Now let's see who can keep hands over ears longer."

I left the room, shutting the door behind me just as more angry words syncopated with breaking dishes. A woman's rage. Then more and more voices joined in. I heard Harry, and Dave. Bunny. I came halfway down the stairs, almost tripping over my blanket train.

A tableau: Harry with his arm around Kate. Kate's face distorted with anger. Dave holding on to the girl I'd seen him with last night. Awake and standing, she was incredibly beautiful, tall, with thick coils of black hair to her waist, slim but full breasted, even in a man's shirting. Porcelain skin, barring the high color edging each cheekbone. Who was she? And where was Paulo, and Daisy, for that matter?

"Not a very nice welcome home, Kate dear," the exotic girl said.

Dave gave her shoulder a squeeze. "Come on, Celia."

Celia. Celia Gillam. The photojournalist whose daring battlefield photographs for the *New York World* had earned her an international reputation. Honored by the French government. Friend of Reed's and Louise Bryant's. What was she to Kate? To Fordy?

When my gaze drifted to Fordy, who stood amid shattered dishes and a large valise, I understood.

"All right." Kate spoke in carbon steel. "Go. But don't think you can come back." She broke away from Harry and withdrew to the kitchen.

"If you're determined to do it, chum," Harry told Fordy, "this would be the right time."

I couldn't tear my gaze from Celia Gillam. Slowly, as if my concentration compelled, she glanced about the room, came to the stairs, traveled up. Our eyes met. The air between us vibrated.

With perfect timing, Paulo, full of good cheer, came tramping in, arms hugging wood for the fire. He had no idea what he'd interrupted. We watched him set down the logs and brush the snow, wood fibers, and leaves from his jacket.

Celia broke the silence. "Let's go." She didn't wait for Fordy but opened the front door and stepped out.

Fordy picked up his valise, shrugged an apology to us. The door sprang closed behind him.

"Where's Kate?" Paulo said.

Dave tilted his head. "Kitchen."

Paulo went after her.

I came down the rest of the stairs. I felt sorry for Kate, sorrier for the children. But permanence was not our world, either way. Celia Gillam and Fordy didn't seem a good fit to me. He was so passive. And Celia? She was magic. A month from now Fordy would be back in Kate's arms.

A shout came from outside. Harry raced past me and flung open the door. I followed. Kate, a carving knife in her hand, glided like a sleepwalker toward Celia and Fordy, who were crossing the road toward Dave's house. We all yelled for Kate to stop, but she didn't. Paulo tackled her, knocking her into the snow, but she held tight to the knife, slashing the air. Then everyone was there.

"Stay back," Paulo ordered as we gathered round them like a Greek chorus. "Kate, don't do anything foolish. Give me the knife." Bunny's Daisy started to cry.

Kate lay flat out in the snow, sobbing and flailing. I looked back at the house. Two frightened little faces were squashed against an upstairs window.

"Kate, think of the children," I said, which was when Paulo grabbed for the knife and Kate, lurching out of his way, sliced through his gray flannel shirt. The darkening seam of blood was immediate. Paulo, stunned, sat in the snow, staring down at his arm.

"Oh no," Kate cried. She dropped the knife and scrambled to her knees, staring at the blood. "I'm sorry, Paul, I'm so sorry."

"Nobody died," Harry said. He brought a handkerchief from his pocket.

I rolled up Paulo's sopping sleeve to reveal a thin slash about four inches long oozing bright red. My fingers, pink and sticky, got a quick wash in the snow.

Harry applied his handkerchief bandage with pressure, and the flow of blood began to ease, but Paulo had turned gray. I threw my blanket over his shoulders, and with Harry gripping Paulo's good arm, we all trooped back to the house, where Kate, contrite, rebandaged Paulo's wound with more tenderness than I cared to see.

She and I went upstairs and got the little ones dressed and brought them down for their lunch. Dave had put the kettle on and made us hot toddies.

All in all, we managed to get through the crisis. And when a short time later, Jig Cook and his wife, Susan Glaspell, arrived in a sputtering, ancient town car they'd wheedled from an enthusiastic subscriber to the Provincetown Playhouse, the party went on, albeit somewhat dispiritedly.

But I'd had my fill of house parties and the company. I wanted to go home to my own room in my little house, in my own Village with its narrow, crooked streets, where I could write and wouldn't have to see or talk with anyone except my sweet Mattie if I didn't want to.

I put on my coat and went out to the backyard. Brittle sunlight colored everything the palest of yellows. The duck pond was frozen over.

Circling the house, I came upon Harry standing in the middle of the front lawn, head bowed.

"Praying?" I asked.

"Did you bring the knife in with you?"

"No. Didn't you?"

"No." He toured the area, taking short steps. "It's not here."

A few lazy flakes of snow drifted down on us. Across the road I saw Celia and Fordy in front of Dave's house. They waved to us as if nothing had happened.

"Cowards," I said softly, waving back. I fell in behind Harry as he searched for the knife. "What do you think?"

Harry didn't answer. So I asked another question, the one that had been on my mind for the last few hours. "Were Kate and Paulo lovers?"

"Do you care, Oliver?" Snowflakes caught on his pale eyelashes.

"I wouldn't be asking otherwise," I said, yet I knew he was right. Did I care? I blew a puff of smoke in the air and watched it hold for a moment, then dissipate.

"I thought poets have intuition," Harry said grumpily, kicking at the freezing snow.

"Women have intuition," I said. "Poets are intuitive."

The snow became thicker, coating us white. We walked back and forth a little longer, but we both knew someone must have taken the knife. The only testament to what had occurred here was the red stain slowly fading into the soft powder of new snow.

Chapter Six

Jig, who never had an opinion he didn't articulate, drove us to the train, filling the empty spaces with words and words and words. No one listened. Harry was muttering under his breath. Paulo was edgy. I kept trying to isolate myself from the extraneous so that the new poem in my head would sort itself out. We had all drunk too much. The events of the day had given us license, had they not? Though I must admit we needed little excuse to get tight.

With no warning whatever, the car went into a skid. Jig applied the brake, and suddenly we were an out-of-control carousel, spinning, spinning . . . then tipping over, we slid sideways into a snow-laden ditch.

For a moment, we were shocked into total silence. Even Jig stopped talking. He struggled with the door but couldn't get it open, as we were upended, his side down, Harry on top of him.

We untangled ourselves, and our screaming laughter shattered the Sunday-quiet countryside. No one was hurt but for a few sore knees and elbows and the bump on my head. We climbed out of the disabled town car. I sat aloft the fender and looked about. We faced the wood, only a short way from the farmhouse.

A train whistle shrilled. The boys looked up at me on my perch. Jig laughed his booming laugh, and its echo came back at us.

"So much for the train," Harry said. He took out his pocket flask and we passed it round as we contemplated our situation. The gin was icy cold to my lips but warm in my throat.

Paulo reached up to me. I shook my head. I was quite comfortable. A stiff wind came up and dusted us with fine powder. The farmhouse, the entire setting, was one of those glass globes that you shake to make the snow fall.

"Won't you swing down from your treetop and join us, little monkey?" Jig said.

I didn't answer him. I was considering the word *monkey*. That was the word the children had used when we asked about Adelle. *Monkey. Tree. Adelle playing monkey in a tree?*

Harry gave me a quizzical glance. Reading my mind again? He did this now with increasing frequency.

"We must go back." I motioned urgently to Paulo, who lifted me from the fender but held me so my feet didn't touch the snow.

"What is it?" he asked. "Did you forget something?"

"There won't be another train for a couple of hours, so we might as well," Harry said, fixing me with knowing eyes.

I wriggled in Paulo's arms. "Put me down, Paulo. We must go back to the house. The children said Adelle was a monkey."

"Monkey business," Harry muttered.

"Who's a monkey?" Paulo looked confused, but he cleared a space in the snow and set me down. I clenched my toes in my thin shoes to keep them from freezing.

"Hold on there, Oliver," Jig said. "Come on, chaps, let's get this buggy on her feet."

There ensued an event of low comedy. Just imagine those zany vaudevillians the Marx Brothers trying to right an automobile lying on its side in a snowy ditch. First Harry slipped and fell; afterward, Jig and Paulo. Then they had an argument on how to do it, whose method was the proper one.

I couldn't help laughing, at which point

they all growled at me. "Get a horse," I yelled, cheering them on with more laughter.

Finally, with all three pushing, the machine came lurching onto all fours, though listing badly.

Once righted, however, the car refused to leave the ditch.

The ceiling of the sky sank lower and lower until I swear I could have reached up and touched it. I'd had my fill of jiggling from one foot to the other and began walking, never mind my unprotected shoes.

I am intuitive, but I hoped I was wrong.

Harry followed practically on my heels. "I'll get Dave. Don't do anything without me."

Woods are lovely in twilight when the dying sunlight streaks the trees and leaves with a pale yellow afterglow. But there was no dying sunlight to speak of this afternoon. All was gray and eerily shadowed. Snow-covered evergreens, their branches like voluminous skirts, curtsied to us as we nine, single file, marked a path where no path was. And where no path would be soon enough.

"I don't understand any of this," Kate

kept saying. She was holding tight to Paulo's coat. "Children make up stories."

I plodded along just behind Natty Bumpo, also known as Harry Melville, who held the flashlight. "Harry, the trees," I said.

The beam of light revealed draperies of snow, thick folds shifting anew and anew.

"I'm going back," Kate said. "The rest of you may stay out here and catch your death, but I don't have to."

The others all murmured agreement.

"I say it's time for a martini," Dave called.

Their voices became distant, muffled. Well, let them go. I poked Harry's sturdy back. "Keep going, please, Harry. Just a little farther."

"Hold on a minute, Oliver," Harry said. Like the line of a fishing rod, he cast the light into the trees, to the right, to the left, back to the right. The beam shivered an instant. Harry said, "Bloody hell!"

I came up beside him and, hand shading my eyes, squinted against clinging snow-flakes. Swathed in ethereal light, an angel floated in the tree, stunned by exposure. "Poor angel," I whispered.

Harry swore again. "Where did everyone go? I'm going to need help."

I shook my head, blinked the snow from my lashes.

He handed me the flashlight. "Keep it steady, Oliver. It's been a long time since I climbed a tree."

Chapter Seven

It seemed to take Harry forever to cut Adelle's frozen corpse from the tree. Once done, she became dead weight and, ice-sheathed, slipped from his arms. Facedown in the snowy undergrowth, she could well have been a fallen log. We would have walked right by and not seen her.

I crouched near Adelle's body and cloaked her with light. "What have we done?"

"Don't touch her." Harry scrambled from the tree.

I was remotely aware of the wet cold clinging to my skirts, the tingling in my knees. My eyes were drawn to the remnant of the death-tie round her neck. The light danced to my shudder. I heard myself say, "She may still be alive." Of course, that was ridiculous, which Harry was quick to inform me.

Harry lifted his flask to his lips and took a mighty swallow. When he handed the flask to me, I finished what remained.

Reclaiming the flashlight from my unresisting hand, he raised it in the air and flashed it on and off and on and off, calling, "Haloo!" Dot. Dot. Dash. Dot. Dot. Dash.

"Haloo." Dave's voice was faint. His haloos came closer until he was upon us. "Give it up," he said. "It's a wild goose."

I got to my feet and Harry stepped aside.

"Cripes," Dave said.

"See if you can rouse the constabulary," Harry said.

"We have to bring her in," I pleaded.

"Is it Adelle?" Dave bent down and, before Harry could stop him, turned her over.

The gin came back on me. I reeled away. It was horrible. What I'd thought was the look of surprise on the angel's face was what came of a hanging, the bulging eyes and the gaping mouth.

She'd said, "It really doesn't matter." But it had. It did.

"I was going to let her go. She must have heard me tell Fordy . . . what was the point in having her here? I told Fordy there was no point." Kate's prattling was hollow. Daisy sobbed pitiably in Bunny's arms, then excused herself and went upstairs to the bathroom. Kate set a replenished tin of cigarettes on the table, and we each took one. "I was going to let her go. I never would have hired her in the first place. It was Fordy's idea. Fordy said it was a favor, that she'd be good for us. But to do something like this . . . to kill herself . . . she must have had a crazy streak. How will I explain to her people?"

"You know the family?" Dave'd brought over two bottles of wine from his place, and we made fast work of them.

"Well, no, but Fordy seemed to know where she came from. She must have family. Doesn't everyone?"

"No, Kate, not everyone." I was testy and not at all ready to accept suicide.

Dave went back out to relieve Paulo — the boys were taking turns keeping watch over Adelle's body.

"What am I going to do?" Kate said. "Fordy is the one who hired her. He can't leave me with this."

How selfish we all are, I thought; Adelle's death was a mere inconvenience in our lives. I brushed back a tear with the side of my hand.

"Are you all right, Oliver?" Paulo burst into the room as if he'd run all the way.

"I think I'll lie down for a while." I edged away from everyone and went slowly up the stairs. Perhaps Adelle had left a note. The Vaudes had given Paulo and me the children's room, which Adelle had shared with them.

Someone was in the room. I could hear small movement, a creak, a chair moved. I went down the hall to the bathroom, expecting to have to dislodge Daisy, but the bathroom was vacant. I grabbed the plunger and came back. What sort of damage I could do with a plunger I never considered. I put the toe of my shoe in the slant of open space and pushed the door ajar, plunger at the ready.

It was Harry. "Looking for something?" I said.

He turned slowly. "Now isn't that a picture for *Vanity Fair*. Famous woman poet with her instrument."

"Bother, Harry." I set down the plunger. "I suppose you are looking for the suicide note, too."

"I'll eat my shoe if that was a suicide, Oliver." Harry doesn't wear a hat.

"When she played Truth with us last night, it got fairly vicious . . . unreasonably, I thought."

"Isn't that the purpose of the game?" was my cynical friend's comment.

"No, it's not. But hear me, Harry, one of

us attacked her as a Judas. I could feel the menace, and I'm sure she did, too. After everyone was asleep, I happened to see her picking through the ashes —"

"You'd come down to get a glass of water, of course."

"Well, of course. And while doing so, I thought I might —"

"Take a little gander among the ashes yourself?"

I grinned at him. "You have a way with words, Harry."

"So did you find anything?"

"No. But maybe she did. Did you find anything here?"

"One drawer is hers, the usual girl stuff. A dress and a pair of shoes in the closet."

"A purse? Personal letters?"

"No. Nothing. Someone's already been through her things. All I found was . . ." He held it up. "A book of poetry. John Donne."

"That's mine, Harry. I must have for-gotten to pack it." I took the book from him. "You know what's really strange? Adelle walked away and left the children outside alone. She didn't strike me as the sort who would do that."

Harry looked thoughtful. "The chil-dren . . ."

It was at this point that the sheriff's deputy, one Amos Hook, made his appearance, and our suppositions went no further. Hook, a gangly Ichabod, arrived in an open, quivering Ford and took statements from us all. The sheriff, it seemed, had broken his leg coming out of his house. Telephone lines were down all over the county. Deputy Hook was able to go round and alert the local doctor, who also did the autopsies, that an ambulance was needed at the Vaude place.

The snow had ceased by the time Amos Hook drove us to the train station. Although Paulo had wanted to stay, Kate insisted she was fine. Besides, Dave was across the road, and Susan and Jig would stay the night, the roads being treacherous.

"Looks to be a suicide." Amos Hook had a slyness about him that made me think he was fabricating.

"Look again." I shivered in the open car.

Paulo took me by the shoulders and stared into my face. "What do you mean, Oliver?"

"Yes, miss, what do you mean?" Hook asked as we pulled up to the station.

"I think you already know, Mr. Hook."

"Talk to the children," Harry said. "They were probably the last to see Adelle except . . ." He let his words fade off. I could finish what he'd left unsaid: *except for the murderer.*

For Harry had noted, as had I, that the death-tie binding Adelle's throat was a man's brown leather belt.

Chapter Eight

When we boarded our train back to the city, I declared I wanted to work and so took a seat to myself and kicked off my overshoes — Reed's overshoes — with which I'd absconded. Behind me, Paulo's and Harry's voices became incoming surf, now and again. The rhythmic reverberation of the car, the faint whistle from the engine, worked with me.

When I was done, I closed my eyes, and slowly the murmuring surf behind me became words again and the words took on meaning.

". . . don't know where she came from. Kate said she was the daughter of one of Fordy's friends. Yale. Were you there at the same time?"

Harry was being Harry, or Sherlock, as the members of the notorious Greenwich Village street gang, the Hudson Dusters, called him. I listened for Paul's response.

"He was a senior. I never said two words to him, though of course everyone knew who he was because of the paintings."

"Ha, I'd forgotten about those." Harry actually chuckled. "He never did graduate, did he?"

"I think they sent him his diploma, but they wouldn't let him stand up with his class."

I wanted to interrupt them, demand to know about Fordy's paintings and why he wasn't allowed to graduate with his class, but I kept my silence. Harry might be a man of few words, but he always had a plan. I would wait and see what it was.

"Boola boola," Harry said.

And I laughed out loud. Harry can be such a card.

Paulo leaned over the back of my seat and tousled my hair. "Do we have a poem?"

"We do."

Harry said, "Well, let's hear it." He passed me his flask.

I shook it. It made a nice, liquid sound. "Thought we were dry."

"Fordy's got an interesting cellar."

I took a generous swallow of gin and returned it to him.

"So let's hear the poem," Paulo said.

"And wake up all these good people?" For a small person I have rather a resonant voice. And I am not shy.

Harry got out of his seat and stood in the aisle. He was very tight. "Ladies and gentlemen, we have with us the famous poet Olivia Brown."

Of course, I could have been mistaken, but I swear there was a little stir. A gentleman in a smart hat lowered his newspaper and stared.

"Bohemians," someone said from the rear of the car, as if that explained all.

"Miss Olivia Brown has written her latest poem in this very railroad car as we travel back to New York. With your permission, she will now give us a recitation." Harry ended with such a grand flourish, the motion threw him unceremoniously back into his seat, from which he called, "I give you the celebrated Miss Olivia Brown."

In truth, the railroad car was sparsely filled, it being a Sunday evening. Still, an audience is an audience, even if it is one person. I stood in the aisle and recited my "Elegy to Jack Reed" as we rumbled toward Grand Central Terminal and home.

Just one last cigarette, and I'll be gone.
I have wing-ed feet that urge me on,
No, it is not Helen who beckons me

To noble wars that make men free.
How can love compare to this?
You think to hold me with your kiss,
That your siren song will make me pause
And drink the potion, cast off the Cause.
My soul will pine for freedom, waste
  away
Within your loving fetters, until one day
I will be dust, nothing there to look
  upon.
So, one last cigarette, my dear, and
  I'll be gone.

There was a smattering of applause, and a gentleman even called, "Brava!"

I made a modest little bow and took my seat again.

Paulo leaned over the seat and kissed me. "Brilliant."

"God damn, Oliver," Harry said.

Harry doesn't impress easily, but it pleases me to say I rendered him speechless.

"Come sit with us," Paulo said.

So I came and sat on his lap. He lit my cigarette. "Tell me about Fordy's paintings," I said.

"They called them pornography," Paulo said, locking his hands about my waist.

"You've seen them?"

Paulo and Harry exchanged a grin. "Hasn't everyone?"

"I haven't. What are they like?"

"I pass to the gentleman on my right," Paulo said.

"Nudes," Harry said. "Girls."

"So, Renoir painted nude women."

"Not with their sex on display."

I was intrigued. Fordy was the last person I would have thought involved with pornography. But then it struck me that the beautiful, celebrated Celia Gillam would not have gone off with someone as ordinary as Fordy had always seemed. "Is that what he does in that studio of his on Washington Square?"

"Have you been there?" Paulo asked Harry.

"No. Have you?"

"No."

"Well, I say let's all go together," I said. "I want to see the real man Celia Gillam went off with, not the suit, vest, and tie."

Harry said, "Celia won't be around for long. She'll hear about an insurrection somewhere in the world and grab her camera and be off. Just like last time."

Paulo's thighs tensed beneath me. His hands fidgeted at my waist. I removed them. "What last time? Don't tell me she's gone off with Fordy before?"

Harry raised a skeptical eyebrow at me. "Not Fordy, Oliver. Kate."

"Really? Kate? How delicious. She's had them both."

Paulo had become an uncomfortable lap, so I went back to my seat and curled up once more. I tried to keep listening, but they began to talk about the War, and I slept.

Chapter Nine

Because Paulo had to teach an early class in New London, where he was professor of English at Connecticut College for Women, the three of us parted in Grand Central Terminal, leaving him to await his connection. I felt an odd sense of relief. Though incredibly handsome and a gentle lover, I'd come to the realization that Paulo was detached, a beautiful shell, while his thoughts were often somewhere else. Not with another girl, but the blasted War, its aftermath hanging like a pall over all of us.

Harry shook Paulo's hand and strode off. I turned my cheek from the urgency of his lips. We'd all had too much to drink and inhaled too much of each other, I think.

I was tired and Harry was grumpy. No, we were both grumpy, and I couldn't say exactly why. Grumpy and silent.

Harry seemed in his own world, even to the point of walking two or three paces ahead of me when we stepped off the trolley in the snow-dusted Village. I had to hurry to keep up, somewhat difficult in Reed's galoshes and on sidewalks, swept in daylight, now reclaimed by the snow. Muted light from the street lamps met snow-coated fences, gates, and trees and melded, creating a virtual fairyland.

The rich smell of burning logs drifted from white-rimmed chimneys. I wanted to stop and exalt in our homecoming, but Harry would have none of it.

"Are you angry with me, Harry?" I asked his back, which gave no response.

The cold prickled my cheeks, brought tears to my eyes. I could smell new snow in the air. I lifted my face to the charcoal sky and walked smack into Harry. We were in front of No. 73½ Bedford Street. Home.

Home was a small three-story house of red brick and, I grant, peeling white trim. We will see to that in the spring. Shrubs, tonight pearl-glazed, filled a handkerchief-size area behind a once black, now bloated with snow, wrought-iron fence. A fine oak door with brass trim led to a small vestibule. Harry occupied the flat on the ground floor, and the rest of the house with its lovely, tall windows was mine.

"Want a nightcap?" Harry said. His offer seemed half-hearted, his tone forced.

Ordinarily I would have respected that

he wanted to be alone, but something took hold of me. Maybe I didn't want to go upstairs to my empty flat. Mattie, my housekeeper, my dearest friend, would not return till tomorrow.

I made a measure with my fingers. "Maybe a wee geneva."

A lone bottle of gin rested in Harry's bathtub, the block of ice long melted. We stared down at it. "Last bottle," he said needlessly.

"I hate warm gin. Come upstairs and make us martinis."

"Not tonight, Oliver."

"Okay, I can take a hint." I picked up my small valise but didn't leave. Harry's skin had a yellow cast. Sometimes he was given to black moods. "Are you all right, Harry?"

"Beat it, Oliver." He hooked his coat on the bathroom doorknob, rolled back his shirtsleeves, and splashed his face with water.

Light trickled from under my door. At first I thought Mattie had returned earlier than planned, but then I saw she had left the hall light on for me so I wouldn't come home to a dark house. So, too, the furnace; although the house was chilled, it was not uncomfortable. I dropped my valise at my feet. A stack of letters awaited me on the marble-topped table of the hall stand. It was good to be home.

In the kitchen I found half a bottle of wine. I took a glass from the shelf and carried both to the hall, unlatched my valise and stuck the bottle in, propping it upright by closing one latch. I put the glass in the pocket of my coat, tucked my mail under my arm, picked up my valise, and went upstairs.

I turned on the light beside my bed and emptied my pockets, setting the glass on the night table. I shrugged out of the old fur and let it slip to the floor. My limbs felt so heavy. Retrieving the wine from the valise, I filled my glass and set the bottle on the table.

The wine warmed me, eased me. I sat on the bed and lit a cigarette. Good, so good. I lay back, and Jack Reed came floating above me.

My poem. "I'll read you my poem, Jack," I said.

I sat up and inverted the valise onto the bed, looking for my poem. On top of the small pile of soiled clothing was the leather-bound volume of John Donne's poems that Mama Danenberg had pressed into my hand. I placed it on the table next to the bottle of wine and my empty glass. I refilled my glass, then rummaged through the rest.

At the bottom of the heap I found my poem. It was lying under a second leather-bound volume. I picked it up and read the binding. It was an exact duplicate of the book of Mr. Donne's poetry that rested on my bedstand.

Chapter Ten

"I do believe you are fonder of Joan Brophy than you are of her son, and that's why you've agreed to marry him," I told my very agreeable Mattie as she stood in my doorway with a tray of coffee and fresh scones. She'd spent the weekend in Washington with her soon-to-be mother-in-law, to champion — now that we had the Vote — equal rights for women.

Mattie colored, as was only proper. "Olivia Brown, you have no shame." She set the tray across my legs.

"Come now, admit it," I said, my fingers trying to tame the snarls from my hair and not succeeding.

"I'll admit nothing of the kind." She drew back the draperies. The sunlight was cold and mean and might as well not have been there, for it hardly gave us a glance. "Gerry Brophy is my sweetheart. It's God's good luck I love his mother, too." Her gaze took in the empty bottle of wine and the glass, the two copies of John Donne on my bedstand. "We've finished the wine."

"I know. It's off to Signore Dionysus for us. I hope there's a check or two in the mail." I patted the bedclothes, looking for my cigarette case, found it. It was empty. "Sans cigarettes."

Mattie removed a tin from the pocket of her apron, and we had our smoke. She sat on the bed and watched me dawdle over the scone. I was not very hungry. My head, nagged by a small but persistent thumping, felt twice its size. Even the very bones under my eyes complained.

When I was a lonely, motherless child of nine, Mattie, a spirited Irish girl a mere ten years my senior, had come to work for my guardian, Jonas Avery. And seeing immediately how much I was in need of a surrogate mother and a friend, Mattie had slipped easily into those positions, and so remained.

"I heard about that poor girl . . . the nanny." Mattie began gathering up clothing and mail that had fallen from the bed as I slept. With the letter opener from my desk, she sliced open the envelopes and handed each to me one at a time.

"Harry told you?"

She nodded.

"It was the nasty finish to a thoroughly unpleasant house party." I muted my coffee with a dollop of cream and sipped it.

"I expect you ate very little and drank a great deal," Mattie said, disapproval in the set of her shoulders.

Mattie insists on thinking I'm frail as a kitten, when I'm not. I'd been ill after the War, as many had, devastated by the loss of those dear to me, my fiancé, Franklin Prince, whose plane had gone down in the English Channel, and then Jonas Avery, my guardian, and my beloved tutor, Miss Sarah Parkman, in the influenza epidemic.

"We must live life to the fullest, Mattie, for we are only young once," I said. "Oh, look, here's an invitation to speak to the Gramercy Poetry Club next month. We'll accept with pleasure, as it brings us twenty-five dollars." Another envelope held a letter from an academic admirer. I set it aside to be answered. The cursive writing on the third made my heart beat a little faster. I turned it over in my hand. It was from Stephen Lowell, the poet and a dear friend. Truly, I love him more than the others, but he's married, with a child, and Chicago is far from the Village. And we have never been lovers. His letter deserved to be read at twilight with a glass of wine. Later.

The last letter produced a delicious check for fifty dollars from *Vanity Fair*. I gave it a tender kiss and turned it over to Mattie. "For Signore Dionysus, the bootlegger." I moved the tray from my legs. "I've rehearsal today. And I must make more time for my work or I shall never have a book ready by spring."

Mattie set the empty bottle of wine and the glass on the tray. She collected my soiled clothing into a roll, tucked the roll under her arm, then picked up the tray. "I've run you a bath, but Harry said not to go off. He needs to talk to you."

Harry, it happened, had a visitor, whose enormous galoshes were parked outside his door. A client. A new case. I was exhilarated. I adjusted the pair of John Donnes on my hip and gave his doorbell a quick twist.

"It's open."

No Murphy bed exposed. Harry's flat was an office again. Harry, in fact, was clean-shaven and dressed for business, not a full suit, but braces and a clean white shirt. The coat was draped on the back of his chair.

Harry's visitor, a tall, gangly man with blond hair and a benign face, stood when I came in. Amos Hook, the deputy sheriff from Croton. He nodded at me. "There's nothing that pleases me more than to kill two birds with one stone."

"I'm not much on killing birds, Mr. Hook," I retorted. I loathe clichéd metaphors, and the feeling came over me that Amos Hook's very harmless manner was in fact a role he played. It is something I know well.

"You'll have to forgive Miss Brown." Harry's eyes sent me a warning. "Yesterday was a long and difficult day, for all of us."

"Of course."

"Of course," I repeated. I nodded gravely at my fellow actor.

"Have a seat, Miss Brown, if you don't mind. I won't keep either of you long. There are just a few questions to ask."

I set the two Donne volumes on the floor next to Harry's broken-down sofa and lodged myself on its loose arm, trusting, since I weigh next to nothing, that it wouldn't give out on me. Amos Hook settled deep into the sofa, taking care to avoid one of the protruding springs. Even sitting low as he was, he proved taller than I, and I was forced to look up to him.

"I'm sorry if I've interrupted you," I said.

"Not at all, Miss Brown, I'd only just arrived." Hook took a small notepad from the pocket of his coat, but his attention was on the hem of my skirt, which stopped just below my knee.

I swung my leg, a rather attractive limb, if I may say. I am a wicked girl.

"What did you want to ask us?" Harry said, trying to get the train back on the track.

"Oh? Ahum. Yes, well, Kate Vaude." A line of perspiration appeared on Hook's clean upper lip.

"What about Kate?" I asked, tiring of the sport.

"How well do you know her?"

Harry said, "I know Fordy better than Kate. He lived in the Village before the War."

"Miss Brown?"

"I hardly know them at all. I met them through Harry and Paulo — Paul Ewing." Actually, I'd met everyone I knew in the Village through Harry, who'd taken me under his wing and introduced me around. Harry knew Paulo from somewhere, and Paulo knew the Vaudes, and that's the way it went. It was like putting a light to a single match in a row of matches and watching one catch fire, then another and another until the whole parcel was ablaze.

"Ewing's not at the address he gave me."

I covered a yawn. My head continued to complain. "When he's in town, Jig and Susan put him up, or other friends do. But he's in Connecticut at the college today."

"Ewing told us he knew Fordy from Yale, though not well." Harry found his cigarette case under some papers and offered it.

We lit up, and very soon a nice smoky haze filled the room.

"How did Mr. and Mrs. Vaude meet?" Hook asked.

Harry rubbed the side of his nose. "I don't know. After the War Fordy went into his father's business, and we didn't see much of him in the Village."

I wondered why Harry hadn't mentioned Fordy's studio on Washington Square South. "Harry, was Kate in the Village before the War?" I asked.

With the faintest flicker of surprise, Harry said, "I don't remember her, but that doesn't mean anything. There were a lot of girls then, who just showed up one day. Some stayed; others were gone the next."

"Maybe Fordy met her in the War," I said. I smiled brightly at Deputy Hook.

"How am I doing? Don't I make a good detective?"

"I understand from Mr. Melville that you and he work together when you're not writing your poems, Miss Brown."

"We do, though not as often as I'd like." I grinned at Harry and gave my hair a good fluffing.

Amos Hook struggled to his feet. "Is there anything else you can tell me about Mrs. Vaude? She has not communicated with you?"

"I'm curious," Harry said. "Why all these questions about Kate?"

"And what of poor old Adelle?" I asked.

"All in the same basket," Hook said.

We waited for him to explain, but he didn't.

"What's this about, then, Hook?" Harry said.

Hook wrapped a long wool scarf round his neck and retrieved his cap from the tilting hat rack near the door. "If you hear from Kate Vaude, I'll thank you to telephone me." He reached into his pocket and took out a business card, handed it to Harry.

"Well, sure." Harry dropped the card on his cluttered desk.

"If you want to know about how Kate

met Fordy, why not just go over to the farm and ask her?" I said, a trifle snippy as Deputy Hook hadn't seen fit to give me a card.

"Ah," Amos Hook said. "You see, we have a small problem. There was no one at the farmhouse this morning. Kate Vaude, and her children, have vanished."

Chapter Eleven

Propping himself against Harry's doorjamb, Deputy Hook pulled on his rubber galoshes one giant foot at a time.

"Have you asked Dave Wolfe, across the road?" I said. "He'll know where she's gone."

"He doesn't, or so he says."

"She'll turn up," Harry said. "After all, where can you go towing around two kids?"

I left the arm of the sofa and approached Hook. "It's about Adelle, isn't it? You've discovered it wasn't a suicide. That's why it's urgent that you find Kate?"

"You're right, Miss Brown. Adelle Zimmer did not commit suicide. She was murdered."

Harry lit a new cigarette from the butt of the old one.

I said, "Zimmer? That was her last name?"

Hook studied us, a deep frown between sprawling brows. "You're not surprised that she was murdered?"

"No chair or ladder kicked over. The limb she hung from was too high for her to climb. . . . Unlikely suicide." Spoke just like a detective, Harry did.

"And a man's belt round her neck," I said.

"Kate had nothing to do with it." Harry looked at me. "It would be difficult for a lone woman to subdue Adelle and get her up on that branch."

"Perhaps," I said. "And why would Kate do it? She had no motive."

"You two want to come up to Croton, maybe the sheriff'll give you my job," Hook said.

I fluttered my fingers and flashed my green eyes at him. "Oh, dear Mr. Hook, you are such a kidder."

He flushed. "I'm not saying she did it. There are questions that have to be asked. If either of you should hear from Mrs. Vaude, I'd be obliged if you'd let me know." With a "Good day to you," he took his leave.

We waited until we heard the outside door slam shut.

"What do you have in the wine cellar?" I asked.

"Couple of swigs of warm gin. I meant to pay a call on my bootlegger, but first

Fordy, then Hook —"

"Fordy? Harry, you didn't say anything."

"Hook was asking about Kate, not Fordy. There's a party in his studio tonight."

"How inappropriate, unless it's a wake."

"I shouldn't think so." He pointed to the floor near the sofa. "What do you have there?"

"Where? Oh, good heavens, I've forgotten entirely why I wanted to talk to you." I scooped up the books and planted them on top of the papers on his desk, next to his feet.

In a distracted fashion, as if he were trying to think of something other than the problem I was introducing, he picked up the top book and read the spine. "*The Poetry of John Donne*. Your book, you said."

"I know what I said. I thought it was mine because I have one just like it, and I'd already packed that one."

He took up the other book. "*The Poetry of John Donne*, it says here. What are you doing with two exactly the same books?"

"That's what I'm trying to tell you, Harry. One of them must be Adelle's."

"Which one?"

"I don't know. I took a cursory look

through each, but —"

"Coincidence."

"I don't think so. I received my copy as a gift from Mama Danenberg, who —"

"Mama Danenberg, Oliver? Sounds like the name of a fence."

"Hardly. The Danenbergs own a little bookshop in Croton. That's probably where Adelle got her copy."

Harry righted himself and thumbed through one of the books. "I don't know that it means anything." He held the front and back covers and shook. I groaned. Nothing fell out. He did the same with the second book. Still nothing. Shrugged. Looked at the inside covers.

"What are you looking for?"

"See if something's hidden in the binding."

"Is there?"

"No." He put one book atop the other and handed them back to me. "What I said before. Coincidence."

"Well, I guess one should go to Adelle's next of kin. If we ever see Mr. Deputy Hook again . . ." I'd lost Harry's attention completely now. His feet were back on his desk, and his fingers made a drumming sound. "So, Harry," I said, "after I killed her, I hung her up in the tree . . ."

His eyes glanced at me. "Right."

"Harry!"

"What?" Now I had his full attention.

"You didn't hear a word I said. Here I tell you I killed Adelle and hung her in the tree and you say, 'Right.' Where were you?"

"I picked up a new client this morning."

"You were thinking about a new case. I forgive you."

"Well, not exactly a new case, Oliver. Daisy telephoned this morning."

He seemed to think I knew her, but at first the name meant nothing to me. Then came a trickle of light. "Not Bunny's friend — she who was particularly broken up about Adelle?"

"Yes."

I was nonplussed. "She's the client?"

He nodded. "It appears she's uncommonly interested in the death of Adelle Zimmer."

Chapter Twelve

I had never been to the lair of the gentleman I always referred to as Signore Dionysus, but I wanted to hear more about Daisy and the new case. And God knows, we were in desperate straits without either gin or wine.

"Get your coat and overshoes," Harry said, and out we went in the hoary noon.

The sunlight was a pale and bleary haze, as if the sun, too, had imbibed immoderately, and under our feet, the deceptive sidewalks, their slick ice hidden by a thin coverlet of snow. When we crossed Houston Street, heading south, we entered another country. Unlike the western tip of the Village, where warehouses faced the Hudson River, these warehouses seemed to incline across the narrow streets, making sunlight an infrequent visitor.

"Harry," I said, shuffling along in Reed's galoshes, "everyone, present company excepted, thinks Adelle's death was a suicide."

"Daisy doesn't know it was murder, at

least she didn't let on."

"Are you going to tell her?"

"Why not?"

"Okay, I have another question: Why would Daisy, of all people, hire you — us — to investigate Adelle's death? What was Adelle to her?"

"You think I didn't ask her? She whispers to me into the telephone that she has to know what happened to Adelle. Claims she knew Adelle from Vassar."

I dodged a fireplug, and in spite of Harry's quick move, almost brought us both down on the icy pavement. "Call me Doubting Thomas," I said, "but neither Daisy nor Adelle let on that they knew each other. Why the charade?"

"She said she was shocked to see Adelle there working as a nanny."

"If they knew each other, why didn't they let on?" I stopped and let out a breath. "Wait, Harry. I did see them talking on the veranda Sunday morning. Daisy was holding on to Adelle, seemed to be pleading with her, and Adelle's face was contorted. Then Adelle gave her a shove, a very angry shove."

Delivery wagons and trucks were being loaded and unloaded by dark-haired, dark-eyed boys and men. The men wore brimmed hats and drooping mustaches and smoked thin, acrid cigars. They called to each other in Italian.

"And how can Daisy," said I, "a poor secretary, afford the likes of H. Melville, Private Investigations?"

"Don't know." He patted the pocket of his overcoat. "But she sent over five hundred bucks."

"Via an office boy from *Vanity Fair*?"

"You guessed."

When we turned east onto Broome Street, a cart rolled slowly by loaded with wooden cases stamped TEA. We'd entered paradise. Everyone, even the cops, knew "tea" was the sobriquet for booze.

Of course, I paused to admire and narrowly missed being run down by a truck backing into a loading dock.

An apparition jumped out of the truck, yelling, "Wyancha watch where youse goin', goilie." Pale blue, pin-dot eyes ogled me. The stump of a cigar wedged in his mouth hardly moved when he spoke. "Lookahere, if it ain't Olwer." Red Farrell doffed red cap; his hair was a conflagration.

Red Farrell was a member of the notorious Irish street gang the Hudson Dusters, and the first time I'd met him, he'd scared me half to death. It had turned out that Red Farrell, and the rest of the Dusters, were keeping an eye on me for Harry, who thought my life was in danger.

For some reason, which Harry had never explained, the Dusters treated Harry with respect, called him Sherlock, and were always available to him when needed. They thought my name was Olwer because when Harry introduced me, he was recovering from a terrible beating that affected his speech. So Oliver became Olwer, and so remained.

"I am delighted to see you again, Mr. Farrell," I told him.

"Youse wouldn'a be if I'da run youse down," he said, pulling his hat over his hair and putting out the fire. "Lucky it were me drivin' and not Jack."

Harry materialized from behind the truck. "Hey, Red."

"Sherlock!"

"We gonna sit here all night while youse make goo-goo eyes?"

The Duster known as Circular Jack, a dandy in a coat of scarlet velvet and a black bowler, got out of the truck and jumped up on the loading dock. He pounded on the door, which was opened cautiously by a man whose proper clothing and prudent manner marked him for one of the bosses. The man stepped out and looked up and down the street. His eyes rested on Harry and me, and he stepped back into the warehouse and started to close the door, but Jack had stuck his foot in it.

"Dey ain't cops," Circular Jack growled, motioning to Red Farrell, who waved us to the side, jumped into the truck, and backed it closer to the loading dock.

Harry took my elbow. "Come on, Oliver. So long, boys."

"Just a little friendly extortion," I murmured to Harry.

At the Palm Café, a dive near where Broome and Chrystie meet, I saw the owners had made little allowance for its reincarnation as a tearoom. A crudely printed sign on the glass-and-wood door announced a variety of Dutch and Scottish teas. Prohibition has given everyone inspiration. Dutch for gin, Scottish, of course, for Scotch.

Inside, it might as well have been night. Dull ceiling lamps barely lit the dingy place, which was just as well. Behind the bar was a squat, barrel-chested man in a derby hat. His sinister mustache was waxed to knife-like points.

"Long time no see, Harry," the sinister mustache said. He gave me a good once-over. I countered with my radiant smile, and he blinked.

"I've been by, haven't seen you."

"Been traveling some. What'll you have?"

"The usual." Harry steered me to a scarred wooden table on unsteady legs. "Don't contribute anything," he told me. As if I would. I was totally intimidated. I sat down at the table, and Harry returned to the bar.

Slowly my eyes became accustomed to the dark and I was conscious of an odd shuffling sound coming from somewhere behind me. It was then I realized that someone was sitting at a table in the back of the saloon. His face was in shadow, but his hands were lit almost theatrically under the ceiling light. Deft hands, they were, whose thick fingers shuffled the cards with casual authority.

I turned my chair so I could observe his hands. They ceased their shuffling and began to lay out the cards. He was playing solitaire. I like a good game of solitaire. I wandered over to watch.

As I came closer, the card player paused, then continued his game. There was a bottle of whiskey to his left, and a half-filled glass. A large ginger cat lay across his shoulders like a fur shawl, purring.

"A glass for da lady," he called suddenly, sweeping his hand at a chair. Another cat, gray this time, leaped onto the table and, eyeing me with something like insolence, snuggled under the cardplayer's hand.

From the front of the saloon I heard Harry's, "Bloody hell!"

I sat down. The sinister mustache arrived immediately with a glass, and the cardplayer filled it and handed it to me. Which was when I saw his face. A terrible face, prominent jowls, a broken nose. A thin white scar ran from the right side of his mouth to his ear. Hair the color of tar. Heavy-lidded eyes, a pale gray, lips decidedly sensuous.

"Monk," Harry said, right behind me.

"She yers, Harry?"

"I'm nobody's," I said. "I belong to myself."

Monk smiled, and the scar puckered into a dimple. I wanted to touch it, touch the muscles moving under his silk shirt. "Yeah," he said, not taking his eyes from mine. "Youse get whatcha want, Harry?"

"Yeah," Harry said.

"Anodder glass," Monk said. This time

85

the sinister mustache filled the glass and handed it to Harry.

Monk raised his glass. *"L'chaim."*

The Scotch was smooth, lush even. I wanted to stand up and sing. "Lovely," I said.

"So what's yer name, nobody's goil?" Monk said.

Harry's unhappiness was palpable, which seemed to amuse Mr. Monk or whoever this very peculiar man was.

I held out my hand. "Olivia Brown."

He lifted my fingers to his lips. "Da poet?"

I was mightily pleased. Even here among the bootleggers, I was known. "Yes. You read poetry, Mr. er . . . Monk?"

"I read yer pomes. How does a goil like youse know so much about love?"

Well, if that wasn't an invitation, I don't know one when I hear one. But that's as far as it got. The next thing I knew I was on the street and Harry was pulling me along. I could still hear Mr. Monk's laughter as Harry rushed me out of the saloon.

When I caught my breath, I stood my ground and would go no farther. "Why did you drag me out of there, Harry?"

"You were making a play for each other,

Oliver, and it won't work."

"Why? Because he's a bootlegger? All right, he's strange looking, but he's educated. He reads my poems. You have no right to interfere." I stamped my foot, and my legs flew out from under me and I landed flat on my derriere. Having lost my dignity, I let Harry help me up.

"Baloney, Oliver. You want to get yourself killed? That was Monk Eastman you were talking poetry with. He has a lot of enemies. Sooner rather than later they're going to find him and whoever he's with gunned down in some alley."

Chapter Thirteen

Our wonderful experiment with theatre, for which the Provincetown Players had come together, was shaken by the stunning success of Gene O'Neill's *The Emperor Jones*. We'd been discovered, it seemed. Everyone wanted tickets, and since we were by-subscription-only, we suddenly had a thousand or more new subscribers.

The critics hadn't even reviewed our November first opening because a musical called *The Half Moon* had opened on Broadway the same night. But that hardly mattered, as Broadway held no interest for us. We were not members of the newly formed professional actors association, Actors Equity. Except for our leading actor, Charles Gilpin, who'd been hired specifically to play the Emperor, we were dedicated amateurs. We performed three times a week for love, not money. We were devoted to experiment, the creation of something new.

When the critics came several days later, Kenneth Macgowan in the *Globe*, Heywood Broun in the *Tribune*, and Alexander Woollcott in the *Times*, each wrote ecstatically about the play, about Gene. Audiences who'd never been south of the Times Square theatre district flocked to our Playhouse.

Offers to move *The Emperor* with its star, Charles Gilpin, to a Broadway theatre and cast the rest of it with professional actors came in almost immediately. It seemed unfair to all of us amateurs who'd given it birth. But the pressure was enormous, and now real negotiations were in progress to pick up the production, lock, stock, and barrel, and bring it uptown for a short run in a larger theatre.

We were divided. If the play went to Broadway, we would share in the box office receipts, so there would be money for more experimental plays, and those of us who performed would be paid. But we were such a small company; even for a short run, who would continue the work at the Playhouse?

It was Gene's play *Diff'rent* that I was rehearsing now. I was playing Emma Crosby, a girl in a whaling town, who's in love with a whaling captain named Caleb. Emma thinks that their love is *diff'rent* because it's based on sexual purity. A perfect role for me, wouldn't you say? Emma refuses to marry poor old Caleb when she finds out he's violated their love by sleeping with a native woman on his last voyage.

The second act is thirty years later. Emma is a bitter old spinster, with Caleb still her suitor. She's flirting with a terrible young man who happens to be Caleb's nephew. Needless to say, neither Emma nor Caleb, who is too loyal to make another life for himself, comes to a good end.

Edward Hall had the part of Caleb. When Edward was the editor of the now defunct magazine *Ainslee's*, he'd been the first to buy my poems. Now that he was at *Vogue* he wanted to do the same, which was a problem because I had a very nice relationship with *Vanity Fair*, *Vogue's* biggest competitor. For a short time Edward and I had been lovers, and we were still very fond of one another.

We worked for the better part of an hour, reading the play through and blocking it, but our formidable leader, Jig Cook, was distracted by the Broadway negotiations. Tomorrow he would have to travel up to the Cape and talk with Gene again about the fate of *The Emperor Jones*.

"I'm of two minds," he proclaimed, hustling me over to Eighth Street and Sixth Avenue to the Working Girls' Home, which was our tarty name for Luke O'Connor's saloon, Columbia Gardens. It was here that Jig and Susan Glaspell, his novelist wife, started planning to do plays in Provincetown, Massachusetts, that first summer. Jig's booming voice echoed down Sixth Avenue.

"I only have time for a quick gin," I said. "Aren't you going to Fordy's party tonight?"

"Later." Jig twisted one of his shaggy white locks round his fingers and resumed his oratory. "Don't misunderstand, our triumph makes me proud of us and what we've accomplished, but success like this pushes us where we never wanted to be: bourgeois Broadway." He shouted, "Bourgeois!" into the night, like an expletive, which it was to us. We'd come to the Village to live the unconventional life.

Luke O'Connor, ruddy faced in his stiff white collar, greeted us with his usual blarney. "A good howlin' evenin' to you, Jig, Oliver."

The saloon was filled with the usual locals this night, it being too cold for the tourists, who'd begun to appear with more and more frequency to gape at us bohemians. Luke served his booze from chipped teacups, making that one concession to Prohibition. Once in a while the cops would raid the saloon, albeit halfheartedly, but Luke was rarely closed down for long. He paid his fine with good humor and reopened.

Wouldn't you know, the first person we saw was Whit Sawyer. Whit and I'd been lovers once, but I'd had to end it when he got too serious. Whit was sitting by himself, a notepad next to his teacup. A half-filled teacup sat in front of the empty chair opposite him. He waved us over. "Pull up a couple of chairs," he said, looking at me expectantly. "You're radiant, Oliver."

"Thank you, Whit." I lowered my lids, determined to be demure and not let him goad me.

Jig grabbed two chairs and set them at Whit's table. "Gin, Oliver?"

I nodded and Jig stepped up to the bar, leaving me with Whit, trying to decide whether to stay or go.

"You look like a sparrow ready to take flight, Oliver," Whit said. "Perhaps you'll let me provide ballast." He took hold of my arm and pulled me down onto the chair.

"Where's Paul tonight?"

"Do you have a cigarette, Whit?" I lifted the half-empty cup to my nose and sniffed. Juniper. "Whose is this?"

"Bunny's, but drink up. He won't mind."

I pulled my old raccoon closer round my shoulders, then made fast work of the bit of gin Bunny'd left in his cup.

"I bet you've given Paul Ewing the old heave-ho."

Drawing myself up with superb dignity, I said, "Oh, you think you know so much."

"I know you, Oliver."

I really hate to hear someone say he knows me. They all think they know me, and they don't. They have no idea.

"Here we are, here we are," Jig roared, setting down our drinks.

"I hear *The Emperor* is going to Broadway," Whit said.

Jig's face sagged in dejection. "We're selling out to the bourgeoisie."

"Oliver!" There was real joy in Bunny Wilson's voice as he came upon us. He placed a kiss in my palm, then wrapped my fingers round it. "I'm writing a short story about poor Adelle, the suicide of a lonely nanny," he said. "Do you think she had a lover? How are you, Jig?"

"Embattled," Jig said.

"Where's Daisy, Bunny?" I asked.

He looked blank. "Daisy? Oh, you mean Daisy."

"Not that stick Daisy from the office?" Whit said. He and Bunny were both editors at *Vanity Fair* now, and very competitive. Bunny had made no secret of his love for me.

"I took her to Fordy and Kate's," Bunny said. "She wasn't very good company."

My sharp little nose twitched. "How so?"

"She just wouldn't stop blubbering after —"

"You're being a little hard on the poor girl," Jig said. "We were all rather upset. Susan couldn't sleep at all that night."

"I heard all about it," Whit said, and added with a smirk, "But how about Fordy and Celia?"

I stared at Whit. I couldn't understand how I'd ever been attracted to him. He was cold and shallow, with little sympathy for anyone. A girl had died tragically, never mind he didn't know her, he knew us, and he had to know her death had upset us. Well, most of us. "Whit, a girl is dead, and all you're interested in is Fordy and Celia."

"What do I care about the girl? I didn't know her," Whit retorted.

"You have no soul," I told him, "and not a speck of human kindness."

I could tell by the deep flush on his face that I'd drawn blood. Turning my attention to Bunny, I said, "Then you're not bringing Daisy to Fordy's tonight?"

"I'm picking her up at her place in a couple of hours."

"I'll see you all later, then." I finished my gin and got up to leave. The men stood. On tiptoes I gave Jig a kiss on the cheek. "Don't be distressed, my dear," I told him. "There's definitely good going to come of it. Think of all the new plays! I shall write one for us."

He wrapped me in a bearish hug. "Do it, Oliver."

Whit then, charitably, had to kiss me on the lips, and Bunny, jealous, did the same.

"I'll walk you home, Oliver," Whit said.

"You'll do nothing of the kind. I do not need an escort, thank you."

I stopped to say good night to Luke O'Connor, and there he was down at the far end of the bar, the darkest spot in the room, talking to a woman with a scarf wrapped round her head. "Night, Luke," I called, in a hurry to leave.

Both he and the woman turned toward me, and I changed my mind about leaving.

I sashayed down to the end of the bar.

"Hello, Oliver." The woman gave me an enigmatic smile and let the scarf slip to the fur collar of her coat.

"Hello, Kate," said I.

Chapter Fourteen

I sat beside her and said not a word till I'd taken a sip from the teacup of gin Luke had set in front of me. For all his Irish joviality, Luke was a discreet man. He listened well and kept everybody's secrets. He let us run up tabs, and we paid him when we had the money. He never offered advice. So after he set down the drink, he took himself off to the front of the bar and left Kate and me to each other.

"Luke's an old friend," she said, finding something fascinating in her drink so she could avoid meeting my eyes.

"Everyone's looking for you."

"Everyone? I doubt that." She offered me a cigarette from her case, and we smoked. A little taller than I, voluptuous, thick honey-colored hair in waves to her shoulders, a soft, tender chin. About her, the subtle scent of peaches. Kate Vaude was an attractive woman.

I found her odd tranquillity riveting. "Well, certainly that quaint sheriff's deputy is. He paid a call on Harry this morning, and I happened to walk in on them. You've vanished, is what he said."

"He's a twerp. I didn't vanish. My step-father drove over last night and took us back to Hartford."

"The twins?"

"They're with my parents." At last she looked directly at me, the hazel eyes with a trace of defiance. "I've taken a room on Twelfth Street."

"Just you?"

"The twins will be happy in Connecticut with my mother. The experiment is ter-minus. I need to be free to finish my novel."

"What experiment?"

"Domesticity."

Well, we might have something in common after all, I thought. "You know where I live. Perhaps you'll come for tea." I held out my hand. Her handshake was firm, her palm warm against mine.

She smiled and clasped my hand between both of hers. "You won't tell on me, Oliver, will you?"

The poem — I shall call it "Domesticity" — prodded me as I walked home, my mind pondering the fate of women in this modern world. I have looked around me, and I have seen no satisfaction for a woman in marriage, unless, of course, having children is the end-all, which for me it is not. And obviously, for Kate it wasn't enough. Although they'd hate to admit it, these clever boys we love think our creative work is a pastime, something we can put aside because we're girls and only men do meaningful work.

Perhaps Fordy's leaving Kate was the catalyst. She looked at what her life had become and realized that we must — each of us — find our own way to express ourselves.

My reflection carried me up the stairs. A truly intoxicating smell emanated from the kitchen.

"Mattie? I'm home," I called, hanging my hat and coat on the rack.

"You're just in time," Mattie responded.

Gerry Brophy, Mattie's intended, rose when I came into the kitchen and greeted me with the kind of smile that crinkled his eyes so that they were almost lost on his face. He's a going-to-orange redhead with loads of freckles. "Miss Olivia." The taciturn fellow hoards words like a miser.

Gerry's a detective with the New York Police Department. I keep telling him to stop calling me "Miss," but he seems constitutionally unable to be what he feels is improper. There's a winning sweetness about the man. If I were casting him in a play, he'd be the priest, not the policeman.

Two big bowls of soup were already on the table, and Mattie was at the stove, ladling a third for me.

I inhaled the exotic aroma. "What is it?"

"An Italian soup. Mr. Santelli gave me the recipe. I added some stewing beef and a marrow bone. Sit down. It's good for you."

I said, "Then I shouldn't like it at all." But I sat down, as did they. "What is this floating on top?"

"Italian cheese. Parma John, Mr. Santelli said."

I finished the bowl of hearty soup, to Mattie's delight, as I hardly eat enough to feed a bird, she always says. She's right. I would forget to eat at all, especially when I'm writing, if she were not here to keep me fed, which is why I suspect she has not set a date for her wedding.

"There's a party tonight," I said.

"There's always a party," Mattie responded. "Who's giving this one?"

"Fordy Vaude."

A flicker of interest surfaced in Gerry's

deep-set blue eyes. "You're going back to Croton?"

"Fordy's studio on Washington Square South. Mattie's told you what happened?"

"About the suicide, yes."

"It appears it wasn't suicide. The Croton deputy sheriff, Amos Hook, came to see Harry this morning. He says Adelle Zimmer was murdered."

Mattie breathed a pale, "Oh."

I said nothing about Daisy having hired Harry because clients and their business are confidential. I might confide in Mattie later, but only after swearing her to secrecy.

"Adelle Zimmer?" Gerry said, rubbing the side of his nose. "What'd she look like?"

We both stared at Gerry. Mattie said, "Oh, my," expressing exactly what I felt. Could Gerry possibly have known Adelle?

"Olivia?" There now, he'd dropped the "Miss."

"Tall. She was quite a bit taller than I. Dark hair in a tight bun. Eyeglasses. Tense, like a tight wire. You can't have known her, Gerry. It would be altogether too odd if you had."

"I'm not sure there's any connection, but I'll soon find out. What was the name of that deputy? Hook?"

"Amos Hook. Croton Sheriff's Department. He left his business card with Harry. He's looking for Kate Vaude, who seems to have, as he said, vanished. Are you going to get in touch with him?"

"Not yet. I want to check something first." Gerry got up. "I'll be back in an hour," he told Mattie.

Mattie and I looked at each other. "Come on now, Gerry," I said. "Tell us how you might know Adelle Zimmer."

"I don't know anyone named Adelle Zimmer, but I know an Adeline Zimmerman who fits that description."

"How on earth — ?" Mattie was amazed, but with an element of pride.

"It would truly be a small world," I said. "Who is this Adeline Zimmerman?"

"I met her on a case last year. She's a Pinkerton."

Chapter Fifteen

Of course, I wanted to rush right downstairs and tell Harry, but I thought better of it. I would get dressed and muse on the possibility — the probability — that Adelle was a Pinkerton, working undercover, as they say.

Mattie came to talk as I pulled my shabby black dress over my head. "This Adeline Zimmerman might not be the same girl," she said, brushing the lint that clung to the worn fabric of my dress. "You're skin and bones, Olivia. . . ."

"I have this feeling . . ." Sitting, I pulled on new silk stockings with the embroidery down the front, fixed the elastic, and rolled them à la mode, just below my knees. I slipped my feet into my new gold-and-black-silk satin shoes, fastened the narrow straps, and stood up on their little Louis heels. They quite outshone my dress.

She tilted her head at me. "That dress has passed its prime."

"True, but we don't have the money right now."

"I could alter another of those dresses in the attic."

"Miss Alice's, yes. I don't think she'd mind. I'd like to have something quite diaphanous that I could wear for my readings. Could you do that, Mattie? I think it should be very romantic and yet dramatic."

Mattie looked thoughtful. "There were all those lovely silk scarves . . . I'll see about it tomorrow. I just might be able to make something elegant for you."

"Hey, anyone home here?" Harry's voice came from below.

Mattie giggled. "Nobody here but us chickens."

We came down the stairs laughing. The parlor gave off a heady perfume. Roses. Impossible in the winter. We looked at each other, perplexed.

"You might keep your door locked, girls," Harry said, the cigarette hardly stirring in his lips. A mild reproof. He agitated the cocktail shaker a bare smidgen, then poured martinis into three glasses.

"Oh, dear," Mattie said. "It wasn't locked? We'll have to be more careful." She took the glass from Harry.

Actually, it was only recently that we'd begun locking our door. There had been

"Monk Eastman himself," Harry said. "Give a taste of his finest."

"Tattletale." I took the glass from Harry's hand. "He's a very intelligent bootlegger, Mattie. He knew who I was. He'd read my poetry."

Mattie, dear Mattie, shook her head at me. "Olivia, I don't know. You are never cautious."

"Life shouldn't be lived cautiously. Besides, he served his country honorably, didn't he, Harry?"

Harry said, "And he served time, which is where he could take up reading poetry."

"And maybe he came back from both a better man."

"Unquestionably."

Harry's irony made me laugh. I raised my glass. "To love."

We all drank to love.

"To health and happiness," Mattie said.

We all drank to health and happiness.

"To booze," Harry said.

"To gin and wine," said I. "And bootleggers."

And we drank to that.

"To poetry," the poet said.

"To crime," the detective said.

We finished our martinis on that toast.

We waste no time on Bedford Street, I can tell you.

"Speaking of crime," said I. "Gerry rushed out of here because the name Adelle Zimmer and my description of her were strikingly similar to that of a girl Gerry knows by the name of Adeline Zimmerman."

"Are we ready to go or shall I make another?" Harry asked.

"No, let's go," I said. "Don't you want to know who Adeline Zimmerman is?"

"Go on, tell me, you're dying to," Harry said.

"She's a Pinkerton."

"Well, well, whaddaya know? Get your coat."

"Not before I see my roses."

They were bloodred, plumply sumptuous on long stems, a dozen at the very least. I sank my face into their tender blooms.

Then wouldn't you know Harry said, "Watch out for the thorns."

The night was exquisitely cold, like fragile crystal that any movement would shatter, the sky a concave dome of black velvet with rhinestone stars. I tucked my hand into the crook of Harry's arm.

you know that she's here in the Village."

" *'Eye of newt, and toe of frog,'* " Harry muttered. I tried to see his face in the slanting light of the street lamp, but it was in shadow.

" *'Like a hell-broth boil and bubble,'* " I agreed, holding up my crossed fingers against the curse of the Scottish play.

We paused in front of No. 42 Washington Square South, where Fordy had his studio. "Well, at least we won't see Kate here tonight," I said.

But I was wrong.

Chapter Sixteen

Trust stuffy old Fordy Vaude to have his studio in 42 Washington Square South, the least stuffy place in the Village. The red-brick building near the corner of Mac-Dougal Street was part of the history of our time in the Village.

Before the War, because it was a cheap rooming house, it had attracted a group of young Harvard graduates led by Jack Reed. The proprietor was delighted to fill the house with artists and writers who occasionally paid rent, and the residents were delighted that no one complained about the wild parties, the drinking, and the comings and goings of all the pretty girls who were drawn here by these brilliant, open, exciting young men.

Having arrived here only this year, I'd missed that exhilarating time entirely. Those beautiful young men had gone off to the War, and those who returned were subliminally less carefree, more circumscribed. They never quite recovered the lightheartedness that had marked them before the horrors of war.

Yet the rooming house remained cheap, with quite adequate furnishings, and continued to attract free-thinking writers and artists, as before.

Fordy's studio was on the third floor, rear, of the building, and the gaiety extended all the way down to us. My little gold shoes fairly danced up the uncarpeted stairs. I was in the mood for a party.

The festivities had spilled out into the hallway, and the guests, smoky blue cocktail glasses in hand, milled about or leaned against walls direly in need of paint or paper. From the studio came the sound of a Victrola playing a popular *Follies* tune.

"Oliver!" Edward Hall left the company of two pretty girls in somewhat gaudy plumage and was at the side of drab little me in an instant. "May I get you a cocktail?"

"That would please me so much, Edward dear," said I. Before he left he lit my cigarette.

Seeing that Harry had stopped to talk to Edward's fair nymphs, I drifted into the studio, which was practically throbbing with people. A hand reached out from the crowd and gave my arm a tug. The hand belonged to our dinner-jacketed host, Fordy Vaude. He bent and kissed me, rather lingeringly, I thought, on the lips and murmured, "So glad you came, Oliver," or something like it. "Where's your cocktail?"

"Edward's gone off to get me one, thank you, Fordy." I tried not to be obvious as my eyes searched the room looking for . . . well, I could tell you I was looking for Daisy, but it was Celia Gillam I wanted to see again.

A large corner room, the studio was lined with tall windows, many facing north. Whiskey and turpentine and the varied perfumes of the party-garbed vied for supremacy. Furnishings consisted of a divan, upholstered in spotty green velvet, a number of spindly chairs, one of those French hand-painted screens. Behind the screen was a bed suitable for a grand affair or Napoleon on a campaign. Or perhaps both.

One whole wall was mahogany bookshelves, in front of which was parked a paint-spattered wooden ladder. This last I fixed my eye upon.

I had barely gotten, somewhat unsteadily, to the second rung of the ladder when someone put a cocktail in my hand. "You look rather naked without one," Celia said in her husky voice.

My smoke rings went askew and dissipated into the hazy air. I took the cocktail glass and lifted it to my lips. It was an exquisite gin. "Thank you. We've not met formally."

"I suppose." She studied me as she would a painting in the Louvre. "Oliver."

Drink to me only with thine eyes.

I was oddly elated. She was lovely. A gold turban barely contained the stream of dusky hair framing her angular face and spilling over her shoulders. She wore a long coat of gold and amber that had Oriental overtones and trousers of amber silk that enhanced her tawny eyes.

Had I not been on the ladder, she would have stood a full head above me. As it was, I felt her magnetism tug at me so that I had to hold tight to my perch to keep from swooning into her arms. And all the while she smiled.

And I shall pledge with mine.

I became conscious of how plain I looked in my shabby black dress.

Or leave a kiss but in the cup,
And I'll not look for wine.

"Oh, there you are, Oliver." Edward presented himself, carrying two drinks. The spell was broken.

"Celia, you do know Edward Hall?" I

113

finished the drink in my hand and traded glasses with Edward, almost dislodging myself in the process.

"We're working on a layout for *Vogue*," Celia said, giving Edward a seductive smile. Oh, intoxicating predator. Ben Jonson betrayed.

"Indeed," Edward responded with a positive preen.

The slavish look in his fawn eyes unsettled me. It was usually reserved for me. I glanced over the crowd. There was Harry across the room in rather intimate conversation with a mature, though striking, brunette. I wondered fleetingly if this was the woman in his life he managed not to talk about.

"Oh, Miss Brown. You are Olivia Brown, the poet?" A beautiful young man held his hand up to me. "I so admire your work. I saw your recitation at the Murray Hill Readers Society. You were wonderful." He wanted to help me down from the ladder, but I liked my suspended position. "Will you do a recitation tonight?"

"I might," I told the young man, but it was his friend, who stood head and shoulders above him, whom I smiled at. "Why, Mr. Danenberg, how delighted I am to see you again."

The first young man was stunned. Carl Danenberg flushed, red as a beet. "You see, Richard, didn't I tell you I knew Olivia Brown?"

Then I saw Kate. Actually, it was her blue jersey dress that caught my attention first. It clung to bosom and thigh as she cut a provocative path across the room, heading either for the serving table on which a bar had been set up or perhaps the toilet in the hallway. And there was Paulo separating himself from the throng in the doorway and following Kate.

I granted the admiring young Richard my hand and let him help me down from the ladder. It was quite unintentional, and though I gave Carl Danenberg an apologetic smile, I saw that by bestowing my attention on his friend, I had, in fact, wounded Carl.

When I caught up with Paulo and Kate at the bar, Whit Sawyer and Dave, in his usual brown corduroys, had joined them. Jig, playing the role of bartender, was pouring straight gin into proffered glasses.

Paulo greeted me with an emotion that took me by surprise, wrapping me in his brawny arms. I rested my head on his breast for a moment, listening to the rapid thumping of his heart, then pulled back in time to catch him and Kate exchanging glances over my head. How discomfiting.

Remembering clearly her anger at Fordy and Celia, and the knife, I said, "I didn't expect to see you here, Kate."

"I'm —"

I never got to hear what Kate had to say, as Bunny and Daisy sidled up to us and our conversation veered to the success of Floyd Dell's first novel, *Moon-Calf*, and thence to *The Emperor Jones* and the fate of the Provincetown Players. We all seemed intent on avoiding any mention of Adelle. Too much so, I thought. What went unsaid filled the space around us. I tried to catch Daisy's eye, but she contrived to be mesmerized by the lazy vapor emanating from her cigarette.

With Harry amorously involved, it seemed up to me to corner Daisy alone and ask some straightforward questions.

As luck would have it, the little fox-trot playing on the Victrola lost its spirit. "Come, Daisy, let's find some bright melody." I took her hand with some insistence.

She stiffened. Her hand struggled mildly in mine, but combat was not her mettle.

"Harry and I have some questions before we can go forward with our investigation,"

116

I said. "You do know we work together?"

She gave a barely perceptible nod as I propelled her toward the Victrola, but someone else had got there first, and it was back in service with another tune.

We idled for a moment, then settled ourselves near a window and looked out into the night. " *'The moon shines bright: in such a night as this . . .'* " The line from *The Merchant of Venice* had come quickly to mind.

"In such a night," Daisy said with bitter wrappings. "As if she never existed at all."

"It is subtext, I think. You knew her well?"

Daisy blinked her eyes rapidly, pressed her lips together. Thin lips, they were. Sad lips. I could hardly hear her "Yes."

"Adelle Zimmer? Or Adeline Zimmerman?"

Her hand flew to her lips. "How do you know?"

I shrugged. "And she was a Pinkerton?"

"Oh." It was a small moan. "It was all an adventure to Addie. She never thought about the danger."

"You hired Harry to find who killed her. We must know these things. You should have told him this morning. The more we know about . . . Addie, the better it is and the faster we can do our job. Will you

117

come and talk to us tomorrow?"

She nodded. "I can come at noon."

I realized then that I hadn't asked her the most important question. "Are you a Pinkerton, too?"

"No, never." She couldn't control a shudder.

"You told Harry you were at Vassar with . . ." But suddenly, there it was looking right at me. I knew why Daisy had been so devastated by Adelle's death. "Oh, my dear —"

"Yes," she said. "Addie was my sister."

Chapter Seventeen

"Oliver?"

I turned from Daisy for a moment to respond to Whit Sawyer, who'd placed his proprietary hand on my shoulder.

"Whit."

"I'll be leaving shortly, and thought you might like me to see you home."

I resented his subtle claim of ownership, but I confess it was rather nice to know he still cared for me. "I thank you kindly, dear, but I'm not ready to leave just yet."

Whit put on a sullen face. "Have it your way. You always do."

"How about a poem, Oliver," Fordy called. His request was echoed by others.

"Yes, do," said my young admirer from the ladder. He stood with several other young men, but Carl Danenberg wasn't one of them.

"Well," said I, modestly. "All right."

"Your latest, Oliver," Paulo suggested. "The 'Elegy to Jack Reed.' "

I looked for Daisy, but apparently she had slipped away when Whit approached. No matter, she would come to see us tomorrow. I made my way to the ladder again and climbed three rungs so I had my little stage, precarious though it was. My audience gazed up at me expectantly, and as I began I saw my lofty Celia, her elbow on the mantelpiece, smoking a dark cigarette, watching me with a half-smile.

Fordy shut down the Victrola, and a hush fell over the room. Almost everyone here had known and loved Reed. When I finished, there were shouts of approval; I bowed graciously, a hazardous choice considering my platform.

"Another, another!" my young admirer cried, and his entreaty was echoed by others.

All except Celia, whose knowing smile had not altered.

So I said, "I offer a silly little quatrain that's been teasing my brain this evening that I haven't yet consigned to paper."

"Go on, Oliver," Bunny said. "We'll take both for the magazine."

I smiled down at Bunny. "I'll start with Ben Jonson's verse, and you'll quickly see why.

Drink to me only with thine eyes,
And I will pledge with mine;
Or leave a kiss but in the cup
And I'll not look for wine."

"Aha!" Dave shouted. "Not look for wine. Clearly not anyone we know."

We all laughed, and I said, "Clearly."

"Go on, Oliver," Bunny said.

I looked at Celia. "My response to Mr. Jonson is:

Thine eyes embraced another this night,
So falsely pledged, O lover mine;
Leave me no kisses in the cup
I'll put my trust in wine."

"Huzzah!" someone yelled as laughter filled the room. Those who knew Ben Jonson's poem was titled "To Celia" loved my little conceit.

Celia herself seemed amused. As for me, I had shown my colors and was ready to go home.

Bunny helped me down from my perch. "Have you seen Daisy?"

"Not for a while," I said. "Do you want to walk me home?"

"She must have left with someone else," Bunny said, a bit irritated.

I squeezed his arm. "Cheer up, old dear. We are both alone tonight. Take me home and I'll ply you with gin as good as Fordy's."

"There now." Bunny gave the fresh log one more poke, and the fire caught hold with a shower of sparks.

My sultry-scented roses in their Chinese vase were not to be ignored.

"Who sent the roses?" Bunny asked, a frown ranging across his broad forehead.

"An admirer."

"Of course."

I made vamp eyes at him as I filled our glasses and handed his over. "And do set down that poker. You look downright militant." I huddled in my coat, feet curled under me, waiting for a little warmth.

He put aside the poker and stood facing me with his back to the fire, a petulant expression on his face. He was like a stiff little teddy bear, a bit round, a bit haughty.

"Tell the truth now, Bunny dear, what is it between you and Daisy?" I patted the cushion. "And do come sit here, as you're absorbing every bit of heat."

Instead he collected the woolly blanket from the back of the chair and tucked it about my legs. Then he sank down beside me on the sofa and took two cigarettes from the box on the side table. Handing one to me, he waited patiently while I put mine in the holder, then lit both, sighing dramatically. "Daisy? She's nothing to me. If only you could think of me — Oliver, you know it's you I love. There could never be anyone else."

He was a dear, Bunny was. And he was brilliant, the best of us all. Our one most likely to succeed. I touched his cheek. "You know I care for you, Bunny, but I cherish our friendship and would not want anything to harm it."

We drank and smoked in silence for only a short while and began to talk, as we often did, of Catullus, whose work we both loved. And so we moved on to T. S. Eliot and Ezra Pound and free verse. And would I ever . . .

"I will never say never."

We talked through the night, Bunny refilling the glasses, our talk so rich with literature that we'd hardly noticed the dawn, except for the sound of the milk truck, which brought us up short. The parlor was cozy, and sometime during the night I'd laid my head on Bunny's shoulder.

I stretched and covered a yawn. "And so

to bed for me." I wagged my finger at the hopeful look in Bunny's eyes. "Alone. Off you go, my dear. But not before you tell me about Daisy."

"I know nothing at all about her, not even where she came from. She was just there one day. Crowny must have hired her." Bunny squashed his cigarette in the ashtray and stood. "She's to assist Whit and me, but she can't type and is not very clever. Whit detests her."

Crowny was Frank Crowninshield, an elegant gentleman, editor in chief at *Vanity Fair*. We were all in awe of him, so it made sense that neither Whit nor Bunny would question anyone Crowny hired.

"But you're squiring Daisy around," I said.

"I feel sorry for her. She's got a flat on Sixteenth Street and wants to be part of the Village life. She'll be gone soon enough."

"You're a good egg."

"I am."

I walked with him to the door. "I was surprised to see Kate there."

"Oh, don't you know?" He tapped his forehead. "Of course, you wouldn't know. I forget sometimes that you haven't always been here."

"What don't I know?"

"This is their scenario. They've been doing it for years. Whenever Celia is back in town they act it out. Last time it was Kate going off with Celia; this time it was Celia and Fordy. Next time it'll be Kate and Celia again."

I was nonplussed. "Forgive my naiveté, but did we not see Kate go after them with a knife?"

"That's so." He was thoughtful. "Each time the game becomes a trifle more real, more violent. Last time Celia was here, Fordy had a gun." Bunny held his thumb and index finger an inch apart. "The girl tried to stop him, and he came that close."

"You mean Fordy almost shot Kate, or was it Celia?"

"Oh no, Oliver. Too much gin makes me careless. It was poor Adelle who tried to stop Fordy and almost got herself shot."

Chapter Eighteen

"I suppose one of your many suitors told you." Harry looked at me with bloodshot eyes.

"You suppose right," I replied. I felt cotton headed myself but would never have let on to Harry. "Why didn't you tell me?"

"Wasn't there. Besides," he added, a ghoulish grin at Mattie, "don't all married people play games like that?"

"What would you know about it, Harry Melville?" Mattie retorted. The percolator began to gulp. Mattie, always alert to fluctuations in my health, set a bowl of oatmeal before me. "Eat, Olivia, or I swear I shall never marry Gerry Brophy." A pitcher of cream appeared near my hand.

I screwed up my face like the spoiled child I was and slid the bowl to Harry. "I just can't, Mattie, dear. I'm feeling a bit queasy this morning. And one dish of oatmeal not eaten will not stop your wedding."

Harry snorted, but I knew he would eat the oatmeal. He always did when Mattie made it. I wondered aloud, not for the first time, how in the world he'd gotten along without us.

I compromised with buttered toast and marmalade and Mattie's strong coffee. "I can confirm the Pinkerton girl, Adeline Zimmerman, that Gerry thinks he knows, is indeed Adelle Zimmer. Have you spoken to Gerry?"

"No one had any information as of last night," Mattie said. She poured herself a cup of coffee and sat down to have a cigarette with us. "The poor girl. It upset Gerry to think she might be this Adeline."

I blew a smoke ring in the air. "Do I detect a smidgen of jealousy?"

"Not at all," Mattie said, but the color in her cheeks told me different. "Murder is a terrible thing."

"If she was a Pinkerton working a case undercover, she had to be aware of the danger," Harry said.

"As a prime example of the New Woman, I say more power to us. I'm happy to know there are Pinkerton women. I'll wager that Pinkerton has more women agents on the payroll than the New York Police Department has women detectives."

"You'd be right," Harry said. He finished off the oatmeal and tackled the toast that remained on the rack.

"I could be an undercover agent," I said. "Don't you think, Harry? It's simply a matter of acting a part."

Harry rolled his eyes at Mattie. "Forget it, Oliver. You could never blend into the woodwork. One passing comment and you would raise your swan-like neck and flash those green eyes. And of course there are all those opinions."

Mattie laughed.

"Oh, you two," I said. "I'm going upstairs to dress. I arranged for Daisy to come see us at twelve, and it's nearly that now."

Mattie set the dirty dishes in the sink and followed me. "I want you to try on a dress," she said, smiling like the cat that swallowed the canary. "Shut your eyes now. It's a surprise." As she slipped the dress over my head, fairy feathers whispered against my skin. "Now you can look."

It was the loveliest thing. Chiffon in the delicate colors of a rainbow floated round me. About six inches of a train trailed along the carpet behind me. When I let my arms flow out as I would were I reciting, the chiffon flowed with me. The whole image was almost astral.

"Do you like it?"

"Oh, Mattie, how can you ask?" I hugged her. "It's perfect."

"Careful, mind the pins," she said, but she was pleased with my reaction. "Now I can finish it. Raise your arms." She lifted it over my head. "And I intend to marry Gerry Brophy whether you eat your oatmeal or not."

I was feeling very jolly when I traveled downstairs. It was nearly twelve. I gave Harry's bell a twist and listened to the sharp ring.

"Door's open," he shouted.

I stepped into his flat and immediately smelled shaving soap.

The bathroom door open, Harry, wearing trousers and a singlet, was patting his face dry. I watched him throw down the towel and reach for his gray shirt, which as usual he'd hung from the doorknob. For a man his age, he had nice shoulders and strong, muscular arms.

"I could button your shirt for you," I offered.

He raised a quizzical brow to which clung a hairbreadth of shaving cream.

"Forget it," I said. "You have lather on your eyebrow." As I wiped it off with my fingertip, Harry's doorbell rang. It was exactly twelve noon.

Daisy wore a mannish suit of brown wool and a brimmed hat with a small veil that danced in front of her eyes. Her curved-heel shoes were very stylish and showed off attractive ankles. I could see Harry thought so as well.

"Have a seat," he said, indicating the broken-down sofa.

"I'd advise you to choose the chair," said I. "It would take too long to chart you a course round the springs on the sofa." I shoved aside some of the papers and sat on the corner of Harry's desk.

Harry said, "Amusing, Oliver."

Daisy almost smiled, and being no fool, she didn't need another warning. She sat prim in the chair, her small pocketbook in her lap. "I don't have much time," she said.

"Okay, it's your nickel. Tell us what you want us to do."

"I told you over the phone." She looked at him apologetically. "I want you to find who killed my sister. Did you get the money?"

"Yes, and that's not what you told me. You said you want to hire me to find out how Adelle died. You didn't say anything about murder —"

"I didn't know."

"And you didn't tell me she was your sister."

Her gaze under her veil seemed to shift to me. "I told Oliver."

"I had to pull it out of you, Daisy," I said.

She looked at Harry. "I didn't think you had to know."

"We have to know everything about her. Oliver tells me her name was not Adelle Zimmer, but Adeline Zimmerman."

"Yes." Daisy opened her purse and took a cigarette from her case. Harry leaned across the desk and lit it for her. We watched her take several short, jerky drags, then stub it out in the ashtray on Harry's desk. "I have no other family." She spoke in a stilted voice. "I am the only one left now."

Harry studied her for a moment. "She was a Pinkerton?"

Daisy nodded, fidgeting with the clasp of her purse, then opened it and withdrew an envelope.

"Then the Pinkertons have cause to be looking into it themselves," he said.

"Have they notified you as her next of kin?" I asked. My question was reasonable, demanded some response, but Daisy was writing the story her way.

"I had no idea she was working for the Vaudes," she said. "I hadn't heard from her for months, but when she was on a case, I never did." She handed the envelope to Harry. "You will find another five hundred dollars here. Is that enough?"

"More than enough, at least for now." He took the envelope. "We'll send you a weekly report."

"Thank you." She stood, shook my hand, shook Harry's hand. At the door, she turned back to us. "Even if they found out who she was, there was no reason to kill her."

After Daisy left, I lay on the sofa, and Harry and I smoked our cigarettes without speaking, each of us deep in unsettled thought.

"What is it, Harry?"

"Don't know." He opened the envelope and shuffled the five hundred-dollar bills. "Something."

"I know." I stopped abruptly and got to my feet because I heard the squeak of the outside gate, which protested from time to time though the hinge was oiled. Opening Harry's door, I saw Gerry Brophy.

"Olivia." He doffed his hat.

"Come in and talk to us, Gerry," I said. I didn't have to persuade him. He had something on his mind.

"Detective Brophy," Harry said.

"Mr. Melville."

"Gerry, meet Harry," I said, impatient with their formality. "Gerry, we know that Adelle Zimmer is your Adeline Zimmerman and that she was a Pinkerton and was working undercover on a case."

He looked surprised. "How do you know all this?"

"Her sister, Daisy, told us."

"Well," he said. "The dead girl may very well be Adeline Zimmerman, but if it was, she was not a Pinkerton, no matter what the sister says."

Using his smoked-down stub, Harry lit a fresh cigarette. He jiggled the bottom drawer with his foot. I knew he had a bottle of whiskey there.

"But didn't you say last night that the Adeline Zimmerman you knew was a Pinkerton?"

"I did, and she was. But she resigned from the Pinkertons six months ago and no one's seen or heard from her since."

Chapter Nineteen

"Might I ask," Gerry Brophy said, "what your interest is in this?"

"Aside from the fact that we found the body?" I asked, wondering how much Harry was going to give away.

"That is a fact," Gerry agreed.

"We've been hired to find her murderer," Harry said.

"And might I ask who your client would be?"

"Now, Detective, you know I'm not at liberty to tell you my client's name."

"Well, it's your business, but it's also police business. The Croton deputy sheriff — a chap by the name of Hook — has paid a call on the commissioner. It seems the sheriff, currently laid up with a broken leg, is brother-in-law to the commissioner. Although the murder took place in Croton, almost everyone involved is from the city."

"Not everyone," I chimed in. "What about the townspeople?"

"Hook is seeing to them. Meantime, the

sheriff's asked the Department for cooperation."

"I see," Harry said. "And he's getting it."

"He is that. I'll say good day to you now, but I caution you to watch you don't tread on Lester Nolan's toes."

"Nolan?" Harry sat up. "What's Nolan got to do with this?"

"Who's Lester Nolan?" I asked.

"He's doing the commissioner a favor, so to speak. Just this once."

"I wouldn't have thought he'd need much persuasion," Harry said.

Gerry Brophy grinned. "There is some good out of this."

Harry growled. "Oh yeah, what?"

"I won't have to work with him." With that, Gerry departed.

Harry gave his bottom drawer a vicious kick. When it opened, he lifted out the bottle of whiskey, unscrewed the cap, and took a long draft.

I tried again. "Who is Lester Nolan?"

"I heard he bought a fishing boat and was living in Florida. The reporters love cops like him. And he loves the attention. It'll be like working the case under the lights, in front of an audience."

"Bosh, Harry, we'll just go about our business. We know everyone. Our friends'll talk to us sooner than they'll talk to a cop."

"You don't know Nolan."

"You mean he's like Charley Walz?" Charley Walz, retired now, was the nasty cop who'd been Gerry Brophy's partner.

"No." Harry closed up and took another drink. He stared hard at me. "Maybe I should work this job myself."

I was hurt. "What are you talking about, Harry?"

"You have a book of poems to produce."

"Which is more than half-written. That's not it, is it, Harry?"

"Let it go, Oliver."

"No." Fists clenched, I stood and faced him across his desk, poised, stamped my little foot. "This is the perfect case for me to work with you. Go on, tell me I'm wrong."

"You're not wrong."

He offered me the whiskey. I shook my head. He knows how willful I can be. "Come on, Harry. Aunt Evangeline would have approved."

"Vangie had little patience for amateurs, but she was a redhead and I should know better than to argue with a redhead and her niece to boot."

I gave him a brilliant smile.

"Okay, okay, you can turn it off now," he said. "We'll start with Fordy and Kate. They hired Adelle, Adeline, whatever her name was. You've already talked to Kate, so I'll have a go at her and you take Fordy. We'll see what we get."

"G—" I started to say "Good," but the raw sound of Harry's doorbell cut into our conversation.

"Yeah?"

"Lester Nolan, Melville."

"Hold on a minute." Harry jumped up, waving at me, pointing toward the bathroom, then he grabbed me by the arms and practically carried me there. "Do what I say, Oliver," he rasped in my ear. "I'll let you know when to come out." He shut the door on my protests.

I closed the toilet seat and sat down, left alone with a bathtub full of bottles of gin and beer nestled among two cakes of ice. Not too bad a place to be. I lit a cigarette and plucked an open bottle of gin from the lot.

Lester Nolan had a rich baritone voice. I imagined him as dark haired and incredibly handsome, perhaps with a tinge of gray at his temples. Intrigued, I put my ear to the door. Wouldn't you know, they were talking about the War.

Then Harry said very clearly, "So you're back in harness."

"A favor, is all. The sooner I clean this up, the faster I get back to my boat."

He was moving about Harry's small flat.

Harry asked, "So what brought you here today, Nolan?"

"Hook — I understand you've met him — gave me the file. Saw you'd found the body. Thought we could renew our acquaintance."

"Ha! So you can build a phony case against me again?"

This was news to me. I'd have to get Harry to come across on Lester Nolan.

"I met Brophy on the street just now. He tells me you've got a client who's hired you to find the murderer."

"Oh, yeah?"

"Who's the client?"

"You know I'm not going to tell you that."

"Why, Melville, we always worked well together."

"Sure we did."

A silence ensued, and I pictured each trying to stare the other down.

"You were muddying the waters."

"Maybe getting too much attention?"

I took another swig of gin. They were

circling each other. Nolan's voice was honeyed, Harry's angry. I knelt and peered through the keyhole. Couldn't see anything. It was as if someone had his hand over it. Had Harry hung his jacket there?

Now back on my feet, I leaned on the door. The next thing I knew, the door was thrown open. Unmoored, I was on the floor, the bottle clutched to my breast, and throughout, Harry swearing to beat the band.

"May I help you, Miss . . . ?" From my humiliating position I saw dark trousers and two-toned shoes.

"Brown," I said with as much poise as I could muster from my present posture.

Nolan took the bottle of gin I was clutching and helped me to my feet. Harry swore under his breath.

When I looked up at Lester Nolan, I saw why Harry hadn't wanted me on the case.

Chapter Twenty

As I imagined from his voice, Lester Nolan was incredibly handsome. I was wrong about his hair, which was blond, streaked with gray. He bore a striking resemblance to the moving picture actor Richard Barthelmess. His rugged physique and leathery skin were indicative of someone who worked outdoors. On a fishing boat in the Florida Keys, perhaps? His eyes, blue as a winter sky, assured me. Everything about him inspired trust.

Yet instinct told me he was too good to be true. How could Harry think I'd fall for him? Because I saw now that's exactly what Harry had been afraid would happen. Was it possible that Harry hadn't wanted me involved because he knew, though free love was my credo, I trusted very few, perhaps only Mattie and him, and he liked it that way?

It followed logically then that Harry said, "Oliver was just leaving, weren't you, Oliver?"

"I do have an appointment." I smiled at

Lester Nolan, trying to remember what I'd overheard Harry saying. Something about Nolan's once falsifying evidence to get Harry thrown into jail?

"Miss Brown," Nolan said. He was still holding my hand, petting it as if it were a small animal. "I wanted to hear your own thoughts on the murder in Croton, so be it now or another time . . ."

The man's presence was so extravagant, I couldn't find words, which is astonishing in itself. I wanted to tell him my every intimate thought, confess my every indiscretion. "Another time. Yes?" I murmured.

Clever old Harry cleared his throat and pointed his index finger from me to the sofa. I intuited there'd be no "another time," if he had anything to say about it. I reclaimed my hand and sat down. Nolan remained standing.

Methodically, Lester Nolan reviewed the events of the weekend. He asked me to describe several times the twins running about without Adelle when I came back from my walk, what the twins had said about Adelle in the tree, which I hadn't understood until too late.

"Hasn't Hook talked with the kids?" Harry asked.

"I think there's some question of just

where Mrs. Vaude and her children are," Nolan said. He paused, as if waiting for us to fill in the missing information. When we didn't offer anything, he asked Harry to describe how we found Adelle. Asked me if Harry'd left anything out.

"Not that I can think of." I kept my answers spare, for which I felt Harry's tacit approval.

"And you don't know where Kate Vaude and the children have gone?"

"Why not ask her husband?" Harry said. Speaking to me, "I say, Oliver, didn't Hook tell us he was heading over to talk to Fordy?"

Nolan watched our performance with icy eyes. "Hook talked to him. Vaude says he doesn't know anything."

"About Kate or about Adelle's murder?" I asked innocently.

The winter-sky orbs settled on me for a long moment. "You told me that Mr. Vaude wasn't present when the girl's body was found."

"That's true," Harry said. He leaned back and put his feet on his desk. I guess I was holding my own with the notorious Nolan.

Nolan drew a notepad from his back pocket. "He had left with one of the other

142

guests, a Miss Celia Gillam. That's the journalist, Celia Gillam?"

As there was only one Celia Gillam, we both said yes. I admit to a short attention span except when I'm writing. Now I wearied of the pretense and began to find Nolan's aura of benevolence oppressive.

I made a show of looking at my tiny gold wristwatch, whose hands I noted had stopped at six because I invariably forget to wind it. "Oh, dear, I do have that appointment." I directed my feet to the door. "I'm sure Harry can answer the rest of your questions, dear Mr. Nolan, but you may call on me whenever you like. If I'm not working, I'll be happy to speak with you."

"Working, Miss Brown? What sort of work do you do?"

Harry guffawed, and I took my leave in something of a snit.

The seat of my chair, in spite of the cushion, had grown uncomfortable. My head ached and my eyes burned. No visit from my Muse. *Muse, have you deserted me? Perhaps I'll conjure up Reed and let his spirit be my Muse.*

Conjure your divine Reed.

I laughed. My Muse does not like competition.

I gave it up. Somehow I'd managed to squander the whole day without a single word on paper. This wouldn't do if I were to have a book ready by spring. I covered my typewriter and emptied my overflowing ashtray. I felt a heaviness settle in my limbs. Without a by-your-leave, the striking visage of Lester Nolan loomed up in my conscious mind. Were it not for Harry, I fear I might have put my trust in him. I confess, I'm a poor judge of character.

I dragged myself from my chair and opened the window, drawing deep breaths of the cold, dry air. On Bedford Street, the noise of daytime traffic, the spontaneous burst of Italian from delivery people and shopkeepers of my little Village, the shrieks and laughter of the children, all worked to revive me. My lungs seemed to expand with every breath I drew, sweeping away the cobwebs in my brain.

"Olivia, you'll catch your death," Mattie said. She had brought tea and tiny butter-and-jam sandwiches. "Are you still working?"

I shook my head. "Not a good day. Stay and have tea with me."

"I want to finish your dress," she said, closing the window and stoking the fire.

"And it wouldn't hurt you to rest."

She was right. I was overtired. That's why I couldn't work. I couldn't blame that on Lester Nolan, though I would have liked to. I lay back on my bed and let Mattie mother me. She filled my teacup, added sugar and milk, and passed it to me, then insisted that I try a sandwich. I had two. Smoothing my unruly hair from my face, Mattie kissed my forehead and tucked me up with the woolly blanket.

"I'll read for a while," I said, taking one of the two complete John Donnes from the bedside table.

Stephen Lowell's unread letter was in the book where I'd left it earlier. I removed it and gently sliced it open with my fingernail. I knew what was in it. We'd been sending each other love sonnets for some time, since before we'd actually met. Here was another.

I always read the sonnet first before his letter. His sonnets kindled my hopes that we might have a future together, but his letters always dashed them. He was, after all, a married man, with a child, and his letters were filled with banal news of the family. This one was no different.

Stephen's new sonnet, however, induced the same old thrill, filled me with a terrible yearning. He was, in truth, my inspiration, the mate of my soul. We would go on exchanging love in fourteen lines, and maybe one day . . .

I buried my face in my pillow and wept. I must have slept, and deeply, too, for when I awoke it was quite dark. The tea tray was gone. I got up and washed my face, fluffed my hair with my fingers. My mirror showed a green-eyed child whose elfin features were still swollen with the effects of sleep . . . and tears.

From Mattie's room came the reassuring hum of the Singer machine. I came into her room, sat myself down in the soft slipper chair, and watched her work, as I had since childhood, her lips holding tight to pins. The cloud of rosy chiffon brought a bloom to her face. I rose and stood behind her, wrapped my arms round her soft frame. "I love you so, Mattie."

She lifted her feet from the treadle and looked up at me. "You've had another letter from Stephen Lowell." It was a statement, not a question.

"He is not leaving his wife, he has no plans to come to New York. But he sent me another sonnet. I suffocate in his ambivalence." I sank back into the chair. "Shall I make us martinis?"

"Yes, do," she said.

The very act of making a batch of martinis restored me somewhat, and then the appearance of Bunny and Whit, determined to take me to dinner at Polly's, restored me even more.

After all, a girl does need her admirers.

Chapter Twenty-one

Polly's, on the ground floor below the Liberal Club at Fourth Street and Sheridan Square, was only a short walk from Bedford Street. Tonight, as almost every night, the little tearoom reverberated with wild talk and raucous laughter, enough to crowd out all transient thought. Every table was occupied and the overflow were standing, drinks in hand, heckling the diners. Usually I preferred Christine's over the Playhouse, where one could find good conversation at lower decibels, but Polly's was what I needed this night.

"Helas, bébé!" Hippolyte Havel, Polly's tiny but fierce-looking anarchist lover, as well as chef and waiter, shouted his usual greeting to one and all above the noise. My own personal welcome came when he clutched me to his bosom, tickling me with his pointed goatee and wicked mustaches as he slathered my face with kisses. Behind his spectacles, his eyes were truly mad. He shouted at me, "What do you want here, Oliver, with all these bourgeois pigs?"

Polly Holladay, a quiet girl from Illinois, was also an anarchist. She accepted Hippolyte's enthusiasms and loved him for, or in spite of, them. I could never be certain. What was certain: We could get a very nice meal at Polly's, Hippolyte being in a fair mood, for thirty-five cents.

It was only because Hippolyte liked me that we were seated at a table ahead of those waiting. "Reserved! Reserved!" he snarled, pushing everyone aside. "Finished!" he yelled at the couple who were having coffee after their meal at the table he meant for us. "Pay up and get out, bourgeois pigs!" He held out his palm, and the intimidated gentleman put two silver dollars into it. The woman's mouth hung open; her eyes, like saucers, gawked at us.

"I'm so sorry," I told them as they tried to slip away. "Really I am."

My escorts placed me between them and immediately vied for my attention.

"I'll get your drink, Oliver," Whit said.

"A Booth martini," Bunny said. "Oliver will have a Booth. And so will I." Bunny had a particular affection for Booth's gin.

"It would be nice if you asked me what I want," I said.

Bunny looked chagrined. "Of course, Oliver. What do you want?"

Truly, I wanted a martini, Booth's or otherwise, but I didn't like people to take it on themselves to make decisions for me. "I'll have wine tonight, thank you."

Eventually, amid the noise and throng, Hippolyte, in a vile temper, reappeared. He dumped our plates on the table and, muttering imprecations, left us. I picked at the stewed beef while my two admirers picked at each other. After Whit went off to get another cocktail and didn't come right back, Bunny asked if I wanted to go upstairs to the Liberal Club.

I demurred. "I'm not in the mood for fervent debate tonight."

"Then we shall go to the Brevoort for a nightcap," he declared.

The café in the cellar of the Brevoort Hotel was the place we frequented when we had the dough, which meant our visits were infrequent.

I had to make a stop at the washroom, where I found the usual line, as it was for boys as well as girls.

When I came out, I didn't see Bunny at all.

"Oliver! Over here." It was a woman's voice, and a hand waved an Isadora scarf at me over the heads of the revelers. I followed the signal and came to a table toward the rear of the room where Celia sat with Margaret Anderson and jane heap, the two women who published *The Little Review*. Jane insisted that her name always be in lowercase, so we complied. The fourth woman had a lovely face but was considerably older than the rest of us.

"Join us," Celia said. It was a command.

"Girls," I said. I rested my hand on Celia's shoulder, aware of her arm round my waist, her fingers dancing on my ribs.

"Oliver," Margaret said. Pretty and blonde, she hardly looked the zealot, yet she had started a celebrated literary magazine with nary a cent to her name and had enlisted Ezra Pound and Hart Crane to help edit and provide material. They'd published *Ulysses* in installments until the obscenity patrol told them they must stop.

Jane heap dressed mannishly and was not at all as charming as Margaret. In fact, she hardly ever contributed to conversation.

"We have not met," I said, holding out my hand to the older woman. "I'm Olivia Brown."

She had a firm handshake and a callused hand. "Virginia Champion," she said. "I knew Vangie and Alice quite well."

"You did?" I was thrilled. Harry was the

only other person I'd met who had known my great-aunt and her friend well.

"I made the bird fountain sculpture for them for their twentieth anniversary."

The beautiful sculpture to which she referred was that of two nude lovers — women — seductively entwined that had been mounted in the garden behind my house. It had been viciously destroyed last month, but that's another story.

"I loved that sculpture," I said. "You know —"

"I know all about it." Virginia had pale blue eyes, fine skin, and a frizz of snowy hair. "My studio is on Commerce Street, above the Cherry Lane Theatre. I can see into your backyard."

"I've wanted to replace it, but I had no idea —"

"Oliver! I might have known." Bunny shoved his way to us. The look he sent Celia was that of one rival to another.

Celia smiled and, with a flick of her wrist, spun me into Bunny's arms.

I couldn't hide my laugh, and Virginia's eyes flickered. She spoke very softly, so that only I heard. "Call on me."

"I will," I said, and waved adieu.

Bunny hailed a taxi and quickly negotiated our transport to Eighth Street and

Fifth Avenue for the grand sum of twenty-five cents.

We were arguing about something, I've forgotten what, when we climbed out of the cab and made our way to the door of the hotel. A group of tourists, as we call those who come to the Village to view us bohemians, were leaving. They couldn't help but nudge each other, giving us the eye, for we were what they had come to see.

"Tell yourrrr forrrrtuna, meeess?" I said in an outrageous Hungarian accent, hunching over and leering gnomishly at one of the beautifully dressed uptown oglers. With a mad squint, I reached for her hand.

Shocked, she backed away, staring at me as if I were a rara avis, which we all know I am. "Er — I — I'm, er —"

Bunny laughed.

"Come along, Nan," her escort said nervously. "Don't you see they're having us on?"

I became the poet Olivia Brown again, and we stood aside to let them out.

"You are quite the funniest girl, Oliver," Bunny said. "Come along. That was a Champagne performance, if ever I saw one."

We were guffawing, holding on to one another as we finally entered the lobby of the Brevoort, where we encountered another group of tourists.

Bunny began, "Now behave your . . ." then his voice trailed off. "Daisy!"

Yes, it was indeed Daisy, in her fur-collared coat and brimmed hat with its little veil. When she saw us a curl of dismay slipped across her lips.

"Daisy," Bunny said again. He seemed shocked, hurt, outraged to see her, as if she had somehow betrayed him.

"It's late," Daisy said, holding her gloved hand in front of her face. To ward off further unspoken recrimination from Bunny?

I was confused. There was that same possessive reaction from Bunny about Daisy that I'd noticed at the Working Girls' Home.

What was between them? And why was she at the Brevoort unescorted at this time of night?

"Rats," Bunny said under his breath, because it had suddenly become obvious Daisy was not alone.

Her companion had stopped to light his cigar, which was why at first we hadn't placed him with her. When he looked up and saw us, Fordy Vaude was just as stunned as we were.

"If she was a Pinkerton, Harry, what was she doing working as a nanny for Kate and Fordy?"

"We'll have to ask Daisy, won't we?"

I'd forgotten all about Daisy. "Maybe she's a Pinkerton, too."

He patted my hand. "You have a grand imagination, Oliver."

"And thanks for the roses, Harry . . . really. It was sweet of you."

"Monk sent you the roses, Oliver. Where would I get money for roses in winter?"

I stopped and made him stop. "You don't have to worry about me, Harry."

"Oh, I don't? Well, that's very nice of you to let me know."

And so we walked in companionable silence, and as we got to Washington Square, I remembered Kate.

"You'll never guess who I ran into at the Working Girls' Home after rehearsal."

"I'm all ears."

"The vanished Kate Vaude. She's boarding the twins with her parents in Hartford and rented a room on Twelfth Street."

"Did she now? She knows Hook is looking for her?"

"She knows now. She asked me not to tell on her. And I won't. I'm only letting

Chapter Twenty-two

I tried to work, but with my thoughts ricocheting, I started, stopped, crossed out, tore paper from my typewriter, until I was surrounded by crumpled morbid couplets and bleak quatrains. How was I to write a love sonnet to Stephen Lowell without declaring my love? And, then, how wondrous strange the mind is:

> *My Ardor comes in fourteen lines*
> *As form, my dear, to us proscribes.*
> *Thus no imag'ry of love designs*
> *Intrusion into other lives.*
> *I press upon the metrical fence*
> *With torrid words that feed the flame.*
> *I give you measured reverence,*
> *In such cadence I see no shame.*
> *So wrestle I with grace and Bard*
> *To versify within this bond,*
> *I am pentam, my boulevard.*
> *And how in truth will you respond?*
> *Within my sestet, resolution;*
> *But for our love, no absolution.*

My fingers rested on the keys as if they wanted to proceed, but I had nothing left. I laid my fevered forehead on the cold metal. The fire, now barely glowing embers, gave off no heat. In the cold of my room I was a raging inferno. I left "My Ardor" in the typewriter and crawled into bed.

"It's from Fordy." I waved the formal notepaper in front of Harry. Having fallen asleep to the sound of the milk wagon, I hadn't awakened till noon. "He's invited me to supper, on his best stationery. What do you think?" I'd just finished telling Harry about last evening.

"I think he's going to try to explain what he was doing with Daisy. Is there more coffee, Mattie?"

"More than enough," Mattie said. "Why not ask Daisy herself?"

Harry put out his cigarette. "Maybe I'll just drop in on her at *Vanity Fair*."

"Celia was at Polly's with *The Little Review* girls and a Virginia Champion."

"Champ," Harry said. Beaming was not a description anyone would ever use about Harry, but he was doing just that.

"She did the garden sculpture," I told Mattie.

"The old girls helped her get started," Harry said. "Haven't seen her since Vangie passed."

"Maybe I'll commission her to redo it, what do you think, Mattie? As a memorial to Aunt Evangeline and Alice." I suppose now I'll have to work extra hard to finish the poems for my book, else where's the money to come from?

"That would be a nice thing." Mattie refilled our coffee cups and sat down with us. "I rather miss it."

"Talked to Kate while you were out on the town," Harry said. His dark eyes were clear under their pale lashes. No hangover.

I was neither clear-eyed nor sharply focused, which is why my reply was a spare, "Oh?"

"She said Fordy brought Adelle home one evening, saying he'd hired her to look after the children so that Kate could write. Supposedly Adelle had graduated from Vassar and needed a job while she decided what she wanted to do."

"But how did Fordy find Adelle?"

"I'm getting to it, Oliver. Detective work is about patience, of which you have little. Fordy told Kate that Adelle's uncle had been one of his professors at Yale. She'd come to his office with a letter of introduction."

"I suppose they never checked her out."

"Well, Kate didn't because the kids liked her immediately and Fordy seemed to know Adelle's family."

"Do you think any of that is true?"

"Probably, from Kate's side. You'll have to see if Fordy's story fits into the puzzle."

"Did Kate say that Adelle's behavior was odd in any way? After all, she was a Pinkerton, even if she wasn't working for Pinkerton anymore. Maybe she'd gone into business as a detective for herself." I grinned at him and patted myself on the back. "We New Women are an ambitious lot."

"Sure," Harry said with his most dubious expression. "And that and a nickel will get you on the subway."

"So go on, did she do anything out of the ordinary?"

"She was there only three months, but Kate said she settled in fine and even found herself a boyfriend."

"Astonishing." I stubbed out my cigarette. "A boyfriend. And no one's brought up this boyfriend till now? Do you think Deputy Hook knows about him, or Nolan?"

"I think they might have asked us about him, if they'd known he existed."

"So who is he and how do we find him?" My questions seemed to amuse Harry.

"I thought you might be able to help us out here, Oliver," he said.

I couldn't help being irritated. "Let me in on the joke, please."

"Well," said Harry, "it seems the boyfriend lives right in Croton. His folks own a bookshop."

Chapter Twenty-three

We had supper at the Yale Club, where our Fordy was known as Fordham Vaude III, no less, class of '12.

Picture a large, undistinguished building on Vanderbilt Avenue in the very shadow of Grand Central Terminal. The dining room, on the twentieth floor, is the size of a ballroom, an elegant presentation, with crystal chandeliers and acres of tables covered with white linen.

Our host was a formally dressed gentleman, whose girth and shag of white hair and noble beard bespoke the halls of academe. The waiters were all tall, distinguished-looking Negroes, servicing tables so discreetly positioned that private conversations could not possibly be overheard.

I wore my shabby black dress, but Mattie had swathed me in a wisteria silk shawl and pinned it to my shoulder with a brooch of rose quartz, which had belonged to my mother.

At table, Fordy lit my cigarette, and almost immediately the cognac appeared.

While I watched, he went through the process of rolling, clipping, and dipping his cigar in the cognac before lighting it.

While this pretentious exhibition played out, I let my eyes wander about the room, checking out the other diners, the women being considerably better dressed than I, and everyone much older than we. This gracious place represented a whole other world. Fordy fit like a leather glove, but this was no place for a true bohemian. I was sorely tempted to stand up in the hushed, well-bred atmosphere and shout as Hippolyte Havel did, "Bourgeois pigs!" The very thought made me giggle.

"You look lovely tonight, Oliver," Fordy said, drawing my attention back to him. I saw a man with a slightly receding hairline of baby fine brown hair, the beginning of pouches under lascivious eyes, and shadowed jaws. Even seated, I could see the slight bulge of belly, made more pronounced by the drape of his watch chain.

"Thank you, kind sir." I flirted with him, wondering why he'd brought me here, why he thought I'd be impressed with all that it implied. Did he actually think I found him attractive? Or had he brought me here because he was certain none of our friends would ever see us?

"I would suggest the roast lamb, Mr. Vaude," our host said after our martinis arrived and we'd tilted our glasses to each other, *comme il faut.*

So we had the roast lamb with mint jelly and creamed spinach with little potatoes. And while Fordy expounded on the work of an obscure Viennese artist named Schiele, who had died of influenza in 1918, we kept drinking martinis until I quite lost count.

When our custards arrived, I pointed my cigarette holder at him. "Shall we now tell each other the truth?"

"Whatever do you mean, Oliver?" he asked, discreetly beckoning the waiter. "Port." He looked at me, and I nodded. Enough was not in my vocabulary.

"This." I made a small sweep with my hand. "Why?"

"Why does any man take a beautiful girl out on the town?"

"I'm not asking any man. I'm asking you."

He reached for my hand. "I've wanted to make love to you, Oliver, since the very first time we met. Certainly you know that."

His palm was clammy. I removed my hand. "I know nothing of the sort. What I know is that you left Kate for Celia. Now you say you want me. Really, Fordy, are you building a harem?"

His laugh was nasal, high-pitched. "Celia? Celia prefers the company of women."

"So you're looking for a replacement?" I was angry and decided Fordy was quite repulsive.

He laughed again. "I'd like to paint you, Oliver. You have the neck and throat of a sylph, and for a plain little mouse of a girl, when you get angry or do a performance, you're quite beautiful."

Plain little mouse of a girl? What did Kate and Celia see in this buffoon? Still, I was not ready to end the evening. I looked at him over the rim of my coffee cup. "Were you making love to Adelle as well?"

"Adelle? Why would you think that? Adelle was a stiff."

I choked and reached for the port the waiter had just delivered.

"I didn't mean that. I meant she wasn't someone you wanted to make love to." He winked at me. "Like you, Oliver."

I'd had enough, and who could blame me? "Harry and I have been hired to investigate Adelle's murder."

The unctuous expression on Fordy's face evaporated. "Who hired you?"

"I'm not at liberty to say."

"Harry will tell me."

"Fine. You may ask him."

"Don't think I won't."

"While we're waiting," I said, "why not tell me how Adelle came to be your nanny."

"That's none of your affair."

"I'm sure you've told Deputy Hook, so what could it hurt to tell me? I heard she was the daughter of one of your professors at Yale."

"No, she was his niece. All right," he said, resigned. "She brought a letter to my studio by way of introduction. Damn." He hit his head with the palm of his hand. "This is intolerable. I should have telephoned him and expressed my condolences and tried to explain what happened, but with my leaving Kate, it just slipped my mind."

"You can still do it. Not that much time has passed. Go on with your story."

"Having just graduated from Vassar, Adelle was looking for a job with young children until she could find a position as a teacher. She was willing to work for a small salary, and Kate needed time away from the twins to write."

"Professor Zimmer?"

"No. Professor Adolphus. Philosophy. Nice old duck, but a bit eccentric. A real enthusiast of barbershop quartets."

"Are you aware that her name was not Adelle Zimmer?"

"What?" He almost dropped his cup. Coffee sloshed over the lip.

"Her real name was Adeline Zimmerman, and at one time, before coming to work for you, she was a Pinkerton."

"Good God!" His face was pale as the tablecloth. I felt eyes on us and a stir from nearby tables, and Fordy must have felt the same, as he lowered his voice. "I can't believe what you're saying. Adelle, a Pinkerton? Do the police know?"

"Yes."

"Then what was she doing in my house, with my children, in Croton?" He looked so upset, I was beginning to believe not only that he hadn't known, but that he was not hiding anything. "Does Kate know all this?"

"I think Harry told her."

"My God. I must telephone Adolphus immediately. There must be some explanation."

"May I be present when you do?"

"Of course, Oliver. I have nothing to hide." Yet beads of sweat dotted his balding crown and upper lip. "So this would have been what that suntanned detective was hinting around about."

"You mean Lester Nolan?"

"Yes. Looks a little like the movie actor Richard Barthelmess, don't you think? He said he's working the case with Deputy Hook because all of us are here, not in Croton."

"Except for Dave."

"Right, though he's been camping out with me in my studio since yesterday."

"Did you know she had a sister?"

"Adelle, I mean, Adeline? She had a sister? No. Why should I know that?"

"Because you've met her, because you were with her last night. Her name is Daisy. She works at *Vanity Fair*."

He was stunned. "Not that Daisy, the one Bunny's been trotting around?"

"The very one."

"By the way, I wasn't with her."

"You weren't? You could have fooled me."

"I stopped by for a drink and she was at the bar, getting a little smashed, I might add. She asked me to see her home. That's the sum of it."

It seemed a plausible accounting, but why did I think he was not telling me the whole truth? "Did you see her home?"

"I had no idea she was Adelle's sister."

"You spent the night, then?"

"Well, it was convenient for both of us." He leered at me. "Are you just a little bit jealous?"

"Not at all. What d'you think about all of this?"

"I'd like to hire you myself to find out."

"I'll mention it to Harry. Tell me about Carl Danenberg."

"You mean the kid from Croton?"

"Yes. He was at your party. And I had a nice little visit with him and his mother at the bookshop when I was in Croton."

"He's at Columbia. So he sometimes comes by to . . . You met the old girl, did you?" A broad smile spread over his face. "And did she ply you with strudel?" The smile broke into laughter, which he smothered with the napkin. I didn't understand the joke, and I felt myself getting hot. Moving the napkin from his lips, he said, "I don't think you looked at the bookshelves too carefully."

"What am I not fathoming here?" I was downright surly.

"Oh, old man Danenberg travels

through the state with his cartons all right, but they don't really hold books. The Danenbergs are bootleggers."

Chapter Twenty-four

Fordy's yellow roadster had barely reached Twelfth Street when an icy rain started with a few sharp points and ended as a deluge of needling exclamations.

"There's an umbrella in the rumble seat," Fordy said. He started to pull over, but I told him not to trouble himself. Truth was, the rain felt good on my face.

In a minute or so we drove up in front of No. 42 Washington Square South. Fordy turned off the motor, jumped out of the car. He lifted the lid to the rumble seat and collected an umbrella, which he opened, and a roll of canvas. Handing me the umbrella, he helped me out, then proceeded to cover the roadster with the canvas.

There's nothing worse than the bestial smell and feel of wet fur, don't you agree? Fordy hung up my coat to dry and went to work building a cozy fire. I removed my sodden hat, got out of my wet shoes, and curled up on the sofa. With the room less populous, I could see the paintings, many of which were nudes, that hung on every inch of the wall. Actually, though I was reminded of the pornography scandal Harry and Paulo had spoken of, Fordy's work was interesting, if most violent in texture, color, and line.

While I studied the paintings, he left the room and returned in his shirtsleeves, a towel round his neck. He handed the damp towel off to me, got down on his knees, and stuffed crumpled newspaper into my poor shoes. His hair was darkly wet and curled against his forehead. He seemed at once sweetly boyish.

I reached out and touched a wayward wisp. "You can be a nice fella, Fordy, when you try."

He lifted eyes so full of lust, I drew back. "I am, Oliver, if you'll give me a chance."

"I'll think about it," I said, light as I could manage.

"I'll paint you in the nude, a toilette."

In a pig's eye, I thought.

He got to his feet and put on a record and wound the Victrola. The romantic strains of "Whispering" filled the room.

"Gin coming right up." He opened a bottle of gin and filled two glasses, setting them on the table in front of the sofa.

"Wouldn't you like to get out of those wet clothes?"

"Not wet," I said, but I rolled down my damp stockings and draped them over the arm of the sofa to dry. "I thought you were going to call Professor Adolphus. If you're not, I'll thank you for the nice dinner and say good night."

"You are a very single-minded girl, Oliver," Fordy said. He ran his hand down my bare leg and then, sighing, went to the telephone, which sat on its own little table. "Dr. Greeve, my psychoanalyst, says I need someone like you. What does yours say?"

"Actually, Fordy, I'm not about to let anyone meddle with my head."

"A great mistake, Oliver. Psychoanalysis expands the mind. You can't know how creative you can be unless you are analyzed." As he spoke, he thumbed through a small leather address book until he found what he was looking for and asked the operator to connect him.

It was at this point that we heard laughter and heavy footsteps coming down the hallway. The herd of laughing elephants opened Fordy's door and Dave came in with a plump blonde I'd seen round the Village. They were soaked to the skin, very drunk, and singing a decidedly

171

off-tune version of "Blowing Bubbles."

"Thank you, operator," Fordy said. "Yes, that's right."

"Oliver!" Dave threw himself down on the sofa near me and, before I could stop him, hugged me, a bear hug from a drenched dog. His thick wet hair clung to my face.

The girl, bedraggled in sopping wool and stringy hair, giggled and hiccoughed. "Davy," she said.

Dave jumped up and stumbled into the table on which rested Fordy's and my glasses of gin. Everything went flying. "This is —" A confused frown, and, "What did you say your name was, kid?"

"Trudy." She spoke with a lisp and an indeterminate accent. "I need the toilet, Davy."

"Hello?" Fordy's face became animated. "Professor Adolphus, is that you?"

"Dave, do you mind?" I stood up. "Fordy's making a phone call."

"Fordham Vaude, here, sir. . . . Yes. . . . I'm very well, thank you. I'm sorry to be calling so late."

Dave tilted left. "Oh, sure, sorry. Come on, Trudy, I'll show you."

The two of them tottered down the short hall and into the bathroom. The door slammed, and Trudy's giggle turned into a baby shriek, followed by more laughter.

Clearly I hadn't drunk enough to find Dave and Trudy either funny or interesting. What I wanted was to get as much information as I could from Fordy and go home.

"I say, sir," Fordy said, "I'm so sorry about your niece. . . . Niece, yes, Adelle . . . Adeline. Poor girl. I feel awfully responsible. After all, you sent her to me —" He suddenly stopped talking and, as he listened, looked at me, appalled.

"What is it?" I asked, standing close to him, trying to hear what Professor Adolphus was saying.

"Dreadfully sorry, sir. . . . Yes, of course, I'd be happy to." He hung the receiver on the hook and looked down at me but didn't speak.

Another giggling shriek came from the bathroom and then a crash.

I shook Fordy's arm. "What did he tell you?"

"I don't understand, Oliver," Fordy said, bewildered. "He said he has no niece, that, in fact, he has no brothers and his sister has never married, that he is a confirmed bachelor, and has never sent anyone to me for any reason whatever."

Chapter Twenty-five

Fordy brought me home, thinking, I'm sure, that he would be invited up. I pleaded profound fatigue. Truly, I worked very hard to conceal my elation. I wanted to share the news about Professor Adolphus with Harry, but he didn't answer my ring, and I saw no light under his door.

And at this hour I wouldn't have awakened Mattie for the world. There was nothing for it but to retire. After hanging my coat and hat on the hall stand, shoes in hand, I climbed the stairs to my room. I was not ready for sleep. Like the owl, I looked to the night for celebration, and inspiration, and for the plush purple peace it offered.

After coaxing a bit of warmth from the fading fire, I sat at my typewriter in my nightie, shawl round my shoulders, and rolled in a sheet of paper. With the best of intentions, Mattie had left a cozied pot of tea for me. But tea would not do tonight. I groped under my desk for the bottle of wine I'd sequestered there for an incident with an intruder — which I'll not speak of now — and we'd resolved always to keep our front and back doors locked. But we were often lax. This time it wasn't our fault.

"Gerry was in a bit of a hurry when he left," I said. "I think you might find the reason rather interesting." I noted the fresh bottle of gin. "Signore Dionysus delivered?"

"He did. And your case is in the kitchen. By the way, Oliver, you might want to put the bunch of roses in some water."

"Roses at this time of year, Harry? You shouldn't have."

"I didn't. They came with the case I ordered for you."

"I'll see to the roses," Mattie said. "Who sent them?"

I hummed a little of the *Apassionata* under my breath, and Mattie gave me a sharp look. She took a cigarette from the box on the side table and lit one and handed it to me, then lit one for herself.

"Oliver made herself another conquest this morning."

" 'They also serve who only stand and wait.' "

"Not Signore Dionysus." Mattie was speechless.

just such an occasion.

I filled the cup with wine, lifted it to my lips, reflecting on the past few days. I set down the cup. My fingers returned to the keys.

Hear, Death, do not rely on me
To welcome you into my home,
Or go with you obligingly
Before I feel my work is done.
She whose soul you wrenched away
Before her time had not full dower
Of life and love. Nor I. So, pray,
Pale Priest, seek me not within the hour.

In death she was a conundrum, this Adeline Zimmerman. How had she gotten to Fordy and Kate, if not through Professor Adolphus? If she was no longer a Pinkerton, for whom was she working? While she may have appeared to be a nanny, she was, assuredly, involved in something much more dangerous. *It doesn't really matter,* she'd said. *I've played this game before,* she'd said.

Well, it mattered to me. I put a cigarette into its holder and padded over to the window, parting the draperies. The ice storm had subsided. Below, the street lamp made a glistening treasure of everything in

175

its path, except for the dark figure in the derby posited under the lamp, with only his long shadow for company. Cupping his hand, he lit a cigarette, then looked directly up at me. I suddenly realized he could see me, for the light from the lamp on my desk gave me a frame. Looking for the protection of my shawl, I found it not on my shoulders, but dangling from the back of my chair.

As if he'd been waiting for me, the man lifted his fingers to his derby and, seemingly satisfied, disappeared into the darkness.

Then a dark green sedan pulled up in front of my house and Harry got out. He leaned back in, and I saw the creamy hand of a woman reach out to him. Well.

I stood away from the window for a moment but came right back, as I'm an artist and, therefore, a voyeur. But the sedan had driven away, and the shriek of the gate told me Harry was indeed home.

Wrapping my errant shawl round my shoulders, I went downstairs, and downstairs again, and gave Harry's bell a sharp twist.

"Come on in, Oliver."

I opened the door and stepped in. "How did you know?"

"You were standing in the window like a beacon," he said. "Waiting up for me, were you?" He wore dinner clothes, though he'd removed his jacket.

"Really, Harry," I said, affronted. "If you must know, I'd been working. I stood up to stretch my legs, looked out the window, and spied a man under the street lamp. He appeared to be watching the house because when he caught sight of me, he saluted and withdrew. Surely you saw him when your lady delivered you in that fancy automobile."

"Didn't see anyone. An imaginary secret admirer?" He gave me a clownish wink, sat down at his desk, and tilted back in his chair, putting his feet up. "How was your dinner?"

I found his attitude provoking and chose not to sit. "He took me to the Yale Club."

"Of course." Harry acted as if he and Fordy shared some boy-to-boy secret, and I grew even more rankled.

"Why do you say, 'Of course'?"

"Wise up, Oliver, he's trying to get into your knickers."

"Well, he'll just have to get on line with the rest," I retorted.

Harry set his feet on the floor and produced his bottle of Scotch from the drawer. He took a swig and offered it to me. I shook my head and waited, trying to remain blasé under Harry's cool appraisal.

"What is it, Harry?" I said. I smoothed the skirt of my nightie, adjusted the shawl. He was making me nervous, unsure of myself. I looked down at my bare feet. Nothing unusual.

"Forget it, Oliver."

I felt peculiar, drained, as if he'd wrung me through a wringer. I didn't understand Harry when he got like this. "I'll have a taste of that," I said, taking the bottle. I tilted my head back and took a good swallow, returned the bottle to Harry, and, with care, sat on the sofa.

"How did the detecting go?" he asked casually.

Well, what I'd sensed must have been an aberration, as I was myself again. "Adelle, Adeline, arrived with a letter of introduction from Fordy's philosophy professor, a man named Adolphus. Fordy phoned him up while I was there, to offer condolences on Adeline's passing, and guess what?"

"Adolphus had no idea who she was."

"Oh, Harry, you knew."

"Good guess. Do you believe him?"

"I didn't talk to him, Fordy did. Why would he lie about it?"

Harry shrugged. "Maybe we should do some checking on this Adolphus. For example, why did Adelle choose him, true or not, to present her to Fordy?"

"You're right. I'll explore that. Perhaps I can arrange to meet the good professor."

"I have complete faith in you, Oliver."

I eyed him suspiciously. Was he pulling my leg? No way to tell, as his face was expressionless. "Another thing, Harry: Carl Danenberg."

"Adelle's so-called boyfriend and the kid who escorted you most of the way home and then skittered off like a scared rabbit."

"Well, I wouldn't go that far, but he seemed uneasy about being seen by anyone at the house."

"What about him?"

"He was at Fordy's party the other night, the young man with all the freckles. Did you see him?"

"Didn't." Then with feigned solemnity: "Though I admit to a fondness for freckles."

"Not like mine, Harry." I felt my cheeks flush. "His are really large and ruddy."

"So what about him?"

"According to Fordy, the bookshop is not a bookshop. The Danenbergs are accomplished bootleggers." I giggled. "As I remember now, they hustled me through the bookshop. Perhaps the only book they have in excess is *The Collected Poems of John Donne*."

"Sometimes the dog doesn't really have to bark," Harry said.

"Thank you, Mr. Sherlock Holmes. Okay, now you tell me. Did you catch up with Daisy at *Vanity Fair*? Fordy said she was sitting at the bar at the Brevoort last night totally smashed and asked him to take her home."

"Did he now?"

"He was shocked when I told him Daisy and Adelle — Adeline — are sisters."

"Was he now?"

"Why, Harry, I believe you're keeping something from me."

He offered me the bottle again. I passed. He took another swallow. "Our client says Fordy not only knew Adelle was her sister, but he invited Daisy to dinner, ostensibly to offer his condolences. In reality, it was to find out if Adelle had told her anything about life with the Vaudes."

"God, Fordy had me completely fooled. That means he could have been lying about Professor Adolphus, too."

"Don't be too hard on yourself, Oliver. Fordy could have been telling the truth and the fair Daisy could be the one who's lying."

"Why do you say that?"

"Because I followed her home."

I opened my mouth to speak.

"Don't ask me why. Call it instinct." He took another long pull from the bottle of Scotch. "I was interested to find that our Daisy has a lover."

"Ah, a lover. It must be Bunny."

"No, not Bunny. Or Fordy, for that matter. Daisy's lover is an old sport by the name of Lester Nolan."

Chapter Twenty-six

All that we see and seem is but a dream within a dream.

Poe's haunting verse burrowed into my mind. From the moment Harry pronounced that Daisy's lover was Lester Nolan, whenever I closed my eyes, the verse appeared in fire on a wind-whipped banner.

Harry smashed his fist down on his desk, sending papers and ashes flying. "It's a setup. But I can't figure it. Why me — us? For what? And with good money, too."

I picked up a bunch of papers that had landed in front of me and returned them to his desk. "Whose money is it, really? Daisy works at a magazine for peon's wages."

"It's Nolan. He set me up before. He thinks I'm his patsy."

"By the way, you owe me an apology," I said.

I'd caught him by surprise. "For what?"

"For thinking I'd fall for Nolan's phony charm and flashy looks. There's something untruthful about his character, and it comes through."

He tried to keep from laughing, but he couldn't. "Well, then, you have my most sincere apology."

"Thank you," I said, assuaged. "So it appears it's Nolan's money we're working with. Here I thought he's a retired cop."

"Yeah, a retired cop with a lot of mazuma to throw around, and a scheme involving a dead girl. What the hell is he up to?"

"Adeline Zimmerman, Harry. Gerry Brophy knew her, worked with her. And he knows Nolan."

"We're not even sure that this girl calling herself Daisy Zimmerman is really the dead girl's sister."

"We should talk with Gerry."

We agreed that I would see what I could get out of Gerry while Harry worked on Nolan and Daisy. At least I think we did.

The screech of the gate startled us awake.

"Bloody hell!" Harry staggered to his feet.

I'd dozed off on the sofa. We stared at each other. There came a thud from the vestibule. The gate screeched again as Harry threw open the door.

It was not Milton's "dewy-feathered slumber" I roused myself from, but a profound and dreamless oblivion I rarely experienced. So it was with some shock that I heard Harry's hoot of laughter.

"Oliver, come out here and see what you've done."

I was still half-asleep when, at the door, Harry thrust an open florist box filled with long-stemmed crimson roses into my arms. On the floor was a case of gin.

"Oooh, lovely," I cried, inhaling the scent of the roses but infinitely more delighted by the contents of the case. "Didn't we just get our order from —" I processed Harry's cynical expression. "Oh, dear, you think this is a gift from Monk Eastman."

"Don't think. Know."

"And he's showering me with favors?"

"Sooner or later, he's going to want something in return. That's the way it works."

"Well, we can't exactly refuse his gift, can we?"

"We? He's not interested in me, Oliver." Harry shouldered the case of gin. "Come on, I'll carry this up for you, and then I suggest we both get some shut-eye."

"I'll go talk to him, Harry, and explain. . . ."

Harry turned on the stairs and growled at me. "Wise up, Little Red Riding Hood."

When Gerry Brophy came by to see Mattie later that afternoon, I was sitting in the kitchen, filling her in on our progress, while she rolled out a pie crust.

"Did they look like sisters?" she'd just asked me.

Gerry's arrival interrupted us. Mattie's hands were flaked with flour, so I went to let him in.

We settled ourselves at the kitchen table and watched Mattie fill the crust with a tower of sugared-and-cinnamoned apple slices. "You didn't answer my question, Olivia."

"Did they look like sisters?" I pondered that. "Maybe. Maybe not. What do you say, Gerry?" Cunning of me, don't you think?

"You girls want to tell me what you're talking about?"

"This girl Daisy, who works at *Vanity Fair* and was at the Vaudes' with all of us, claims to be Adeline Zimmerman's sister. The question is, did Adeline Zimmerman have a sister?"

Under Gerry's intent gaze, I confess a fleeting streak of shame. Mattie dotted the apples with small chunks of butter, then rolled out the top crust. A long minute passed.

"What makes you think I know, Olivia?" Gerry plucked a leftover slice of apple from the bowl and ate it.

"You said you knew Adeline."

"I worked a case with her about a year ago. Doesn't mean I knew her."

Mattie folded the top crust in half and slashed out a little diamond to release the steam. Yes, slashed.

"Mattie's jealous," I said.

"I am not," Mattie said, crimson faced.

"I'd like it if you were, Mattie." What a dear man Gerry Brophy is.

Mattie rewarded him with a sweet smile, covered the apples with the top crust. After piercing it with the tongs of a fork, she fancy-fluted the top and bottom together.

The exchange between them filled me with so much pleasure, I almost forgot my assignment. It was Gerry himself who brought me back.

"You want to know what I know about Addie Zimmerman, is that it, Olivia?"

I nodded. Mattie painted the crust with a beaten egg and set the pie in the oven. "You knew the real girl, Gerry. The girl who worked as a nanny wasn't real."

"Addie was a good operative, knew her business. Smart. She could have been an actress, she was so good at playing a part."

"What kind of case was it?"

"Can't talk about it, but when we broke it, she should have gotten more credit. It's hard for a girl in this line of work."

"What makes a girl choose police work?" Mattie said, filling the kettle with water and setting up the tea things.

I answered her. "The adventure, Mattie. The danger."

"She never talked about anything personal," Gerry said. He took out his neatly folded handkerchief and, leaning over, dusted a bit of flour from Mattie's nose. "Though I think she felt she could do more if they let her."

"She talked about quitting?" I asked.

"She knew she would never go further with the Pinkertons. She liked being around us cops, but there's no future on the Force for a woman, except as a secretary. Maybe she should have talked to Harry."

"But she must have quit the Pinkertons for some other kind of investigation, Gerry. Do you suppose she was working on her own?"

"If she was, without her files or unless

her client comes forward, we'll never know."

The boiling kettle distracted us. Mattie warmed the teapot, then measured the leaves and steeped the tea.

"Did anyone think to look in the City Directory for a listing of her office?"

"Nolan did, I'm sure. . . ." His voice trailed off, and his attention went inward. "Nolan."

"What about Nolan?" I prodded, making a mental note to check the City Directory myself.

"Funny thing, now that I think of it." Gerry paused, took a sip of tea, rubbed his chin. "Nolan'd retired, moved away, but he came around from time to time. After we closed the case, a group of us took Addie for a drink before she left town — Chumley's, I think it was — and everybody was having a good time. It was getting late when we noticed that Addie was gone, and none of us had seen her go. Joe at the bar told us she'd left with Lester Nolan."

Chapter Twenty-seven

The Chelsea Poetry Circle met once a month in the Chelsea Hotel, a brick structure of some twelve stories, its iron balconies suggesting eclectic Victorian. Edward Hall had arranged a speaking engagement for me this night.

You can imagine my delight when we arrived and I saw the room filled to the rafters. They'd run out of folding chairs. The walls were lined with people, many definitely the uptown sort.

A whole day had passed, and more, since Gerry Brophy had connected Adeline and Nolan for us. Harry and I didn't know what to make of it. It was certainly beginning to look as though Harry were right. In some way, for some reason, we were being set up.

My instantaneous query was, "What do we do now?"

To which Harry'd responded, "Nothing. We need a plan."

I agreed. I'd already searched the City Directory and found no listings for either

Adeline Zimmerman or Adelle Zimmer.

"If she was running her own agency in the city, I'd know about it," he said. "A girl in this business would stand out like a sore thumb."

"Thanks, Harry," I said. A girl poet doesn't stand out like a sore thumb; I went back to work on my book. Or tried to, at least. My mind kept wandering off in different directions, the paths converging on Professor Adolphus. How was I going to arrange a meeting?

"Oliver," Edward said, bringing me back from my reverie. "This is Mrs. Finley Jorgenson, the president of the Poetry Circle. She will introduce you." He took my cloak from my shoulders, and my new dress of rainbow-colored chiffon shimmered round me.

"Oh, my, what a lovely dress!" Mrs. Jorgenson pumped my hand with enthusiasm. She was an imposing, pigeon-breasted woman well into her thirties. A loose-fitting wine wool suit only served to enlarge what was already there. On her head was a beaded black turban. "Such an honor to have you read from your work, Miss Brown. I can't tell you how excited we are to have you here."

Pressing my hands together to keep

them from shaking, I thanked her graciously. My nervousness was routine. I knew from experience, once I began, it disappeared entirely. I thrived on an audience.

At the far end of the room was a platform; on it, in the center, was a lectern taller than I, and two chairs well off to the side. Mrs. Jorgenson showed me to one chair and put some notepaper facedown on the other. "I'll be back shortly to introduce you," she said. "We're having tea and cakes afterward. All of our members are so eager to meet you."

My hostess moved through the audience, greeting people. My gaze followed her, albeit absently. My thoughts were on my recitation. So when my eyes passed over a familiar face, they kept on traveling.

Wait, I told myself. Go back. It was Carl Danenberg. I sent him a welcoming smile. It seemed just the invitation he needed, for he jumped up, spoke briefly to his neighbor, and made his way to the platform.

"Miss Brown," he said, coming right up onto the platform and getting down on one knee before me, almost absorbing me with his eyes.

"Are you proposing, Mr. Danenberg?"

"Oh — I — no — I'm sorry —" His face became so inflamed, I was sorry I'd teased him.

"I'm just razzing you, Mr. Danenberg. How is your kind mother?"

He recovered himself quickly. "She's well, Miss Brown. I told her I was coming to hear you read your poems tonight, and she asked that I send you her best regards."

Serendipity, was it not? A few stragglers were still looking for seats. Though I was the focus of everyone's attention, I might use this small nugget of time to query Carl about Adelle.

Taking up Mrs. Jorgenson's notepaper — her introduction of me in a tiny cramped hand — I patted the chair beside me. "Mr. Danenberg, come sit with me a moment." As soon as he sat I said, "It's so tragic about the Vaude nanny, Adelle, don't you think?"

He stiffened. I waited. When he looked at me, I saw tears in his eyes.

"Why, Mr. Danenberg, did you know the poor girl well?" Apparently he'd been in love with her, and I was being cruel. Harry would say it's part of the job, if you have the stomach for it. I didn't know that I had.

Carl Danenberg was having difficulty

answering me. Flushing again, he looked down at his hands. Then he said in a choke whisper I could barely hear, "We were lovers."

I touched his hand. "Then you knew who she really was."

His stare was so reptilian, I pulled my hand away. "What are you saying?"

"That she was a Pinkerton. Her name was Adeline Zimmerman."

He turned a hideous shade of green. "No!"

"You'd best alert your mother," I suggested, "though it seems no secret what business you're in."

"I loved her and she loved me. I know it. How could it all have been a lie?" he asked bitterly.

Out of the corner of my eye I saw Mrs. Jorgenson heading our way.

"You loved her, someone didn't. Perhaps you know who that was?"

"She broke it off. There was someone else." He stood up.

"Her new lover, who was he?" I persisted, standing as well.

He was almost rigid with anger. "I don't understand why you're asking me these questions. It's none of your business. Adelle was —"

Mrs. Jorgenson stepped onto the platform, inserting herself. "I'm sorry to interrupt," she said, not sorry at all. "Will you take your seat now, sir?"

I handed her the sheet of notepaper and caught up with Carl on the edge of the platform. "Carl, wait, you must have had some idea. Whoever her new lover was may have murdered her. Was it Fordy Vaude?"

His reaction was fierce, ugly. I thought for a moment he might strike me. "You have no right —" Then he said, "It couldn't have been Mr. Vaude. He was never there."

Chapter Twenty-eight

"Ladies and gentlemen," Mrs. Jorgenson said, situating herself behind the lectern. "We're about to begin our program."

I tried to clear my mind of detritus and focus only on my presentation. It consisted of a mixture of talk about my poems, blended with the recitation of approximately a dozen I'd chosen specifically for the evening.

Not only had I hurt a nice boy, probably needlessly, but Carl Danenberg's last words to me kept intruding. What had he meant, Fordy was never there? Where had Fordy been, if not in Croton? Were Kate and Fordy separated and putting on a show for us? It was all very baffling.

After Mrs. Jorgenson's gushing introduction, I rose in a billow of chiffon, made my way to the front of the platform, avoiding the lectern. I would have quite disappeared behind that fortification, and I was aware of the theatricality of my standing before my audience with no barrier between us.

There was nothing so thrilling as holding

an audience in the cup of your hand. Except the poem in its creation.

I began slowly, with a sonnet, holding out my arms to the assembly, come along, come along, on my magic carpet. I could feel them with me, their warmth enclosing me, keeping me in their embrace. When I ended with my "Elegy to Jack Reed," I raised my arms, brought them down, bowed my head. Not a sound came from my audience at first, then explosive applause. I felt light-headed, giddy.

Edward rescued me. I threw so much emotion into a performance, I was usually drained afterward. He sat me down and went to get some tea. I was no sooner sitting than I was surrounded by people, all plying me with questions, or comments, about my poems.

I raised my voice. "I'll be happy to answer any of your questions, if you'll allow me a sip or two of tea." Taking the cup from Edward, I noted his droll expression, then looked at the clear liquid in my cup.

"Take a sip," he said.

I did. Not tea at all, but gin. Lovely gin. "Now I can answer your questions," I said, revived. Where was Carl Danenberg? He'd become a chameleon before my very eyes, and I was intrigued. If Fordy wasn't Adelle's lover, who was? I couldn't help but think, given her background, that she had method in her inconstancy. The girl was working a job.

If she'd cast aside young Carl Danenberg, it may have been because she found him of little use. It was entirely possible that what she was working on had nothing to do with bootlegging. So if not bootlegging, what was it? And for whom was she working?

She'd acquired a new lover, which may have meant she'd shifted her investigation in another direction.

Then again, was I being too harsh on her? Maybe she'd fallen for Carl, and when the romance got in the way of her investigation, she'd ended it. It didn't mean she hadn't been in love with him.

I was a romantic at heart. I wanted to believe she had.

Mrs. Jorgenson made her way to my side, offering me a plate of butter cookies. "Stand back, everyone. Let's not crowd our charming guest. I'll ask the first question, if I may?"

I took a cookie. "By all means."

"We're all curious, when will you publish a book, Miss Brown?"

"In the spring, I think, if I can finish my work."

"Will you ever write blank verse, Miss Brown?" a college girl, by the look of her, asked.

"Perhaps." I smiled at her. "One must never say never."

"What about the sonnet as a poetic form?" asked a gentleman with a meager goatee. "You obviously don't agree with *Poetry* magazine that the sonnet is dead."

"Believe me, sir, the sonnet is very much alive. Ask Stephen Lowell. Ask Edna Millay, Arthur Ficke. It is an exquisite form in which I, in particular, feel very comfortable."

Edward placed his hand on my shoulder and nodded to Mrs. Jorgenson. He carried my cloak over his arm. "The sonnet is far from dead," he said. "In the spring, *Vogue* will publish a two-page feature on Olivia Brown, including six of her sonnets."

"Oh, Edward, what a lovely surprise." It was the first I'd heard.

"We'll look forward to it," Mrs. Jorgenson said. "Now I think we should free our guest to go home. Thank you for giving us such a splendid evening, Miss Brown." She pressed an envelope into my hand.

I got to my feet, and Edward wrapped me in my cloak.

"Miss Brown! One more question." A harsh voice. I looked for the speaker. People fell away and left Carl Danenberg standing by himself.

"Yes?" I said.

"Your poems. So many of them are about death."

"That's true."

"Are you obsessed with death?"

Edward said, "I think Miss Brown has had enough questions for the evening."

"I deserve a response," Carl insisted, coming to stand right in front of me.

"I wish I had one, Mr. Danenberg," I said softly, "but I don't. My poems come as they come. That death intrudes in some is not my deliberate decision."

Even as Edward was hustling me out, Carl followed, hurling last words across the lobby at me.

"Don't think you are immune, Miss Brown. Death walks with you!"

Chapter Twenty-nine

Murder me now lest I forsake thee,
For I will.
Kill me with thy kisses sweetly
While I'm still.
Slay me ardently, else I'll fly away
Sans adieu.
Slaughter me, my love, or this very day
I will you.

It was a fever, raging. Words erupted, one
hard upon the other, without thought. It
had disturbed my sleep, thrust itself upon
me, wakened me before dawn, compelled
me to stand over my typewriter, as if some
mystical force were pressing my fingers to
the keys.

I crawled into bed, shaking, unable to
find warmth even under the mound of
blankets. Eventually, as life returned to the
street below, the shivers subsided and I
slept.

Early in the afternoon, fortified — at
Mattie's insistence — with a breakfast of

sausage and eggs, I dressed, tore my disturbing poem from my typewriter, and went downstairs to find Harry.

The acrid smell of cigar abused me as I opened the door to our common vestibule. Harry's door stood ajar; the doorstop, human.

"Olwer," the doorstop said through the stump of a cigar. He scrambled to his bony haunches, snatching his cap from his head.

I shaded my eyes from the firestorm that was his hair. "Mr. Farrell," I said.

Ding Dong, the chief of the Hudson Dusters, was stretched out on Harry's sofa, never mind the springs, his derby over his eyes, the acrid cigar in his mouth.

"Come in and sit down, Oliver," Harry said. I could hardly find him behind Kid Yorke, who, guzzling a bottle of beer, had planted himself cross-legged atop Harry's desk.

The notorious Ding Dong rose to greet me in an almost courtly fashion, lifting his derby. He wore his usual costume of baggy trousers, long velvet coat, and fringed silk aviator scarf.

I sat on the sofa and fitted a cigarette into my holder. Ding Dong dropped down beside me. He struck a match on his rump, lit my cigarette, and proceeded to study me as if I were a road map. It was disconcerting.

"I've enlisted a little help from our friends here, Oliver," Harry said. "They'll keep their eyes on Daisy, Nolan, Fordy, and Kate, and we'll see what they're up to, if anything."

"Youse can depend on us, Sherlock," Ding Dong said, not taking his eyes off me. "Whatcha got dere, Olwer?"

I'd forgotten I was carrying my poem. "A poem," I said. "I came down to talk to you about it, Harry." And then I blurted out the rest. "Carl Danenberg was at my reading last night." Harry raised an eyebrow. "He's a fan of my poetry, Harry."

"Youse want him glommed, too?" Ding Dong asked. "Here, give us some a dat." He leaned forward and took the beer bottle from Kid Yorke.

"Danenberg lives in Croton, Ding Dong. I think he'd know you were following him. Go on, Oliver."

"He came up to talk to me before the reading, so I asked him about Adelle, and he got angry. Said she broke it off with him, that there was someone else."

Harry gave me a cynical grin. "Sure, our Fordy has a way with the girls."

"No, I don't think so. Carl said Fordy was never there. This boy I thought was so

202

nice turned on me last night. He was like a chameleon."

"A chameleon," Ding Dong offered expansively, "is a lizard what changes color. Ain't dat right, Olwer."

"That's right," I said, working to remain somber. "After my reading I was answering questions about my work, and Carl asked first if I was obsessed with death, and then told me Death walks with me."

"You think he was threatening you?"

"It felt like that, Harry, but now I don't know."

"Don't youse worry none, Olwer." Ding Dong patted my shoulder, his mashed nose close to my cheek. He was staring hard at my poem.

Red Farrell said, "We'll protect youse, Olwer."

"Thank you, boys." I choked up, unexpectedly emotional.

"Okay." Kid Yorke jumped off the desk. "We ready to go?"

"Siddown," Ding Dong ordered. "Ain't youse got no manners? Olwer's gonna read us her pome."

So I read my pome.

"Jeeze, Olwer, dat's some pome," Ding Dong said. "How about it, Sherlock?"

"Yeah, Oliver, that's some pome," Harry

said. He stood up and everyone shook hands. "Thanks for your help, boys."

"Youse can count on us, Sherlock," Red Farrell said, winking one of his pin-dot eyes at me.

The Hudson Dusters took their leave. Restless, I began pacing back and forth in front of Harry's desk.

"That's some poem, Oliver," Harry said again, this time with the proper pronunciation. "Herr Dr. Freud would make hay with it."

"The fury of it frightened me, Harry." I crushed my cigarette out in his near-to-overflowing ashtray. I felt like a spring in Harry's sofa. "And did you notice how Ding Dong was staring at me? He's never done that before."

Harry's eyes rested on me for a moment, then slid away. "Word is out that Monk Eastman's sweet on you."

I considered that as Harry went to the bathroom and brought back a bottle of gin. "You mean the flowers and the gin."

"What else? Martini?"

I shook my head. "I have an engagement." I watched him concoct a martini with practically no vermouth. "What do you think of Carl Danenberg as a suspect?"

"Don't know enough about him."

"He says he was Adeline's lover. My theory is that she took him as a lover because she thought he could tell her something about her investigation. When she realized he was a dead end, she broke it off and went on to someone who could. What do you think?"

He took a swallow of gin. "Not bad."

"So the question is, who is the someone who could? And did he catch on and kill her?"

"Or she?"

"Or she? A woman couldn't have lifted the dead weight of Adeline into that tree, Harry."

"Not by herself."

"Then it's a conspiracy."

"Could be."

"But nothing to do with gin running, otherwise she would have stuck with Carl."

"Nolan knows what she was investigating, or if he doesn't, he's made a pretty good guess. Daisy, too. But for some reason they want us to be point men."

I was feeling better and told Harry so. "Although," I said, "I felt uncomfortable about lying to Carl Danenberg, pushing him into giving me information."

"It's what a detective has to do, Oliver."

I left him on that, went back upstairs,

where I saw Mattie in her hat and coat, carrying her market basket, prepared to go out. "Wait for me a minute and I'll walk a way with you," I said. I ran upstairs, dropped my poem on my typewriter, and worked a comb through my hair. I touched my lips with pink and slipped some money into my pocket.

The telephone rang. I came to the top of the stairs.

"Olivia, it's Paul Ewing for you," Mattie called.

I didn't want to talk to Paulo. But he'd been there that weekend, which made him a suspect, though it was hard to believe any lover of mine could do something so violent. Then it came to me, he'd also gone to Yale, therefore must know Professor Adolphus. How was I going to work this? "Don't wait for me," I told Mattie. I took the earpiece from her. "Paulo!"

"Oliver, I've missed you."

"And I you, my dear, but I've been a very busy elf, trying to earn a living, working on my book. Even elves must eat, alas. I did a reading for the Chelsea Poetry Circle last night that Edward Hall arranged for some small bit of moolah." I paused. "We had such a nice evening together."

"Edward Hall?" There, I'd aroused a spark of jealousy. "He's so repressed." Paulo was being analyzed, too. They all were.

"Well, Paulo, perhaps you could find me a nice reading in New Haven, or even Yale, and then we can spend some time together."

"I'll do it," he cried, his enthusiasm practically piercing my eardrum. "There's the Poetry Society at Yale. I'll see who's president now. I'm sure they'll be interested."

"Paulo, there's a Professor Adolphus at Yale whose work I quite admire. If you can set up a reading for me, perhaps I can meet him in person."

"Old Adolphus? You want to meet old Adolphus? That'll be easy. He was my faculty adviser."

Chapter Thirty

Bleached to but an illusion of blue, the sky above me was distant and impersonal. I had started my trek with a purpose, but as I neared my destination, I faltered.

Having been well brought up, with the most perfect of manners, I knew a girl ought to thank an admirer for his flowers, not to mention his booze. I'd considered writing, but how would I address it? Mr. Monk Eastman, Dionysus, Palm Café, Chrystie Street, New York City. Something told me that wouldn't be wise. Besides, I admit to being curious. I wanted to talk with him again, thank him in person.

I made my way, amid a cacophony of horns, dodging the delivery vans and trucks that clogged the streets and ran over onto what sidewalks there were in front of the warehouses along Broome Street.

In tandem with my rapidly dissolving assurance, the Palm Café materialized much too soon on its Chrystie Street corner. I peered into the darkened window of the door, seeing only my reflection, lurked near the entrance to bolster my courage. He might not even be there.

No one has ever characterized me as timid; I opened the door and slipped inside, then leaned against the closed door to catch my breath. It took a few moments for my eyes to get used to the dim light, and when they did the first thing I saw was Sinister Mustache behind the bar.

"Whaddaya want?" His question was not particularly amicable.

Not thinking, I said "Wine."

"This is a tearoom, goilie. Alcoholic beverages is against the law."

"Tea, then," delivered with some nonchalance.

"Oh, it's youse, is it?"

I let out a relieved breath. He remembered me. "I'd like to see Mr. Monk —" I stared into the murky back of the room, where light was barely a glimmer.

"Wait here." Sinister Mustache came from behind the bar, muttering, "Dames is nothing but trouble." He merged with the darkness, re-emerged very quickly. "Go on back."

I wove my way past empty tables to where Monk Eastman sat with his cards in a solitaire spread. Next to the cards, on the other side of the bottle of whiskey and a half-filled glass, sat the large ginger cat, who contemplated me with yellow eyes.

Monk stood as I approached. He took off a small derby hat and set it down on the banquette beside him. "Miss Brown. Will youse join me?"

"I wanted to thank you for the flowers and the —"

Waving his hand, he pulled over a chair for me. "No need. I enjoy yer pomes."

He sat again and stroked the head of the cat, who arched her neck sensuously under his big scarred hand. Her purr was gaudy.

Sinister Mustache returned with a glass and filled it with wine, deep purple.

"Don't bodder me wid nottin'," Monk said. His face was elongated in the dim light, giving prominence to his scar and his broken nose. Broken, but not mashed, as Ding Dong's. He wore his dark hair long, perhaps in an effort to hide his cauliflower ears.

When we were alone he looked at me directly, and I saw past the strangeness of his features to the world-weariness in his pale gray eyes.

The wine stayed tart on my tongue. "Your flowers are very beautiful, Mr. Eastman," I said. "They fill my room with a lovely scent."

"Youse is like a ray of sunshine, Miss Brown," he said formally, giving me something that could pass for a smile.

I wondered if he was thinking of making love to me. I wondered how it would be to be made love to by a gangster like Monk Eastman who had spent many years in jail. But he'd been rehabilitated, Harry had told me somewhat dubiously. Governor Al Smith had restored Monk Eastman's citizenship the year before because of his bravery on the battlefields of France.

So who was this man across the table from me?

Uncomfortable under his gaze, I pulled out a cigarette. He lit it for me. "You are very kind, Mr. Eastman."

"Monk."

"Monk. My friends call me Oliver."

"Why youse call yerself by a boy's name?"

I shrugged. "It suits me."

"No, it don't. Miss Brown . . . Olivia," he said. "Lemme hear youse say one of yer pomes. Dat's a good enough thanks for me."

Jack Reed. My instinct told me Monk would like that one. I got to my feet and performed it for him, and his cat. My voice, I could see, surprised Monk with its depth and richness. The floor creaked behind me, and I knew I'd lured Sinister Mustache from his place behind the bar.

When I finished, it was a revelation to see Monk's eyes were moist. "Yeah," he said. The cat yawned. Sinister Mustache retreated.

I took my seat again and had a sip of wine. "How do you come to read poetry, Monk?"

"Started in Dannemora. I spent tree years dere." A vein throbbed in his forehead. "Youse I found in France, in a magazine."

"*Ainslee's*, it must have been. No one else would publish me at that time." Something brushed against my leg, and I swear I jumped a foot in the air. It turned out to be another cat, this one white with black markings. She sprang onto Monk's lap and, like a lover, pressed herself against him as, like a lover, he stroked her. In response, the ginger cat flicked her tail against the table, shifting the cards.

"Whaddaya have to do wid Nolan?" Monk asked suddenly.

"Nolan? You mean Lester Nolan?"

"Yeah."

"It's about the murder of a girl in

Croton. She worked as a nanny for the Vaude family. We were all there for a party that weekend. The Croton sheriff asked the New York police for cooperation, and Lester Nolan was brought in to help since most of the suspects live here."

The prominent vein in Monk's forehead throbbed. "A dame gets herself bumped off in Croton and Nolan is into it? Naa. Dere's more to it dan dat."

I hesitated. "Well, I suppose her death might have something to do with gin running and the illegal sale of" — I looked down at my empty glass — "alcohol. There are people in Croton who —"

"Da Feds know all about da Danenbergs." He poured more whiskey into his glass and filled mine with wine.

"The girl that was murdered was using a fake name and had once been a Pinkerton."

Throwing back his head, he emptied the glass of whiskey. "Youse know dis? How?"

"Harry Melville — we — have been hired to find out who killed her."

"Better youse should stick wid pomes."

I smiled at him. He was an old-fashioned man. Probably didn't believe women should have gotten the vote, either.

"Dere's still Nolan," he said.

"You don't like him?"

A harsh laugh. "He sent me up twice."

"The police commissioner brought him out of retirement to help on this case."

"Retirement? Nolan? Da only way he'll retire is —" He stopped dead. The spotted cat in Monk's lap wrapped herself like a furry boa round Monk's thick neck and meowed smugly. With a mighty slap, the ginger cat's tail hit the table, sending the cards flying. Monk gathered up the cards and shuffled the deck with his scarred hands.

I waited, watching the elegance of motion, but he said nothing further.

Chapter Thirty-one

I made my way back to the Village and now wandered into Romany Marie's Gypsy Tea Room in desperate need of warmth for my soul and a glowing fire and Turkish coffee to thaw my extremities. And who should be sitting before the fire, a cup in his hand, comfortable as you please, but Lester Nolan. His companion, long legs in buttery leather riding boots, was Celia Gillam, her wild ringlets hardly docile under a fuchsia scarf. *To Medusa.*

"Coffee!" Marie shouted, not looking up from her anarchist newspaper or moving from her stool behind the counter, on which her enormous bosom rested near her ubiquitous cup of Turkish coffee. No hooch served here.

Once, the Hudson Dusters had invaded the tearoom and demanded Romany Marie serve them her strongest drink. Her strongest drink was coffee, she said. "Okay," they said, "coffee." The tearoom emptied out quickly. After three rounds of coffee, Romany Marie told the Dusters they'd had enough, folded her arms over her formidable bosom, and handed them her bill. They paid it and left, never to return, because, it was said, they respected her lack of fear and because Gene O'Neill, their favorite bohemian, whom they called "Da Kid," asked them not to.

I loved Romany Marie's for the good conversation, the good food, and her generosity. She let chits pile up for hungry artists who couldn't pay the fare.

"Oliver," Celia cried, cadence of desperation underscored. "Come right over here and sit down." The tearoom was near to empty, rarely filling up until much later. By evening it would be crowded and would stay so till dawn.

Nolan rumbled to his feet, the essence of chivalry to the unwary. Which I was not.

"Miss Brown, how appropriate you should arrive just now. Miss Gillam and I were having a nice little chat about the house party at the Vaudes'."

"Were we?" Celia gave him a lazy smile. "I think you were chatting and I was listening. Sit down, Oliver."

Instead I made a detour to greet Romany Marie's husband, Damon Marchand, whose domain was the kitchen.

Marie, swathed in her Gypsy fringes of shawls, skirts, and turban, thrust a steamy cup at me. Nolan motioned me to a chair beside him. I didn't sit.

"Nearrrr firrre," Romany Marie said, rolling her r's extravagantly, her accent thick as the Turkish coffee. Soon she would tell me I was too thin. I set my chair close to Celia's. "You arrre piece ice, no, Oliverrrr?"

"A piece ice, yes, Marie."

"And no flesh on bones. Men like hold something. No, Damon?" she called to her husband.

The cup warmed my frosty fingers. I breathed in the steam, aware of Celia's eyes, the musk of her scent. "I was on my way to the Playhouse for rehearsals." I set down the cup and fumbled with a cigarette. Nolan produced a light.

Marie, deviating from her usual demeanor, hovered over us. "I rrread palm," she told Nolan. "Perrrhaps gentleman would know futurrrre?"

"Not interested," Nolan muttered.

"Oh, do," Celia said.

"No."

"He's afraid," I said.

"Oh, go on," Celia said. "It won't hurt."

We wore him down. He shoved his palm

at Maria, who bent over it. "Hum, huh, hum, huh."

With barely contained fury, Nolan pulled his hand back. "Say it and be gone."

Marie gave him a Gypsy smile, full of wisdom and mystery. "Lucky man, with two beautiful girrrrls." In a flurry of fringe, she returned to her stool behind the counter.

The two beautiful girrrrls were content.

After a long moment, Nolan said, "I was asking, before we were interrupted, who had contact of any kind with Adelle, and what that contact was. Miss Gillam?"

Celia, busy with a cigarette, didn't look up. "As I told you, I didn't arrive until late Saturday night. I was almost blind with exhaustion, been traveling for weeks, Moscow, St. Petersburg, Paris. When I ran into Max in Paris, he offered me his house, as he's done whenever I'm in town," Celia said. "Someone — Dave Wolfe — was already living there, but Max puts many of us up from time to time."

"You didn't answer my question about Adelle."

"What was your question?" she asked with a flare of anger.

"What contact did you have with the nanny, Adelle?"

"I wouldn't have known the girl if I'd seen her, which I did not."

Thawed by the warmth of the fire, I tilted my head back and blew perfect smoke rings. Celia was lying, of course. I'd seen the look she and Adelle had exchanged on the stairway before Adelle had taken the children out and disappeared. Why was she lying about it? Why would she need to?

"What about the argument?" Nolan prompted, watching me, not Celia.

"An argument? Was there an argument, Oliver?" Celia didn't wait for my response. "Oh, you must mean our little charade. It helps engage a fallow marriage. Pretense, is all."

"The Vaudes instigate this . . . charade?"

"Well, of course. We're all in on it." Celia's tone was condescending, meaning, *This is the bohemian way, and you, Nolan, can't possibly understand.* "Isn't that so, Oliver?" Her casual gesture brought — not quite accidentally — her hand to my thigh, where it tarried, luring the blood from my head to the heat of her hand.

"Of course." Light-headed, I placed my hand over hers.

"But you had contact with Adelle, Miss Brown." He watched us through a haze of smoke. Under the table, our hands merged.

"She said, 'There's no hot water,' and, 'Perhaps Miss Brown will read a story later.' Each time she was with the children."

"And what sort of person did you take her for, Miss Brown?"

"I made no judgment of her at all, Mr. Nolan, although she did not give the impression of a person who had enemies. This was before I found out she'd been a Pinkerton."

"Ahh." Nolan lit another cigarette.

Celia's eyes widened. "A Pinkerton? Really? How do you know that, Oliver?"

"I only recently found out."

"Now what would a Pinkerton be doing working as a nanny in the country?" Celia said.

"I think she was no longer a Pinkerton," I said. "Am I right, Mr. Nolan? Perhaps you know what she was doing there. Perhaps she was working for you." What if both Adeline and Daisy were working for Nolan? And . . . what if that was why Daisy had hired us? Any information we provided, she could pass on to Nolan.

"Me?" Nolan's laugh was falsely hearty. "Well now, little lady, that would be difficult since I'm retired —"

"And keeping your bees?" I asked.

Nolan frowned. "Unlike Sherlock Holmes, Miss Brown, I'm spending my leisure time fishing."

"But for what, Mr. Nolan?" Regretfully, I let go of Celia's hand. "I must go now."

"And I," Celia said. She collected her cape from the hooks near the door. "Marie?"

"I'll take care of it," Nolan said, on his feet.

In a confusion of spangles and beads, Marie moved from behind the counter. She took the change he offered. "No forrrtunes today, girrrrls?"

"I make my own fortune," Celia said, "for better or for worse."

"Ahhh." Marie nodded. "Reed said the same."

"Come with me," Celia whispered, touching her cheek to mine.

"Can't."

"Soon." With a small nod she strode off, tall, assured, westward. I had no idea where she was staying, if not with Fordy, and she was gone before I could ask her.

"Oliverrr." Marie touched my shoulder. "Come say au revoirrr to Damon." She steered me toward the kitchen, murmuring, her gold hoop earrings pressing my forehead. "I see evil in that man, anger and pride." She'd lost her heavy accent. "Be careful."

I understood her warning.

"Where you headed, Miss Brown?" Nolan appeared at my elbow.

"The Provincetown Playhouse."

"Then I think I'll just stroll along with you. Mr. Cook and his wife are next on my list."

"But Adelle — Adeline — had already disappeared by the time Jig and Susan arrived," I said. A fine drizzly mist hung over the Village. My words were moist white puffs.

"I'm speaking to everyone who was at the Vaudes' for any time that weekend. The odd bit of information could lead us to the murderer."

"Excuse me, you're saying that one of us killed her?"

"One or more."

"But we had no reason."

"Can you speak for anyone other than yourself, Miss Brown?"

Washington Square Park was winter barren, of grass and people, though women with market baskets hurried along the wet walks. When we arrived at the Playhouse,

Nolan opened the door and stood aside for me to enter. I could hear Jig's booming voice giving orders. Behind us, Edward Hall called to me as he made the turn onto Washington Square.

"What is your interest really in all this, Mr. Nolan?" I asked. He was like some wax model of a hero in human clothing.

"A favor, is all." A rank smell emanated from his rain-damp coat.

"I hear tell that you're a Fed, Mr. Nolan." I did a doggy shake with my fur.

"Now who have you been talking to, Miss Brown? The Gypsy faker?"

"People who know Feds when they see them, Mr. Nolan. Was Adeline working for you?" He moved ahead of me, not answering. "How about Daisy? How long has she been working for you? You know, you can't keep much secret here in the Village."

"Oliver!" Edward rushed through the door. "Didn't you hear me calling?" He looked at Nolan with suspicion. As if I could find the pasteboard Lester Nolan attractive.

"This is Lester Nolan, Edward. He's a Fed, aren't you, Mr. Nolan?" Thus did I finally manage to bring to the surface

Nolan's raw malevolence.

He said, "You do know, don't you, Miss Brown, what happens to little girls who play with fire?"

Chapter Thirty-two

Paulo, very handsome in his teaching tweeds, came for Harry and me in a borrowed Model T, and we motored to the country for "an inquest into the death of Miss Adelle Zimmer, alias Adeline Zimmerman," as stated in the letter from the Sheriff's Department of the Village of Croton, requesting our presence.

It might well have seemed a class reunion were it not for the tragic overtones and the fact that it was held in the small white clapboard, modestly steepled, predictably unheated Methodist church. One could almost hear the hymnal strains of the organ. The cold pew could have been a block of ice. Seated between Harry and Paulo, I drew them close on either side to give me their warmth.

We were all there. In front of us sat Fordy and Kate as if they were a couple again. A haggard Fordy, not at all as I had seen him the other evening, greeted us with a distracted nod. Kate, dressed dramatically in black, doled out anemic kisses, as one bereaved. Sitting beside Kate, Bunny patted Daisy's hand ineffectually as she sniffled into a handkerchief.

"Where's Nolan?" I murmured to Harry.

"Up to no good," was Harry's response.

Paulo's arm crawled round my shoulders. In this dreadful, mortal situation my body surged with life.

Dave Wolfe, next to Celia in the pew behind me, leaned forward; his whisper tickled my ear. "Do you suppose Kate will do the eulogy?"

Celia smiled at me as if we had a secret, which we had.

Across the aisle to my left, separate from the rest of us, were Mama and Carl Danenberg. No Papa.

Seated at a table in front of the altar were Deputy Hook and a stocky, gray-bearded man in a brown suit. The lantern-jawed woman with them wore glasses, a black woolen coat, and a black hat, a huge gray silk cabbage rose attached to its brim. Lying on the table near her gloved hands were a notepad and a pencil.

Deputy Hook got to his feet; his eyes ranged about the room, settling on first one, then another of us, with satisfaction. "Shall we begin?" It was a rhetorical question. "Ladies and gentlemen, thank you for coming here this morning. We're sorry for the inconvenience and promise not to keep you too long. For those who don't as yet know me, I am Deputy Amos Hook. Sheriff Van Buren is gonna be laid up with his bad leg for a while. This pretty lady here is Mrs. Hook, my wife, and she has kindly volunteered to keep the record." Mrs. Hook reacted with a flush of pink and a modest nod; the cabbage rose trembled.

A loud clank came from the back of the church, interrupting Hook's speech. We all turned to see the front door to the church standing open. The hitherto missing Lester Nolan made his grand entrance in a gush of cold wind.

"I'll thank you to close the door and be seated, Mr. Nolan, so we can continue." Hook was curt, his resentment more than slight. "This is an inquiry into the unnatural death of one Adeline Zimmerman, alias Adelle Zimmer, on or about December 5th, 1920, in the wood near the home of Fordham and Kate Vaude."

A small moan came from Daisy, and almost as one, we moved to comfort her, all except Harry, that is. I took note of that. Had Harry's acrimony toward Lester Nolan spilled over onto our client? Or was it something else? Whatever it was, he steadfastly ignored the pressure of my arm.

"I will give my own testimony first and then ask that Dr. Clyde Ebersole, our coroner, sum up his findings, after which we'll take testimony from those who knew Miss Zimmerman and were present in the area at the time of her death." He withdrew a notepad from his pocket and opened it. "I received a call from Sheriff Van Buren at five forty-five P.M. on the afternoon of December 5th, telling me to go out to the Vaude house to investigate what might be the unnatural death of the Vaude nanny. I found Mrs. Vaude and the children, Miss D. Zimmerman, Mr. E. Wilson, and Mr. D. Wolfe, Miss S. Glaspell, and Mr. G., known as 'Jig,' Cook, and Mr. P. Ewing at the house. Mr. Wolfe led me into the wood, where Miss O. Brown and Mr. H. Melville were keeping guard over the frozen corpse of Miss Adelle Zimmer, alias Adeline Zimmerman, which was lying on the ground —"

"No, please!" Daisy rose wraith-like, then fainted dead away across Bunny.

"Oh, dear," Mrs. Hook cried, and rushed over with smelling salts as we all came out of our seats.

After a minute or so, while we milled, Daisy recovered herself.

"Would you like to lie down until we call you, Miss Zimmerman?" Hook asked.

"No, please, I'm quite improved," Daisy said, but she was waxen as death.

"Then if everyone will sit again, we can continue. Where was I?"

Mrs. Hook referred to her notes. "Miss Zimmer's body was lying on the ground."

"Yes. Mr. Melville had cut her down from the tree, where they'd found her hanging, in a failed attempt to revive her. Miss Adelle Zimmer, the Vaude nanny, had not been seen since before noon that same day. Now I'll ask that Dr. Ebersole continue." Hook took his seat at the table.

The man in the brown suit rose and removed a pair of glasses from a breast pocket of his coat, hooked them to his ears, positioned them on his nose. He then unfolded carefully several sheets of paper, which he'd removed from a battered leather briefcase. He began at once in a gravelly voice. "Due to the extreme frozen nature of the corpse —"

Daisy began to sob. Hook said, "I'm sorry, miss, but this has to be done. Go on, Dr. Ebersole."

Ebersole cleared his throat, studied his notes, began again. "Due to the extreme frozen nature of the corpse, it was difficult to determine with any accuracy the time of death. Death was caused by asphyxia due to hanging. The victim had a deep groove, colored black and blue owing to the rupture of small blood vessels, across the upper part of the neck from the noose, which leads me to believe that the victim was alive when the hanging took place."

Kate said, "Oh God."

"However, it is my opinion that the victim was unconscious when she was hanged, owing to a prior blunt-force injury to the skull."

I felt a sudden sharp pain. Paulo's fingers were digging into the fleshy part of my upper arm. I jerked my arm away and saw that he was sweating profusely.

"What is it?" I whispered. His eyes were glazed, and he hadn't even noticed I'd drawn away or spoken to him. I gave Harry a swat with my foot and directed his gaze toward Paulo, who ducked his head, hands over his ears. Harry reached across me and shook Paulo's arm.

Paulo gasped, "Get down! Can't you hear the shells?" Suddenly his hands were on the back of my neck, forcing my head to my lap, holding me there, rigid. I tried to struggle but couldn't move.

Quick-witted Dave, sitting behind us,

grabbed Paulo's shoulder, but Paulo didn't let go, and I was rapidly losing my wind.

"What the hell's the matter with you, Ewing?" Harry growled, breaking Paulo's hold.

Paulo rose, swaying. He looked at the ceiling, shouted, "Stop! No more!" Now with everyone's attention frozen on him, he hunched over, hands wrapped round his head. With another spasm of energy, he moved left, stumbled over our feet, and sprawled in the aisle.

Chapter Thirty-three

After a quick glance to see I was all right, Harry leaped from his seat and crouched beside Paulo, rolling him onto his back. Then we were all on our feet, all talking at once. Although it seemed to have been prolonged, the entire incident had taken place in only a few seconds.

"It's okay, pal," Harry said gently. "The shelling's over."

"Stay back," someone said. "Give him some air." It was the doctor who'd been testifying — Ebersole. He knelt beside Paulo and took his pulse, felt his forehead, and declared, "Touch of the grippe."

Paulo groaned, struggled to sit up. Dave massaged his shoulder. "You tried to choke Oliver, old man," Dave said.

My knees wobbled, and I sank onto the edge of the pew near where Paulo lay. The back of my neck felt bruised. Celia touched her hand to my cheek.

"Oh God, Oliver." Paulo stared at me, appalled, and began to shiver. I forgave him immediately. How could I not? He was ill and, in his delirium, thought he was back in the trenches and we were being shelled. I felt fragile, as if I would break. The War had left its mark on all of us, for better and for worse.

Harry, O blasphemy, held his flask to Paulo's lips and made him swallow a few drops.

Kate, having run out to their car and returned with a blanket, draped the blanket over Paulo's shoulders as Harry and Fordy got him to his feet. "I think," Kate told Deputy Hook, who was standing and watching the whole procedure, "that we should adjourn —"

"Not at all, Mrs. Vaude," said Hook. "We'll just let Mr. Ewing rest on the couch in the rectory while we continue."

"If we must," Kate said. "But I'll have to sit with Paul in case he gets worse."

"It's okay, Kate. I'm feeling better," Paulo said, bless him.

We were all taking our places as before, minus Paulo, of course, when I remembered the Danenbergs. I stole a look at them across the aisle and realized with a small shock that during Paulo's collapse, they had never moved.

The inquest resumed.

Dr. Ebersole concluded his testimony

with: "I certify this as death by criminal violence." He folded his notes precisely and sat down.

"Thank you, Doctor." Hook moved an empty chair to the side of the table. "Now I'll be asking a few questions of each of you, and I want you to answer truthfully to the best of your ability, as there's a murderer been visiting us and we'd like to root him out."

Deputy Hook started with Kate, who told him what she'd told me, that Adelle had arrived via Fordy, was good with the children, and was pleasant to have around, though a bit tense.

"She also seemed to enjoy the country, went for long walks on her time off. That's probably how she met the young man Carl Danenberg, whose parents owned the bookshop."

What Kate did not say was what she'd told us after we'd discovered Adelle's corpse: that she'd intended to let Adelle go.

Fordy reiterated what Kate said, adding, "Adelle had presented a letter from my old professor at Yale, saying that she was his niece, that she was good with children, and that perhaps I could take her on temporarily." He'd developed a nervous tic near his mouth, which on quick glance made him seem to be smirking.

"This professor . . . ," Hook said.

"Professor Adolphus." Fordy looked at me as if trying to decide whether I would tell. I masked any expression. "I called him afterward to offer my condolences, but he said he was the last of his line and knew nothing about a letter or a niece." Fordy admitted to having left Croton with Celia before noon on that Sunday. No, no one had seen them leave.

Celia affirmed that she'd arrived in the middle of the night at Max's house, where Dave was staying, found no one there, and had wandered over to the Vaudes' and, being exhausted from her long trip, had fallen asleep on the sofa with Dave. She did not remember seeing Adelle at all before she and Fordy left Croton.

So she was sticking with her story. Could I be wrong? The picture appeared in my mind again: the exchange of glances. No. I was certain Celia and Adelle had known one another . . . in another context, perhaps.

Bunny said, "I saw Adelle on the last three visits I made to Kate and Fordy. Brought her a book of poems by Elinor Wylie, as Adelle told me she admired Miss

Wylie's work and she'd heard from Kate that I know Miss Wylie quite well." He didn't remember seeing Adelle that Sunday.

Harry, too, did not remember seeing her that morning and allowed he'd never had a conversation with her. If asked, I could verify that conversation is not Harry's forte.

Dave said, "I liked Adelle. She played a good game of chess. I used to go back and forth from my house across the road, to see Kate and the kids. Fordy travels a lot, and when I'm not writing, I help Kate out. I'm pretty good with my hands. I built some bookshelves, and fixed the sink a few times, even chopped wood for them. Adelle and I never talked about anything personal, but I knew Danenberg was her lover and it wasn't good. Don't ask me how, you just know those things if you're around people all the time."

A scuffling noise came from across the aisle, and when we turned, Carl Danenberg was standing, his fist raised and clenched. "You are no gentleman, Mr. Wolfe," he shouted. His mother took his arm and pulled him back into his seat.

"Please, let's not have any more interruptions," Deputy Hook said. "Mr. Wolfe, what time did you see Miss Zimmerman on the last day of her life?"

"I did not see her at all," Dave said.

When it was my turn, I repeated the conversation I'd had with Adelle about there being no hot water and reading to the children. I remembered very clearly, I said, seeing her hustle the children out, having her tell me that there was no hot water, and seeing her "talking" to Daisy on the veranda. I did not mention that they looked as if they were arguing. Nor did I mention, as no one had, the game of Truth or my seeing Adelle sifting through the charred remains of the fire.

"Now let's see if Mr. Ewing is well enough to testify," Deputy Hook said. "Would you have a look, Mr. Melville?"

In less than a minute they returned, Paulo, who seemed to have come around somewhat, leaning on Harry's arm. Slumping in the witness chair, Paulo apologized for his infirmity. He gave his testimony: "I saw Adelle at the Vaudes' over the last few months, gave her the latest edition of *The Little Review*, as she'd borrowed mine once and enjoyed its contents." He said he did not remember seeing Adelle that Sunday.

Then it was Daisy's turn.

"She was my sister," Daisy said. "Her name was Adeline Zimmerman."

"She'd been working as a Pinkerton?" Hook asked.

"Yes, but she left her job suddenly about six months ago and disappeared. You can imagine my shock when I saw her at the Vaudes', working as a nanny."

"I can imagine," Harry mumbled beside me.

I squinted at him. He didn't believe her.

Hook said, "What did she say to you?"

"She refused to acknowledge me."

"But Miss Brown saw you talking on the veranda."

"We were arguing. She told me to leave her alone."

"Well, there's a particle of truth," I whispered to Harry.

"Do you know this Professor Adolphus she used to get the Vaudes to employ her?"

"I never heard of him."

Daisy stepped down, and Mama Danenberg, not wearing pants now, took her place. Her thick calves were encrusted with heavy lisle hose. "I only met the girl twice. My Carl liked her and brought her to see Papa and me. May she rest in peace, we thought she was not right for him. My Carl is a nice boy; she seemed a very . . . I don't like to speak ill of the dead, but she seemed a very modern girl, if you understand me."

His mother's comments coming on top of everything the rest of us had said must have been difficult for Carl Danenberg. When it was his turn, he broke down, confessed he'd been in love with Adelle and that she'd left him for someone else. "After she told me it was over," he said, "I kept pleading with her until she said she wanted me to stay away from her. I never went back to the Vaude place after that."

Deputy Hook remained standing. "I want to say for the record that the crime scene revealed nothing, and even after the thaw and the snow melted, we found nothing. The noose, however, was a gentleman's leather belt. Although Mr. Melville had cut it through with his pocketknife, one could see by its condition otherwise that it belonged to a man of average girth." He looked down at the doctor, who had raised his hand. "Doctor, you have something to add?"

Dr. Ebersole rose. "I want to add only one thing more. The contents of the victim's stomach showed she'd recently eaten a sweet cake, full of raisins and nuts."

"Mrs. Vaude," Hook said, "do you

remember what Adelle — Adeline — had to eat that morning?"

"No, but we were all eating pancakes that morning. I didn't have raisins or nuts in the larder."

I shifted in my seat so that I could see the Danenbergs. Mama Danenberg's strudel was full of raisins and nuts.

Chapter Thirty-four

For all that, we were no further toward discovering why Adeline Zimmerman had taken a position with Kate and Fordy as a nanny.

"The missing piece of the puzzle," Harry said, his cigarette barely moving as he spoke, "the reason she was killed." He gave the batch of martinis he'd just mixed a gentle shake, then poured.

"Which would lead us to her killer." I stood in front of the hearty fire, trying to coax a thaw in my extremities.

The drive home had been unusual in that for once we were each lost in our own thoughts and had little to say to one another. I sat crammed into the narrow backseat, getting a sideways view of the cynical set to Harry's jaw. The lovely nape of Paulo's neck glistened with sweat. Muttering he was not well, he dropped us rather peremptorily on Bedford Street and drove off.

Martinis seemed in order.

"It appears you've developed a jaundiced opinion of Daisy," I said, relieving Harry of one of two glasses.

"No matter what she pretends, she knows why Adeline was at the Vaudes'. And so does Nolan."

"Then why aren't they telling us?" Oh, blessed gin that rushed lickety-split into my bloodstream. Harry made grand martinis.

"They're using us, me, as a stalking horse."

I debated with myself. Should I confess my foray below Houston Street and tell Harry what Monk Eastman said about Nolan, that he was a Fed? Oh well, why not? I was, after all, a free woman of 1920, with full voting rights.

Harry's reaction? Explosive. He swallowed his martini all at once. "If you think Monk Eastman is a regular fellow, you're bloody naive."

"I'm not exactly taking him as a lover, Harry," I said, intrigued by the thought. "I merely wanted to thank him —"

"What's wrong with the U.S. Postal Service?" He lit my cigarette, refilled our glasses.

"Now, Harry, you said yourself that the governor had restored Monk's citizenship —"

"Live by the sword, die by the sword."

"Sez who?" I plunked myself down on the sofa, finished my martini, and set my glass on the table with a thump, releasing the sweet *ping* from the crystal.

"I'd just as soon none of my friends is around when that happens," he said.

I smiled at him fondly. It's not that I didn't take Harry's caution seriously. My smile quickly became a yawn. I'd been up quite late the night before, as had Harry, I was certain. Early mornings were not our finest hours.

"Okay." It was hard to keep my eyelids from drooping. "Can we put Monk Eastman aside and talk about the inquest?"

"What, specifically?"

"You thought Daisy was lying. I thought everyone was lying, 'cept you and me, m' dear, and I didn't tell everything I know. Fordy and Kate, Celia, Dave, not one of them told the truth. They're each of them covering something up. For example, that awful game of Truth we played with Adelle. Even Mama Danenberg, busy talking about what kind of girl Adelle was, but not accounting for the strudel in Adelle's stomach when she died."

"How do you know they're connected?"

"I had her strudel. Maybe Adelle was with Mama Danenberg drinking coffee and eating strudel and someone knocked her unconscious."

"Carl?"

"Maybe. And what is this about Fordy traveling all the time?"

"Must have something to do with his family business," Harry said. "Do you want another drink?" He was concocting another batch of martinis.

"Yes, but no. I've work to do on my book. What is Fordy's family business?"

"Something financial, stock brokerage or insurance. Wall Street."

"Ah, that's why Fordy's always vague about his job. It's so bourgeois. I suppose, then, that he travels to talk to clients."

"Probably." Now Harry yawned.

After Harry left, I poured what remained in the cocktail shaker into a glass for Mattie and put the kettle on to boil. Where was Mattie? I wondered. I gazed down at my desolate backyard. I'd never had the heart to remove the broken pieces of Great-Aunt Evangeline's birdbath. Now that I'd met Virginia Champion, the original sculptress — Champ, Harry'd called her — I would stop procrastinating and replace it.

I fixed a cup of tea and dragged myself up to my room, rolled a sheet of clean paper into my typewriter. Paulo's delirium had taken him back to the War. The hateful War.

Why do men glorify war? My friends had all been marked by the horror in France, but when they spoke of it, it was as this splendid Great War, a wonderful secret society — with Death its honorary member.

I'll not exalt the noble sword
When Death is bravery's reward.

I stared at the paper, hoping more words would appear, abracadabra. Of course, they did not. It is not a perfect world.

Slipping off my shoes, I wrapped myself in my shawl and then took to my bed with Mr. Donne's love poems. I sipped the tepid tea until my cup was empty. The book slid from my hand.

A siren shattered my deep sleep, tore me from a sensuous dream, which waking smashed into a thousand shards, my lover's face lost. Yet the essence of moist sweetness lingered on my skin. I sat up on my elbows, reluctant to let go.

Had I imagined it? Now it came again.

Not a siren, but my doorbell. I heard Mattie's voice, then another joined hers. Reluctantly I left my bed and gazed blear-eyed into my hand mirror. My hair stood out from my head like a mad-woman's, and I'd never changed into my nightie.

I opened my door a crack and caught Mattie, her hand raised, prepared to knock.

"Ah, you're awake," she said, a look of pure mischief on her face. "You've slept clear through the night. I don't know the last time you did such a dreadful thing. And without wine. How was the inquest?"

"It was interesting because not one person, including me, and possibly Harry, with the exception of the deputy sheriff and the coroner, told the truth. Gerry would have picked up on it right away. Harry and I had a few martinis when we came home."

"Joan took me to meet Margaret Sanger." Mattie stepped past me and pulled back the draperies; cool white sunlight filled my room.

"I am envious. Your future mother-in-law travels in the best of circles."

"That she does." She looked at me in despair. "You are totally disheveled, Olivia.

I'd like to take an iron to you."

I giggled. "Would you now?" I took off my blouse and put on another. The skirt would have to do. "Who was at the door?"

She touched her finger to her brow. "There's coffee waiting. And a gentleman caller."

"Who?" I combed my fingers through my hair, bringing a modicum of order. "What time is it?"

"After nine."

I was aghast. "In the morning? No friend of mine would be calling at this unearthly hour."

It turned out to be Bunny. He was pacing my small parlor, looking, in spite of his perfectly assembled suit and tie, as if he'd been up all night.

"Oliver!" His greeting was effusive. A stranger would have assumed he hadn't seen me in a fortnight. "She's ill and I'm in a pickle."

"Daisy?" I said, handing him a cup of coffee and taking mine from Mattie.

"Daisy?" He stopped pacing and took a swallow of coffee. "What does Daisy have to do with it?"

"You said she's ill."

"Not Daisy, Elinor. Elinor Wylie. As she's a friend, I made all the arrangements.

And now she's ill." He paused, waiting for me to say something, but I didn't know what he was talking about and said so. Dismayed, he said, "Paul was supposed to telephone you to make the arrangements last night, but —"

"He didn't. I haven't heard from him. Did Paulo telephone last night, Mattie?"

"No." My house is so tiny, she didn't have to be in the same room to hear our conversation. "Come into the kitchen and I'll give you both some breakfast."

"Are you asking me to stand in for Elinor Wylie, Bunny?"

"Would you, Oliver? It's the thirtieth anniversary celebration of the Poetry Society." He got down on his knees. "I'll be your slave for life."

I laughed and patted his head. "Oh, do get up, Bunny. You'll crush your creases, and Crowny will disapprove and blame me, as always, for leading you astray. When am I to do this, and where?"

On his feet again, almost dancing, seriously relieved, Bunny said, "Friday night. I'll drive you up. Will you do it, Oliver? You can read the poems from your book."

"Of course I'll do it, Bunny. I'm honored to be asked to substitute for Elinor Wylie.

But where is this to take place?"

Bunny threw up his hands. "Oh, forgive me, Oliver. It's the Yale Poetry Society."

Chapter Thirty-five

Ah, felicitous fortune. My life is rich with such.

Paulo finally phoned me late in the morning.

"You're a little late," I said. "But I've told Bunny I will come to your rescue." I extracted as penance, however, a favor. "I'd like you to arrange for me to meet Professor Adolphus," I said.

"I don't have to arrange anything, Oliver. He's president of the Poetry Society. You can't help but meet him. The reception will be in his home. I'll drive you up and back, of course."

"No need," I declared airily. "Bunny has already volunteered."

It brought, I felt, a satisfactory end to our conversation. It wasn't until I joined Mattie in the kitchen that I realized Paulo hadn't pressed very hard to see me. Were the powers of Oliver, the sorceress, waning?

"I'm losing my mystical charms over the male of the species," I announced to Mattie.

"You mean I won't have to sweep them off our doorstep anymore? Now there's a chore I won't miss."

"Oh, you." I gave her a quick hug.

She had just set out a plate of bread and butter and poured a fresh cup of coffee for each of us when our doorbell rang. "It's a busy morning," she said, rising.

This time our caller was Lester Nolan, and he was oozing charm from every pore.

"Sorry to disturb you, Miss Brown. Just had a few quick questions." He insinuated himself into our tiny kitchen and sat opposite me, ogling the half loaf of fresh egg bread and the tub of butter until Mattie offered him some. I could see he made her uneasy and sent her a warning look.

"I answered all of Deputy Hook's questions."

"That hick cop wouldn't know to ask the right question if it bit him on the . . . nose." Nolan buttered his bread lavishly and took a big swallow from the cup of coffee Mattie, with an amusing lack of grace, had poured for him.

Nolan's presence was so oppressive, I fancied I could see him physically swell, closing off my route of escape. One glance at Mattie and I saw she was having the same reaction. He cut himself another thick slice of bread; butter and crumbs clung to his full lips and dribbled on his chin. "A good old-fashioned girl like you, Miss Mattie, who knows how to take care of a man, is hard to find these days."

Mattie's outrage shone from her eyes. "I'm a suffragist, Mr. Nolan, and getting the vote was only the first step. Our job is not finished."

Huzzah! I thought.

Nolan blinked.

"Well, let's get to it, Mr. Nolan. I am working on a book and do not have time to waste."

"A girl is dead, Miss Brown, and I'm no country yokel. When I hear a lie, my nose starts to itch. And my nose was giving me a lot of trouble yesterday."

"Then perhaps you should try scratching, Mr. Nolan. I told the truth at the inquest."

"Perhaps. I was thinking more in terms of Kate and Fordham Vaude and Celia Gillam."

"I can't speak for anyone else. Cigarette, Mr. Nolan?" When he refused, I lit one for myself and passed another to Mattie.

"But you know they were lying about where they were at the time of Adeline's death."

"I know nothing of the kind. Kate was in the kitchen with Paul Ewing when I saw Adelle go off with the children. And Fordy and Celia had already left Croton."

"Had they? And how would you know that, Miss Brown? Did you see them drive off?"

How would I, indeed? I tried to imagine Celia and Fordy conspiring to kill Adelle. And Kate possibly in on it? For what reason? "I didn't see them drive off, so I don't know for sure they left Croton. Is that what you wanted, Mr. Nolan?"

"Thank you, Miss Brown." With his palms on the table, he raised himself from the tight fit of the chair and, once upright, said, "You wouldn't know where Melville is, would you?"

"He's not at home?"

"Doesn't seem to be. If you see him, let him know I was looking for him. I'm also looking for Miss Gillam." He paused expectantly. "She seems not to have an address."

I shrugged. I had no idea where Celia was staying, and even if I had, I felt no obligation to tell Nolan.

Seeing that he would get no more from me, Nolan said, "Good day to you, ladies."

I followed him into my hall, wanting to

make sure he left nothing of himself here. To my astonishment, he was going through my mail, which Mattie had left on the table.

"Are you looking for something in particular?"

He handed me my letters without an ounce of embarrassment and put on his overcoat, took his hat from the rack. I opened the door for him and waited until he'd gone halfway down the stairs. "Oh, Mr. Nolan, if it's lying you're talking about, you don't have to look further than Daisy Zimmerman, or whatever her real name is. But you know that already, don't you?" I shut the door and went back to the kitchen.

"What a dreadful man," Mattie said. "Though he does look a little like Richard Barthelmess."

"He was going through my mail."

"Gerry doesn't like him."

"Nolan's lying, too, Mattie. Harry and I think he knows why Adelle-Adeline took the job as nanny. But he doesn't know what she discovered that made someone murder her. And he thinks one of us did it and we know more than we're saying."

"Do you, Olivia?" She frowned. She knows me better than anyone.

"No, Mattie." Well, not a whole lot.

"If you did, you would be in danger."

"I suppose if I knew who did it, I would be. But I don't."

"It worries me that you are detecting again with Harry."

I smiled at her very serious face. "Because I'm a girl and can't take care of myself?"

"No. Because I love you, Olivia, and I know you can be reckless. Will you promise me you will not go off on your own looking for this killer?"

"Oh, Mattie."

"Promise."

"I promise."

"And if you discover something, you'll take it right to Harry?"

After swearing I would do all those things, with an unspoken *if possible,* I went up to my room and sorted my mail, looking for a letter from Stephen. Alas, none. The sensation was of treading water, not going in any direction. I was drifting toward melancholy when the peripheral scent of Monk's roses engaged me.

I closed my eyes but saw only the snow-cloaked corpse hanging like a Christmas ornament from the tree in the woods. Heard Harry's "Bloody hell." A strange course fate had taken to turn what was meant to be fun, ominous. Yet the portent had been ominous all the time, but we all, rapt in ourselves, had never heard it. The dark side of carnival, as in carn-evil. I sat down at my typewriter.

Hammer the stakes and pitch the tents
And place my bleachers row on row
Set up the stalls for side events
Those games of chance, a penny a throw.
Oh, yes, my pennants conceal caprice
And cotton candy finally cloys,
My carousel spins without release
To organ music, dissonant noise.
My clowns arrive with much fanfare
To pinch and paw and terrorize,
And juggle curses in the air.
I am carnivale, naught but lies.
'Neath finery, I'm flawless vice,
Wagering souls with Death's own dice.

Chapter Thirty-six

A bottle of gin under my coat, I ducked into Mr. Santelli's little grocery and bought a bag of apples. Although the building on Commerce Street that houses the Cherry Lane Theatre is tired, the stairs leading to the flats above were spotless. Along the way, gaslight, more forgiving than incandescent, created compassionate shadows. The sweetness of the apples hung in the air.

"It's open, come in," Virginia Champion called in answer to my knock. "We're in the studio."

I followed her voice to the back of the flat. "I've brought some apples," I said, "and —"

"Don't move," she said. Hands disfigured with clay, she'd sensed I'd frozen in place. She smiled. "I didn't mean you, Oliver."

The studio was filled with ethereal light from a north-facing skylight, and I, so used to the dear, dark cave of my room, was dazzled by flashing lights and angels' voices, a heavenly landscape. My innards shivered, an utterly strange sensation. In a moment, it was over.

Earthbound again, I set the bag of apples upon the wooden slats of a packing crate with foreign labels near the doorway.

Champ's crepe cheeks were dusty and smudged, her white frizz wrapped away in a scarf of deep purple silk. "Come along," she said. "We're finished for today. Artemis has little patience." This last evoked a knowing laugh, not from Champ.

I saw she was working on the torso of a woman, life-size, broad of shoulder, neck long, slender, breasts high and bold. In slipped Greek chiton. The face was still undefined, except for the resolute chin. Artemis, the Huntress. Celia Gillam.

"Here, I'll take that," Celia said, husky voiced, her billow of thick dusky hair her only cover. She relieved me of the bottle of gin in my embrace, set it on the window-sill. Hands on my lapels, she eased my coat from my shoulders. Her touch brought a torrent of joy so intense, I was buoyant. En garde, I told myself. We were well matched, she and I.

I rescued my coat. Celia laughed again, gathering her hair with expert hands, twisting and braiding, her breasts con-spiring, until she thrust her arms into the sleeves of the man's shirt that was her trademark. Taming mane, breasts, all but allure.

Champ, in a flowing smock, brought glasses, my apples in a bowl, and a paring knife. She turned a valise on its side, covered it with a linen napkin, and we made a picnic on the floor, drinking gin, feeding each other slices of apples, and smoking until natural light faded and the tiny specks of our cigarettes flitted like fireflies as we spoke.

"Theirs was a love so deep and pure to the very end," Champ said of my great-aunt Evangeline and her lover, Alice, "that I'm confident it was eternal. I made the marble lovers as a gift for their twentieth year together."

The horror — never truly distant — of my finding the broken pieces, my life threatened in the process, came creeping back to me. A wound from which there can be no true recovery. "Will you create another for us?"

"When I finish this commission." She nodded in the direction of the featureless Huntress, silhouetted now in the sheer moonlight that made ghosts of us all.

We discharged the gin while Celia spoke with passion of the Revolution, the joy, the hunger, cholera, death in the streets, Moscow and St. Petersburg, of Reed and Louise, Jack Reed, the brilliant, naive boy-lover, and his wife, Louise Bryant, whom Celia had loved at least as much as Jack, if not more. And I was with them there as I sat transfixed, arms hugging my bent knees.

A distant voice said, "There's wine. . . ." Champ started to rise; Celia sprang to her feet and helped her up.

"I'll get it," Celia said. She carried off the valise as if going on a trip.

Champ reached down and brushed the strands of hair from my forehead. "You're a lovely, terrifyingly gifted child, Oliver. Beware the archer."

Her garments rustled softly as she slipped away.

Beware the archer. Was Champ saying I should be wary of Celia? My brain was dense with gin. Almost at once, Celia dropped down beside me and filled my glass and hers. We tilted glasses to each other. In the moonlight I could see the planes of her face. She was very beautiful. With the tip of my finger I traced the line of her cheekbone downward. Her lips opened for me, held me enthralled.

Beware the archer.

I broke the spell, ringed my glass with both hands, and drank most of my wine. I lit a cigarette with shaking hands as she watched. The first inhale brought balance; the exhale, strength.

She said, "What would you like to know?"

My head began to throb. "Are you and Fordy lovers?"

"Ahhh." She was pleased. Did she think I was jealous? Was I jealous? "No," she said.

I took heart. "Were you ever lovers?"

"I've had many lovers."

"Kate?"

She smiled.

"Dave?"

Another smile.

"Did you leave Croton with Fordy the day of the murder?"

"Once the game was played, it was over."

"I don't understand. You mean you were still there when we found the nanny?"

"Not at all. I took the first train out and came here."

"And left Fordy in Croton?"

"Why not? I am Hecuba. What am I to him or he to me?" She touched her lips to mine, a brief feathery glance, then away. "He disgusted me. The minute we crossed the street, he began to cry. He needed me, he said, to get away."

"From what?"

"I don't know. I was weary. I'd been traveling for weeks. All I wanted was a little rest. I knew I'd have none if I stayed there."

"So you just walked away?"

"You think me callous? Perhaps. Fordy's troubles could hardly be compared to what I've seen on my travels. He play-acts being a bohemian, but he can't hide his origins."

"So he didn't tell the truth at the inquest. And neither did you. Why were you protecting him?"

Celia shrugged. "Does it matter?"

"Of course it matters. A girl was murdered."

"Of course."

"You knew her from somewhere else, didn't you?"

"You are the fox, Oliver."

"I am."

"Well, little fox, we met in Rome last summer, at the American embassy's Fourth of July party. Her name was Adeline Zimmerman. She was on the staff of the embassy."

Chapter Thirty-seven

The night was still young, too early to abandon. An indefinable rawness, the taste of Celia's lips, kept me moving. It was past midnight when I wandered into the Working Girls' Home and met Jig and Susan on the way out. Jig gave me a crushing hug.

"Seen Harry?" I asked when I came up for air.

"You've come to the right place," Susan said.

The room was crowded, and a group had gathered at the far end of the bar. I stood on a chair and spotted Harry arm wrestling Whit Sawyer while Dave Wolfe rolled up his sleeve, ready to challenge Harry next. The pack, no strangers here, cheered them on.

"What'll you have, Oliver?" Luke O'Connor called to me.

I made a w-purse of my lips, and in no time at all had a teacup of wine in my hand. "To Prohibition!" I saluted Luke with my cup and got a broad wink.

Fordy, in green corduroys, wove his way from the bar, holding two teacups. I followed him. He led me to Kate. From the back, I would not have recognized her. She'd bobbed her deep honey hair, exposing her soft nape for Fordy's tender kiss.

Their laugh was intimate, and I felt the voyeur. Were they together again?

"Oliver!" Edward Hall called out to me from somewhere close by, giving me away.

"I've been following you," I told Fordy.

"You have?" His hand shook as he held a chair for me.

"There's no safe place, Fordy," I said gravely.

An unpleasant sweat gave his face an oily sheen.

"Naughty, Oliver." Kate stroked Fordy's hand as she gave me a warning look. "Now Fordy thinks you've seen him with another girl and I'll be upset with him."

"Followed you across the room, is all," I said, hanging my head. "I'm just an old tease."

"You are a tease, Oliver," he said with a touch of relief. "What are we going to do with you?"

Edward arrived at this moment and joined us. Our talk turned, as it often did these days, to Gene O'Neill and what would happen to the Players without him.

"Winner and *champeen!*" Harry shouted.

"Another round?" Edward said, looking at our empty cups.

"I wouldn't mind," I said.

"Why not?" Kate said.

The boys went off for a refill, and I smiled at Kate. "Together again?"

"Yes." She seemed pleased, gave me a searching look. "You're mellow tonight, Oliver."

I shrugged off her scrutiny. "Going back to Croton?"

"Probably not."

"I heard something interesting today about Adelle."

"I'm not sure I want to hear."

"Okay," I said.

We sat without speaking for a minute, then Kate sighed. "All right."

"Celia told me she'd met Adelle in Rome last July, only she was Adeline Zimmerman there, and she worked at the American embassy."

"I don't understand any of this," Kate said in a strained voice. "Do you?"

"No." I got to my feet. "I'll be on my way," I said, "if I can tear Harry from his victories."

"Don't you want to wait for Edward?" Kate asked.

"Say good night for me."

I couldn't catch Harry's attention, though admittedly I didn't try too hard. I was suddenly impatient to get away; my fingers itched for my typewriter. Luke kept a tab for me. I'd pay him when my next check came in, or someone else would.

I stepped out behind three rowdy college boys, one of whom gave me a drunken leer. The cold was quiet, intense, the sky swarming with stars. A beautiful night.

"Don't tell me a pretty little thing like you is alone tonight." The boy with the beery leer took my arm. The other two surrounded me, playfully, I thought.

"She's not alone," Fordy said, coming up behind me. He pushed the boys aside. "On your way, boys."

Disgruntled, the boys moved off.

"That was sweet of you, Fordy, though I'm sure they wouldn't have bothered me." I looked up at him, then stepped back. Something in his eyes . . . a savage fear. "What is it, Fordy?"

He grabbed me, hands on my arms, squeezing. "You told Kate that Adelle was in Rome in July. What do you know about it?" He began shaking me, hard. "What do you know about her?"

My head snapped back and forward, back and forward, my feet off the ground. His fingers on my arms were torture. I kicked out at him. "Stop! Fordy! Are you mad?" But my teeth clattered, and I'd had too much gin and wine. In a minute I'd be sick.

A thud and a grunt, and I was on the sidewalk, on my hands and knees, Fordy sprawled a few feet away.

"Jeeze, Olwer, what kinda low-lifes d'ya know?"

Red Farrell sat on his bony haunches, staring at me with his blue pin-dot eyes. Fordy groaned, and Red got up and kicked him into the gutter.

"Mr. Farrell," I said, taking the hand he offered, "there's no need to get rough."

"I got me orders, Olwer."

I stamped my foot and fumed. "Why doesn't Harry trust me to take care of myself?"

Red Farrell rubbed his partially chewed ear and grinned at me, his cigar propped where he was missing teeth. "Oh, it ain't Sherlock I'm keepin' an eye on youse for."

I stopped in the midst of brushing myself off. "It's not?"

"Well, well, what do we have here?" Harry said.

"You're a little late, Jack Dempsey. Mr. Farrell came to my rescue."

"It was nottin'," Red said with pride. "Some bum got rough wit' Olwer here."

"Oh yeah?" Harry bent over Fordy in the gutter. Fordy moaned. "Christ. Fordy."

"Gosh, Harry, he's really hurt," I said. "What should we do?"

"I'll take care of him. Red'll see you home." When I hesitated he said, "Go on, go on. I'll talk to you later."

So Red Farrell escorted me home while I tried to pry out of him who'd hired him to watch over me. When we turned onto Bedford Street, it came to me.

"Monk Eastman," I said.

Red Farrell's strange eyes gleamed in the light of the street lamp. He didn't have to respond.

Chapter Thirty-eight

"Oliver."

I woke with my head pressed against my typewriter and a most dreadful headache. What had wakened me? I blinked to clear my sight, if not my brain. My room wore a sepia hue.

"Oliver, are you decent?"

I shifted in my chair, taking care that my head didn't explode. Harry stood silhouetted in the open slit of my door.

"Give me one of those, Harry." He passed his cigarette to me and lit another for himself. "What time is it?"

"After four."

"Come in and shut the door. Let's not wake Mattie."

Taking up the poker, Harry induced some semblance of life into my languishing logs and sat on my bed. The blanket was turned down, but I had not seen my bed this night.

"How's Fordy?"

"Bruised and cowed. Left him with Dave. What'd he do to make Red plaster him?"

"It appears Monk Eastman has the Dusters looking out for me. Fordy got a little rough."

Harry grunted. "Yeah? Why?"

"What do you mean, 'why'? Why Monk or why Fordy?"

"I know damn well why Monk. You must have done or said something to Fordy —"

"Celia told me — do you mind if I crawl under the covers? I'm freezing." I settled myself against the propped pillows and let Harry tuck me in. "That's nice, Harry." The bedding was cool and soothing to my throbbing head. "Where were we?"

"Celia told you —"

"Yes. She told me she met our Adeline at a Fourth of July party at the American embassy in Rome last summer."

"Rome?" Puzzlement brought on a deep frown.

"Adeline was connected to the embassy, Celia said."

Harry jumped up and began pacing. "What the deuce have we got here? I need a drink."

"There's a bottle under my desk."

He reached down and hauled out the bottle of wine, holding it up to the light. "Not much left."

"Finish it. What happened was, I mentioned it to Kate as I was leaving the Working Girls' Home last night, and she must have told Fordy and he came after me. That's all I know."

Harry laughed. "So like you, Oliver. Set something up like that when you have no one watching your back. What would you have done if Red hadn't been out there?"

"I'd have thought of something, I'm sure. Do you really think Fordy would have hurt me? We don't know that he killed Adeline. What did he say?"

"He was beyond saying anything. And yes, I think he could have hurt you. We don't know that he *didn't* murder that girl."

"What about Daisy?"

He drained the small amount of wine left in the bottle. "What about her?"

"We're supposed to be working for her."

"Her money is still good. And we're doing our job. She and Nolan are counting on us to come up with what they need."

"And when we do, will we tell them?" I slid farther under the bedclothes and pulled them up over my chin.

"Daisy's our client," he said dubiously. "We're obliged . . ."

"What if we discover something that incriminates her?"

271

"We'll face that when it happens. I hate doing the coppers' work for them, and that's what I'm always doing." He sat down on my bed and stared at me, but he was somewhere else.

"What do we do now?" I murmured from the cozy warmth of my cocoon. "Talk fast, Harry, Morpheus doth make himself known."

"Cute, Oliver. So, Fordy went nuts when he heard Adeline was in Rome. I'll pay him a visit in the light of day and get tough."

Get tough? Is that what Harry just said? I was losing pieces. "You're going to his office?"

"I don't think he'll be in any shape to go to an office. I'll see him at home."

I couldn't contain a mighty yawn. "Then maybe I should have a peek at his office."

"Don't go alone. Take Ding Dong with you."

"Yes, Ding Dong and I will make quite a pair in the financial district, don't you think?"

"Not funny, Oliver, you just blunder along in your own world and never think you can get hurt."

"Go on, Harry. In broad daylight, what can happen to me?"

Chapter Thirty-nine

I would have gone by myself, but Mattie was not about to allow it. She'd brought me a breakfast tray and remarked with uncharacteristic tartness that I looked like a limp lily, and she was not letting me out of her sight. So what could I do?

I conceded that "limp lily" was a lovely phrase and that I intended to steal it, and that she could come exploring with me.

After rummaging through the cedar closet in the attic, we began trying on clothes. In my shift, there was no hiding the nasty blue remnants of Fordy's fingers on my arms.

"Olivia —" Mattie examined them, shocked.

"Fordy shook me rather hard," I said.

"He may have murdered that girl, and that puts you right in the middle of it."

"Well," I said modestly, "I did inherit Great-Aunt Evangeline's talent for detection."

At last, outfitted as uptown ladies, with dark stockings and curved-heeled shoes with silver buckles, a proper dark green tweed suit for me and soft blue serge for Mattie, we surveyed the transformation. Miss Alice'd had fine taste, so the suits were elegant, if somewhat outdated, the skirts too long, but who would notice? The few women who visited the bastion of men — the Wall Street area — would most likely be rich, conservative widows.

The brimmed-and-flowered hats we found thundered their turn-of-the-century origins, so we compromised with our own cloches. It was a masquerade. When we were done, the mirror presented two eccentric uptown ladies, which was fair enough.

Mattie giggled. "No one would ever recognize us."

I had to agree. "Not in the Village, anyway." Accustomed to the freedom of sandals, I removed my ill-fitting shoes in order to descend the stairs without breaking my elegant neck. "We'll need a cab," I said, slipping my feet back into the shoes.

The support of a cane was definitely in order. I plucked a sturdy-looking umbrella from the stand in the hall.

The City Directory listed Fordham Vaude & Sons, Life Mutual Assurance, at No. 30 Beaver Street, but Beaver Street proved hardly more than a narrow, albeit paved, cowpath, which was what it had been in the seventeenth century, thus impossible to enter by conveyance. Our driver deposited us at the mouth of the street and collected another customer almost at once.

I led the way, with Mattie directly behind me. Fordy's office was in an eight-story, marble-fronted building that had seen better days. A Negro doorman in a shabby gray uniform with gold buttons and derelict trim directed us to the elevator. "Third floor," he said, and alerted the operator. "Passengers, Sheamus. Third floor. Vaude Assurance."

The elevator was ornate but ill-used, the brasses faded and bruised, the woodwork gouged; its operator was bleary-eyed and unsteady on his feet. On his wrinkled uniform one could see threads from empty sockets, where gold buttons had once been. He smelled sour of whiskey, and every breath he took was a whistling wheeze. As soon as the doors closed, the elevator groaned, and continued so in an almost human fashion as we rode up to the third floor. Mattie and I, faced with this ludicrous situation, held hands and didn't dare look at each other.

"Vaude Assurance, to the left," Sheamus announced with a modicum of drunken dignity.

We waited until the elevator moved downward again, then looked about. A dull corridor extended in both directions. Walking left, we heard muffled voices and the clatter of typewriters from behind doors, their businesses handsomely named in gold letters. M. Goldman & Sons, Cotton Brokers. Stewart, Belder, and Fine, Attorneys-at-Law.

At the end of the corridor we found Fordham Vaude & Sons, Life Mutual Assurance, somewhat tarnished on the dusty glass, and under the name: Established 1855.

"Very impressive," said I, trying the door. It was locked.

"Try knocking," Mattie suggested. "There'll be a secretary."

I rapped on the door. I rapped again and put my ear to the glass. No sound. "Not even chickens." I peered through the mail slot and saw only darkness. Giving my co-conspirator a speculative grin, I said, "What do you think?" With my hair bobbed, I had no need of hairpins.

"Well, he did try to hurt you."

"He did."

"Hmmm." Having made her decision, Mattie reached up under her hat and removed a hairpin.

I did the honors. It was an old lock and not difficult to unlatch. When the click came, I straightened, tried the knob. It turned in my hand. "Thank you for the use of your key," I said, returning the hairpin to Mattie with a flourish.

The knob may have turned, but the door didn't open. I stepped back, wobbling on my heels, and let Mattie give it a go. It was stuck.

"Let's both try," I said, and we pressed our shoulders to the door. It shuddered, gave slightly. We tried again, and we were in. A smell of must and mildew surrounded us, as if we were in a mausoleum. I sneezed twice.

"There should be a chain for a light," Mattie whispered, groping in the air. Now she sneezed. "Ugh, spiderwebs. What kind of business is this?"

She was quite correct. No one human had conducted business here for a long time.

"Here it is," Mattie said. Faint light came on from an overhead fixture, dimmer than expected because it was so dusty. An assortment of unopened letters was strewn over the floor. Wary of being locked in, I closed the door gingerly.

Had we broken into an ancient tomb? It certainly seemed so.

The room contained two desks and three tall filing cabinets. On one desk, an ancient typewriter and an adding machine. On the other, a teapot on a tray with three cups, all covered with enough dust to look like an outer skin.

A door led to a second room, smaller than the first, with a large mahogany desk, a library wall of books, so grimy that one could not read the titles. Two carved and upholstered chairs from a previous era were positioned in front of the desk, as if waiting for a nineteenth-century Fordham Vaude to return. Nevermore. The room was very cold, much colder than the first. A terrible, inexplicable sadness came over me.

Mattie sneezed. "Look here, Olivia," she said, then sneezed again.

I turned my back to the room that had washed me with melancholy and returned to Mattie. The drawers of the filing cabinets were open. Mattie was sifting through the files. I looked over her shoulder.

"Everything yellowed with age," she said.

"And all the dates are 1910 and earlier. Nothing recent."

"How do you suppose Fordy earns his daily bread?" I mused, stooping to gather up the letters from the floor.

"What are you doing with those?"

"I thought I'd take them home and look at them in a less creepy place with real light."

"Do you think we should?"

She was nervous, and it was catching. I thrust the letters into the pocket of my coat and grabbed her hand. "Turn off the light, and let's leave this place."

The door to the tomb closed behind us. We hurried down the corridor, taking big gulps of air, and rang for the elevator. We lit cigarettes and smoked while we waited.

No sound came from the elevator. I rang again, heard a scraping noise.

"It's coming," Mattie said. "Here it is."

With a creak and a groan, the car arrived on our floor. The metal door was pulled back. Two bull-shouldered, swarthy men stood there. Thick mustaches hid their upper lips.

"Geddon," one said. He wore a dark suit, a fedora hat down over his low brow. "No smokes."

The other man stared at us with flat

black eyes. A judgment on girls who smoke in public. He had his hands in his pockets.

"Where's Sheamus?" I said uneasily. Mattie pressed herself against me. We were not about to get on that elevator.

"Geddon," the Low Brow said again, shoving a gun in my face.

Chapter Forty

Mattie let out an eardrum-shattering shriek, which would have made me laugh if this were a laughing matter, which it wasn't. I couldn't honestly remember getting on the elevator, but there we were.

"What do you want?" I demanded as the Fedora closed the door and we began to move downward.

"Hello? Hello?" came a voice from above. "Is there a problem?"

Mattie and I held tight to each other.

"Open yer yaps and yer dead," the Fedora told us.

We were as good as dead anyway, so I screamed good and loud.

"Youse shouldna done dat." The erstwhile silent one finally spoke. His monotone was chilling.

The elevator passed the lobby floor and continued downward into the basement, where the Fedora brought it to a stop and ordered us out. Something pressed against my leg. The umbrella. I'd almost forgotten it was hooked on my arm.

My mind began flying in all different directions. They would either murder us here or kidnap us. But why?

"We don't have any money," I said. The acrid smell of a cheap cigar seared the air.

"Or jewelry worth anything," Mattie added.

"So there's nothing to kill us for," I said.

"We don't kill dames," the Fedora growled, "unless dey butt dere noses in where dey don't belong. Da boss don't like it."

"The boss? Who's the boss?" Out of the corner of my eye, I caught a movement near the coal chute. I shook my arm and slid the crook of the umbrella to my hand, ready to use it as a club. My other hand I pressed into Mattie's forearm.

"Move," the Fedora said, pointing to steps that must lead to a service door.

"If you're not going to kill us, what are you going to do with us?" Mattie said, her face ashen, except for two red spots high in her cheeks.

"Eieiei!" came a howl, and a figure leaped out from behind the coal chute, wielding a baseball bat. He clobbered the Fedora, who went down like a wounded bull. The gunman raised his arm, and I smacked it good and hard with the umbrella. His gun clattered to the cement floor. He went scrambling for it, and our rescuer knocked him cold.

"I'll tell youse, Olwer, youse could keep five o' us busy." Ding Dong, in his baggy trousers and red velvet coat, rested on the baseball bat, his high squeaky laugh echoing round us.

"Mattie, this is Ding Dong," I said, my poor heart still thundering in my breast.

"More than happy to make your acquaintance, Mr. Ding Dong," Mattie said. "Now can we get out of here?"

"No problem." Ding Dong rubbed a spot on his mashed nose and flung his fringed silk aviator scarf over his shoulder. He led us out to the street, where Kid Yorke was leaning against the building, smoking, waiting, grinning from ear to ear as he pitched a baseball from hand to hand. Ding Dong handed him the bat.

"We got trouble?" Kid Yorke asked.

"Lupo's boys."

"Lupo?" I said, puzzled. "Who is Lupo, and what does he want of me?"

Ding Dong shrugged. "Let's get youse a hack."

"It's okay, really, Mr. Ding Dong," Mattie said, knowing full well no responsible cabbie would stop for one of the

Dusters, if he could help it. She patted her clothing straight and lifted her arm just as a taxicab rounded the corner. Getting in before he could change his mind, she called, "Olivia!"

"Who is Lupo?" I asked again.

Ding Dong said, "Someone it ain't healthy to bodder."

Chapter Forty-one

A bulky package, somewhat like an oversize football wrapped in brown paper, addressed to MISS OLIVIA BROWN, was propped up against our door. We eyed it skeptically, each still shaken from our brush with Signore Lupo's "boys." I couldn't banish the picture of the ugly muzzle of that gun in my face.

"O brave heart," I said, and gave the bundle a little shove with my stockinged feet. The pockets of my coat each contained a punishing shoe.

Mattie made an anxious little noise in her throat.

Nothing untoward happened, though it did move an inch or two.

Kneeling, Mattie gave it a tentative press and a sniff. She unwrapped the paper, laughing. "It's a smoked ham," she said.

"A ham? Who would send me a ham?"

"Maybe the same man who sent you the flowers." She picked it up.

"Oh."

Right, *oh*. Now Monk Eastman had

added delicacies to the flowers and booze and protection. I rang Harry's bell, jiggled his doorknob. "Harry?" He wasn't home.

Pensive, I took the key from Mattie and unlocked our door. Was Harry right that somewhere along the line there'd have to be a payback?

We hung up our coats, and I set my shoes neatly on the stairs. The bent umbrella would have to be repaired. I returned it to the stand for the time being.

In the kitchen, Mattie left our ham on the counter and put the kettle on. "I'm going to call Gerry." The comedy inspired by the ham had dissipated. She looked ashen again.

"Yes, do." I needed something stronger than tea, and so did she. I poured gin into two glasses. She took hers to the telephone. Mine didn't last a second swallow. As I listened to the murmur of her voice from the foyer, the blessed gin began its good work.

But Gerry wasn't at the precinct. "I left a message for him," Mattie said. Her glass was as empty as mine. "We could have been killed, Olivia."

"They told us to keep our noses out of their business, Mattie. They weren't going to kill us. I think they wanted to scare us."

At least I hoped that's all it was.

"Then they succeeded," she said. She put the empty glasses into the sink. The teapot warmed, she measured in the leaves, filled the pot with the boiling water, and tucked it up in its cozy to steep. "Do you think it has something to do with the nanny's murder?"

"How could it?" Of course that was impossible. Or was it? "It was a warning from this Mr. Lupo, whoever he is. But what is the business we're supposed to keep out of?" I needed to talk to Harry. Maybe this had more to do with Monk Eastman than Adeline Zimmerman's death. This last thought came with a violent shiver; someone had walked over my grave.

Outside, daylight was spent. From our kitchen window I could see blotches of light shining through curtains in the houses behind us. We had our tea with thick slices of ham and bread and butter, and we'd still not heard from Gerry.

"It's not like him," Mattie said, worried. "He knows I would only call if it was something important."

"Try him again," I said. "Maybe they didn't give him your message. And I'll run downstairs and see if Harry's come home."

I padded down the stairs as Mattie told the operator the precinct number.

"Harry?" I called, twisting his doorbell. "Are you there?" I wasn't troubled. After he left Fordy he probably went off to a saloon to spend the rest of the day. Wouldn't you know he'd do that when there was so much I had to tell him. My hand lingered on his doorknob as if I could make him appear.

The door to the street opened suddenly, and Gerry Brophy was as startled to see me as I was him. His face was drawn, his clothing rumpled.

"Harry's not here," I said.

"Olivia." He put an arm about my shoulders. "Let's go upstairs."

"We've been trying to get you on the phone, Gerry. I mean, Mattie has. We had a very strange experience this afternoon —" I stopped, aware that I was chattering. "Is anything wrong?"

"Oh, Gerry," Mattie said, rushing to him. "We had such a nasty — What is it? What's happened? Is it Joan?"

"No. Joan is fine."

We pulled him into the kitchen and sat him in a chair. I poured him a cup of tea while Mattie held his hand. He seemed to be thinking things over, looking from me to Mattie and back to me again.

He stood. "You girls had better sit down."

Confused, we looked at each other and obeyed. Something told me that we should switch back to gin. How right I was.

"Harry Melville's been arrested for murder," he said.

Chapter Forty-two

"He confessed," Dave Wolfe said.

We were all gathered at the precinct house. Not all. But enough of us: a ragged, devastated Kate, a nervously jabbering Dave, and Mattie and I. After Gerry had recounted the shocking events that had led up to Harry's arrest, we'd insisted on accompanying him when he returned to the precinct house. Once there, he told us to wait and disappeared up a flight of stairs.

"Who confessed?" I demanded. "Not Harry, surely."

"No, not Harry, Fordy. Wrote out a confession about Adelle and then hanged himself." The brown of Dave's corduroy shirt matched that of his mustache and short beard.

Although Gerry had told us as much, the news was still staggering. "Then why has Harry been arrested?"

He shrugged.

Kate, her cheeks blotched and chapped from salty tears, said, "Fordy didn't kill himself. He would never. I know him."

Dave said, "When I left the flat this afternoon around two, I met Harry on the stairs on his way to see Fordy."

"Harry was just leaving when I got there — about four," Kate said. She took a handkerchief from her pocket and blotted her eyes.

"And Fordy was okay?"

"He was not himself, but not to the point he'd . . ." Her voice trailed off as she caught sight of the fine-looking man in the excellent suit walking toward us.

I'd inherited Thomas Jenner III along with my house and Harry Melville. Thomas's father had been my great-aunt Evangeline's attorney; Thomas was now mine. I'd telephoned him after Gerry had recounted the disturbing news. Harry had few real friends on the Force, at least that was the impression he'd always given me.

"Good evening to you, Olivia," Thomas said somberly. "Mattie?"

"Not so good," I said. Mattie offered a tremulous smile.

"Harry's been arrested for murder, Thomas. Something he couldn't possibly have done. You've got to clear this up." Thomas's gaze went to Kate and Dave. "May I present Mr. Thomas Jenner, my attorney. Thomas, these are my friends, Dave Wolfe and Kate Vaude. It's Kate's husband, Fordy, Fordham Vaude, whom Harry's been accused of murdering. Dave thinks Fordy committed suicide because there was a note, right, Dave?"

"Yes. Fordy confessed to Adelle's murder."

"I'm perplexed here," Thomas said. "If you'll excuse us . . ." He took me aside. "It's not wise to involve all these people who might have a selfish interest in Harry's guilt or innocence. After all, this woman, Kate Vaude, is the victim's wife."

"Go on, Thomas, we're all friends here."

"Olivia, a wife can murder a husband. How was this man killed?"

"I'm not sure."

"I'm going to present my credentials and talk with Harry. I would like you to keep your own counsel. Don't offer any information. Don't trust anyone."

Don't trust anyone? How could I not trust my friends? But I saw merit in Thomas's advice. Any way you looked at it, Fordy was Kate's husband. I sat down next to Mattie, whose pinched face reflected how I felt.

"What did he say?" Dave asked, his arm tight round Kate's shoulders.

"He's going to talk to Harry."

"Fordy did not kill Adelle," Kate said. "It's a lie. Someone made him write that note."

"You saw it?" Mattie said.

"The police showed it to me, asked if it was his handwriting."

"Was it?" I wasn't offering information; I was gleaning.

She buried her face in Dave's shoulder. "Yes." Dave stroked her hair in a gesture of extreme tenderness.

I caught Mattie making the same observation. "What time did you leave, Kate?"

"I didn't stay long. He said he had some business to do, an associate coming by, so I left. We were to meet later at Polly's."

"An associate?" I said. "What kind of business was Fordy in?"

"You know, assurance and finance," Kate said. "His family business."

"And it's a good business?" I felt Mattie's eyes on me.

"We haven't been living hand-to-mouth, Oliver, if that's what you mean," she said irritably. "But who knows what will happen now." She swallowed a sob.

"Come, Kate, let me take you home," Dave said. "There's nothing more we can do here."

"No, I want to talk to Harry. I must know what happened." She pressed a sodden handkerchief to tear-swollen eyes. "And we shouldn't leave Oliver."

"Oliver has Mattie here, and the lawyer. Besides, Harry might not get out tonight."

"Oh God, Dave," I said. "You really think so?"

"Your lawyer will have to get a bail bondsman. It takes time." Dave held out his cigarette case, and we all helped ourselves, then lit one from the other. And we waited.

Abruptly, without warning, we were in the midst of mad turmoil, people yelling, pulling, pushing, cops all over the place. It became clear that they'd chosen this night to raid the Hell Hole, a local speakeasy favored by Gene O'Neill, so some familiar faces were herded past us. Not Gene, though it might well have been were he not in Provincetown these days. And not any of the Dusters, whose favorite saloon it was. It was not a pleasant sight, especially when someone started retching, which was what finally made Kate acquiesce to Dave's gentle prodding.

They had no sooner left the station house than Mattie nudged me. Thomas was maneuvering his way toward us through the group being booked.

We rose expectantly.

"He's okay," Thomas said. "I've arranged for bail."

"Thomas, Kate just told me she met him as he was leaving Fordy's about four o'clock this afternoon."

Thomas frowned at me. Obviously I hadn't heeded his advice about keeping my own counsel.

"He went back, Olivia. He called the police himself when he found Fordham Vaude's body. They have no reason to hold him."

"Especially since as Kate said, Fordy committed suicide and left a note in his own handwriting." The enormity of what had happened seized me, and sorrow for Fordy, for Kate, for the children, was like a boulder in my breast.

"I'm going to put you girls into a cab," Thomas said, not commenting on what I'd just told him. "It'll be a while before Harry gets home. I'll wait here. You both look as if you could use a good night's sleep."

"We could, but . . . ," Mattie said, caution in her voice because she'd determined, as I had, that Thomas was not telling us everything.

"Not until you tell us the rest," I said. In

addition to being a fine poet, I am a stubborn creature.

"Olivia —" He escorted us out to the street and beckoned to a taxicab.

"Thomas —" I did not move an inch.

He gave up. "This must go no further than we three."

"Agreed. Right, Mattie?"

"Yes."

"Although he was found hanged, Mr. Vaude did not commit suicide. He was murdered." The cab pulled up. "A quarter, to Bedford Street."

"Thirty cents," the driver said.

Thomas gave him thirty cents and opened the door of the cab for us.

"And how do we know it was murder, Thomas?"

"Because," Thomas said, dropping his voice, "the late Mr. Vaude would hardly have slit his own tongue."

Chapter Forty-three

Sleep was furthermost from my mind. Mattie, on the other hand, went off to bed with a hot-water bottle, admonishing me to do the same, even placing one under the bedclothes for me.

But, determined to wait up for Harry, I moved my chair close to the window, pulled back the draperies, curled up, smoked, my eyes on the street below, my mind detailing all the events of the last two weeks.

Was it Adeline Zimmerman's connection to the American embassy that had so disturbed Fordy? Or was it the fact that she'd been in Rome? Neither made any sense at all. Why would he care?

The American embassy. Rome. Fordy. Fordy traveled a lot. By any chance had Fordy been in Rome at the same time as Adeline? Could he have met her in Rome? No. He'd been shocked and fearful to hear she'd been there.

My foot, which I'd been sitting on, went to sleep. I wriggled and flexed my toes.

From below came the distinctive slam of the door of an automobile. I saw the lights of a taxi. Harry was home. Throwing my shawl over my shoulders, I hurried downstairs, all but dragging my tingling limb.

"Har—" His name caught in my throat, for it wasn't Harry who stood in our shared vestibule, but Daisy Zimmerman.

She took one look at me and would have bolted, but I was too quick. I spread my small, not-so-fragile self in front of the outside door. Who was I kidding? Daisy could have plowed right through me, but she didn't. She burst into tears.

"Oh, my dear," said I. A cold *whoosh* of air hit my back.

"I brung her for Sherlock," croaked a voice behind me. Circular Jack. His voice was unmistakable. "Salutations, Olwer." He tipped his black bowler to me. He wore his long black velvet coat with his usual aplomb.

"Mr. Jack," I said. "A pleasure as always. Harry's in the pokey."

"Don't I know it. He tells me go get her as dem dumb flatfoots're takin' him away."

"He should be home any minute," I said. "He's getting bailed out."

"I'd like to go now," Daisy said, sniffling. She tried to edge round me.

Circular Jack leaned against the doorjamb and folded his arms. "Youse goin' nowhere, sister, till Sherlock gives da woid."

The perfect cue.

"I'll take it from here, Jack, thank you very much."

"Sherlock. Olwer." He tipped his hat to me, opened the outside door, and blended into the night.

Harry was home, but certainly worse for the wear. Even in the dim light I could see that his face had been used for a punching bag. Both his eyes were blackened, his nose was raw and puffed. He unlocked his door, opened it, and stood back.

I gave Daisy a not-so-subtle push, switched on the light, and took a good look at Harry. He had blood in his nostrils and a cut and swollen lip.

"I see they made you right at home," I said.

"Sit down, Daisy," Harry said.

She sat on the couch. "You have no right —"

"I've had about enough of this," Harry said, slamming his fist on his desk. Daisy literally rose up in the air and came down like a tired rag. "What the hell is going on here?"

I went into the bathroom, which was like an icebox. Harry kept the window open so as not to melt the block of ice in his bathtub. I stabbed the block with the pick and chipped off some slivers, wrapped them in a dingy towel, and brought it to Harry, who held it to his face. He was a mess. If I didn't already know him, I'd hate to meet him on a dark street.

Daisy said plaintively, "I'm only trying to find out who killed my sister."

"It's how you're doing it that I object to," Harry said. "What is Lester Nolan to you?"

Her face was stained with tears. She looked absolutely pathetic.

"Harry, maybe we —"

He cut me off. "Well, if you're not going to cough it up about Nolan, how about what you were doing in Fordy's flat?"

"When?" I demanded. "When was she in Fordy's flat?"

"Try just before I found him," Harry said.

"Daisy was the last person to see Fordy alive?"

Daisy shuddered. "He was hanging there when I arrived."

"She ran like a bat out of hell and smacked into me."

300

"I was scared."

"Scared enough to get the coppers to come after me?"

"I didn't."

"Well, someone did. I was set up good."

"Let me understand this," I said. "Daisy went to Fordy's, found him dead, ran out, ran into you, and you found him dead? You went back?"

"Yes." He moved the towel of ice to his forehead.

"Why?"

"I had a couple more questions."

I turned to Daisy. "Why were you there, Daisy?"

"Fordy called me at *Vanity Fair* and told me he knew who killed Adeline. He wanted to talk to me."

"And you went by yourself?" I asked, knowing I would have been just as stupid.

Daisy stared at me.

Harry said, "Daisy made a phone call before she left for Fordy's, right?" Harry's voice was full of derision. "You called Nolan and told him what Fordy said, didn't you?"

She started to deny, stopped. The truth was written all over her face.

Chapter Forty-four

"It didn't look as if anyone had conducted anything there in years," I told Harry after he returned from putting Daisy in a taxi. "But the company name was still on the door, and the doorman and the elevator operator knew it was there." I wasn't ready to spew out the rest of it, as in retrospect it had the appearance of bad comedy-farce.

"Someone's got the lease on the office." He lit our cigarettes and retreated to his chair, feet on the desk.

"I'll bet that no one's been near the place since Fordy's father died. When was that, do you know?"

"Before the War, I think."

"Fordy must have been keeping it up. For appearances, I'd say. Still, think of it. He traveled a lot on business, kept a studio here, the office downtown, and a house in Croton. Considering the condition of the family business, where was he getting the money?"

"Kate's family has money."

"Really?" It was something none of us

ever talked about. Actually, it was very déclassé to have come from the moneyed class. We were all supposed to be starving artists. Yet everyone knew Fordy had money because he had the family business. "She told you?"

"No. Can't remember who said it." Harry grimaced as the gin came in contact with his cut lip. "Fordy was murdered between the time Kate left him and the time I came back."

"You're assuming Kate didn't do it."

"She could have, but she would have needed help."

"Kate said Fordy told her he was expecting an associate and would meet her later for supper."

"An associate." He pressed the towel to his face. The ice had melted and was dripping all over him. He didn't notice.

"A lover?"

Harry shook his head. "What the hell business was he in?"

"Something he didn't want anyone to know about, Harry. That made him feel threatened when he found out that Adelle/Adeline was not who she said she was."

"She was an experienced operative. How did Fordy find out?"

"That's just it. Maybe he didn't find out

until after Adelle was dead. When we all did. And therefore he would have had no motive to murder her."

"But he had a pretty good idea who did."

"So Fordy was killed to keep him quiet, about the murder —"

"And about where the money was coming from. Which leads us right back to Adeline Zimmerman: Who was she working for, and what was the job?" Harry sagged in his chair and into a brown funk. Or maybe he was getting tired of it all. I certainly was.

Even when Harry's spirit became dark, which was not infrequent, I would trust him with my life. Though I was a modern, independent girl, I had only my intelligence to work with, no small thing. Harry was my intellectual equal, as well as a tower of physical and moral strength.

I knew for all his ways, he was still something of an old Galahad where girls were concerned. He didn't take kindly to my putting myself in danger. But we were going nowhere with our investigation, and what I had left out of my story would wait. I rested my head for a minute on the arm of the couch. A hush descended on us.

The milkman — who gave no consideration to nightly revels — announced his dawn arrival with the rude clank of bottles. I'd slept what was left of the night away on Harry's dreadful couch. And Harry, snoring through his swollen nose, was still slumped at his desk.

I managed to eject myself from the bowels of the couch and stand, none too steadily. Harry stopped snoring. His eyes remained shut. It was a good time to leave.

"Oliver!" His ghastly eyes were open, staring at me. "There's something you're not telling me." He pointed to his couch. Though disinclined, I sat. "Spill it."

Have I mentioned Harry's telepathic flair?

So I told him everything, my narration interrupted liberally with a litany of Harry's bloody hells.

"Lupo sent two of his bulls after you?"

"They meant to scare us, Harry, because if they'd wanted to, they could have killed us. And by the way, who is this Lupo?"

"Ignazio Lupo, affectionately known as Lupo the Wolf. The boss of the Black Hand." He took a long drink of gin, a contemplative look on his face.

"The Black Hand?" A chill ran through me. What had I, a mere slip of a girl, a poet of enormous talent, done to anger a beast like Lupo?

"He runs an extortion racket on well-to-do Italians, threatening them with bodily harm."

"And it works?"

"Better than you'd think. The Black Hand's an ancient Sicilian blood brotherhood, specializing in extortion, blackmail, and murder." He gave me a hard look. "Lupo's no friend of Monk Eastman's, either."

"But there's nothing between Monk Eastman and me."

Harry wasn't listening. Something was percolating in his brain. "Wait a goddam minute," he said. His feet came off his desk with a thud and he stood, rubbing his chin, grimacing. "Lupo's also a contract murderer. He leaves his calling card on his victims."

"Very classy," I said glumly.

"Not that kind of calling card." He dropped back into his chair. "What a simpleton I am."

Now I was thoroughly lost. "What on earth are you talking about, Harry?"

"Lupo slits his victim's tongue."

Chapter Forty-five

Bunny had a curious way of speaking: a low, breathless whisper as if his throat were closed off. His conversation was a combination of long pauses interspersed with sharp little bursts of words emerging all tangled up in his ideas. This characteristic extended to the gas pedal of an automobile, which could be very disconcerting when he was driving. I had not looked forward to his escorting me to Yale for my reading.

As it happened, it was Dave who drove us to New Haven in an old black Reo touring car that belonged to Bunny's uncle, and Bunny produced his conversation from the commodious backseat. He'd given himself a bad sprain of arm and shoulder while trying to move a filing cabinet in his office and now eased his pain with swigs of gin from his silver pocket flask.

"I will navigate," he said flatly when Dave and I both assured him that he didn't have to come with us. "Neither of you has been to New Haven." This was true.

We hardly spoke after that, each to our own reflections, until I decided to vocalize what hovered in the air. "Dreadful about Fordy."

Bunny groaned as he shifted in his seat. He patted my back with his good arm. "Never took him for a murderer."

"Shut the hell up, Bunny." Dave's hands gripped the steering wheel, knuckles white.

It was clear we could not continue on the subject of Fordy. We talked instead about the success of Larry Langner's inspired Theatre Guild company of professional actors. The Washington Square Players had disbanded, leaving the Provincetown Players as the only really experimental amateur acting company in the Village. And with Gene looking more and more at Broadway, how long could we continue?

As the conversation drifted, Bunny began to enumerate the idealistic goals of the Guild and what it would mean for the American theatre.

The day was uncharacteristically mild under warm sunlight, but cold gusts, reminding us it was December, knocked the car about. We'd been driving over two hours, and all the while Bunny's monologue had continued without letup. He'd moved on from the Theatre Guild to Djuna Barnes, her innovative writing and clever drawings, and Sherwood Anderson, and Tolstoy, and Jack Reed and Louise Bryant and Celia Gillam, my Celia.

Every now and again, Dave and I'd exchanged a conspiratorial smile, but most of the time I studied his hirsute profile as he drove.

"You've missed the turnoff," Bunny said, interrupting his monologue.

Dave winked at me, made a wide U. "I could use a cigarette," he said.

I lit one and, gliding closer, placed it between his lips, which I noticed for the first time were full and sensual, something I'd quite missed because of his beard. My fingertips brushed his lips on departure. He caught my wandering hand on the seat out of Bunny's line of sight and covered it with his.

"How is Kate?" I murmured, trying to make a voice.

"She will move on," he said. Dark haired and dark eyed, he was a fatalistic Jew who spoke little of his origins. He'd come down from Harvard with Jack Reed, had joined up in Canada early in the War. It was said he'd survived gas and shrapnel in his shoulder, but he never spoke of it.

"It's a fine novel," Bunny said. "Make a left."

"What novel is that?" I asked.

"Dave's. Make a right here, go through the town, and you'll see the college."

"You've finished your novel?"

"Only the first draft," Dave said.

"That's wonderful, Dave."

"I'd be honored if you'd read it, Oliver."

"I'm honored that you ask."

"You need to give your characters more definition," Bunny said grumpily. "It's the white brick Colonial on the corner."

We were late; the reception had started without us. Everyone seemed in great spirits, thanks in good part to the free flow thereof.

And here was Professor William Henry Adolphus. Except for his pince-nez, he looked more like a lumberjack compressed into formal evening clothes than a professor of philosophy. His thick mane of hair and beard were gray, streaked with white. With his stentorian voice and gracious manner, I was made to feel not the stand-in, but the esteemed guest.

A trifle hard of hearing, he shouted, "Mary," at a sweet-faced woman standing at his side, "show Miss Brown where she can freshen up."

So we went upstairs, with "Mary" introducing herself as William's sister and, in response to what I hoped were my innocuous questions, my hostess, as neither she nor her brother had married. I told her I'd be delighted if she would call me Olivia. She left me to unpack my recitation costume, flowing streams of rainbow silk with the small train, and my gold satin shoes.

In a corner of the room were a sink and guest towels. I splashed water on my face, stepped out of my blouse and skirt, and pulled the gown over my head. The gossamer fabric settled on my body with a whisper. I gazed into the mirror over the chest of drawers. The door opened behind me. Paulo's reflection appeared in the mirror.

"Oliver." He took me in his big old arms, and I won't say I didn't like it.

"Just in time to hook up my dress."

He found the small hooks. "I'm good at unhooking, too."

Why hadn't he mentioned Fordy? How could he not have heard? Now I would have to be the one to tell him. "There's this business with Fordy —"

"What?" He held me at arm's length, face blank. Wouldn't Kate have telephoned him? "What?" he said again, giving me a little shake.

"Oh, Paulo, you haven't heard. It's dreadful. You'd best sit down."

"Tell me."

I hesitated. There was an odd fragility about Paulo since his collapse at the inquest. "He's hanged himself —"

"No. No." Paulo sat heavily, stunned and pale.

"He's left a note confessing to the nanny's death."

"When?"

On the marble-topped table near the door, where Paulo must have set them when he came into the room, were two glasses of Champagne. Without comment, he handed one to me and drank deeply of the other.

Quavering, chilled, I said, "Yesterday." The Champagne was welcome.

"I've been ill since the inquest." He looked ill now. "He wouldn't have, not Fordy."

"Killed the nanny? Or killed himself?"

"Either. Neither. He's Catholic, as am I."

"I think he was in some sort of trouble, Paulo."

"Old Adolphus didn't mention anything.

312

He doesn't know, either."

Paulo seemed planted in the chair, brooding. I wanted to look over the poems I'd chosen to read. And I had a plan of sorts. My news had quite destroyed all notion of romance. He didn't protest when I hurried him out.

Quickly, I slipped my feet into the gold shoes and fastened the straps, added a touch of rouge to my lips and cheeks, and stepped out of the room. No sound up here. It was the perfect moment to have a little snoop.

Across the hall, I found what looked to be Mary Adolphus's bedroom. Someone was coming up the stairs. I closed my hostess's door and scuttled back to my room. The front bedroom was undoubtedly Professor Adolphus's. This was confirmed moments later. It was he who had climbed the stairs. He went into his room and shut the door.

There was no point in waiting for another opportunity. I took the long route down to the reception, by way of the back stairs, and came out into the kitchen. A motherly-looking woman in a huge white apron was rolling pastry dough into circles on a wooden table. The room smelled of roasting meats and sugared apples.

"Good heavens, miss, you startled me," she said when she caught sight of me.

"I'm so sorry, I've gotten turned round. I should have used the other staircase."

"You can go right out that door and down the hallway, and you'll find yourself." She gestured in the general direction with her dusty rolling pin.

A girl could get lost in such a big house.

Here was a hallway with doors branching off. Of course, to be sure, I would have to look in one at a time. From a distance came the high-spirited sounds of the reception.

The room I entered was large and imposing and smelled richly of tobacco. A gentle fire gave wavering light and moderate warmth. I saw glass-enclosed bookshelves, leather-bound books, a library table, a desk, comfortable chairs, footrests, and books and journals stacked everywhere. Handsome oils of Hudson Valley scenes hung on the walls. It was very inviting.

I sat in one of the comfortable chairs, but I knew I couldn't stay long. Shortly, I would be missed. What I wouldn't give for a library like this. It was only when I was leaving and about to pull the door shut that I noticed the cherry side table beyond

314

the fireplace, partially obscured by a standing globe of the world. On it was a collection of framed photographs.

Family photographs, it seemed. Many of them. Varied sizes. Silver frames. Something caught my eye. I picked up the photograph.

A group of fresh-faced young men in the striped shirts and straw hats of a barbershop quartet. One sweeping glance, and I knew a beardless, gaunter Adolphus. But in the sweep, I'd also recognized one of the other men in the group.

Seated in front of Adolphus, Adolphus's hand on his shoulder, was Lester Nolan.

Chapter Forty-six

Although Jack Reed was Harvard through and through, I concluded with my "Elegy," let my voice trail off, bowed my head, and said, "Thank you." A more than respectable round of applause came from my audience. It was thrilling. Thrilling also was the number of people who'd filled the auditorium.

A young man came down the center aisle carrying a bouquet of flowers and laid them at my feet. I answered questions graciously presented, including the usual one: whether the sonnet was an archaic form now that free verse was rampant and T. S. Eliot had achieved acclaim for his free verse.

"Not at all," I said, and gave my usual homage to my favorite form.

I could have answered questions well into the evening, but the good professor appeared, saying that he had to save me from myself or I'd spend the night on the stage. And supper awaited.

Paulo and Dave joined us as we came

outside. It was snowing, big, fat, floppy flakes, and beginning to mass. Above us, the moon wore a gauzy shawl.

"Where's Bunny?" I asked. He liked to hear me read, and I hadn't seen him.

"Left him at the infirmary to sleep it off," Paulo said. "Doc there gave him a hypo for the pain. He'll be out cold the rest of the night."

Supper was at the home of the chairman of the English Department, a wee old gentleman with crisp white hair and a faded English accent. His wife was a watercolorist of some renown, and her work was evident everywhere. The food and conversation were pleasant enough; the martinis were extraordinary. I was my most charming. The snow continued to fall.

Dave came round with my coat over his arm. "We ought to start back to the city."

"Oh, yes," I said, rising. "Where has time flown?" I thanked my host and his wife.

"But you cannot leave tonight," the massive Adolphus said, blocking our way both figuratively and actually. "The roads are quite unpassable. Tomorrow you can take the train. Tonight, Miss Brown, you will be our guest. What do you say, Mary? I brook no protests, Miss Brown." He gave me a firmly furrowed smile.

I hadn't stood a chance. I daresay no one contradicted William Henry Adolphus and lived to tell the tale.

So Paulo and Dave headed for the Faculty Club, and I was virtually abducted by Professor Adolphus.

A sight to behold in Mary Adolphus's stifling, frilly flannel, Victorian nightdress, I lay on the four-poster as the princess and the pea lay on the many mattresses.

And I was about as sleepless as the pea-besotted princess.

When I closed my eyes, macabre visions assaulted me. Foolish, vain, almost impossibly harmless Fordy. Why? Why? I found the low stool needed to get in and out of bed and climbed down.

The house was silent as the grave. Drawing back the draperies, I blew hot breath on the frozen landscape etched in the windowpane and rubbed its essence away so I could see outside.

We might have been in Russia. A blue white sheen covered everything, and the snow floated in the air like rice powder after a sneeze.

A pastoral scene on my windowpane
Of small farmhouses, peaceful glens.
Fingers exploring the icy terrain
Find Death beneath benevolence.

Lucidity. Morbidity. Fordy would have made a comment about the good Herr Doktor and the influence of the subconscious in my poems. Ah, dear Fordy. He was a sweet old thing.

I released the draperies and dried my eyes with the hem of Mary Adolphus's flannel nightdress. Lighting a cigarette, I considered. Had there been a typewriter in the library downstairs? Had there been gin? Well, I would just have a look. And while I was at it, I would have another peek at that photograph.

A wan night-light in the hallway guided me to the back stairs, which were stale with trapped air. I gathered up Miss Mary's nightdress, so as not to trip over the hem, and felt my way down slowly, passing through the kitchen with nary a rattle.

Without incident, I arrived at the library. Now a cigarette, and light. The switch was just inside the door. No typewriter. I helped myself to writing paper and a pencil, sat down at the desk, and set my poem to paper.

I became aware I was shivering. Would there be gin in the kitchen? Or here? I am a poor guest, I thought, but a desperate one. I opened the drawers of the desk. Not even a medicinal bottle of brandy.

It was back to bed for me, then. But first, one last look at the photograph. I wanted to etch the faces of the barbershop quartet, of Nolan and Adolphus, into my memory, so that I could describe them to Harry.

I sidled over to the table cluttered with framed photographs. If I were a different kind of girl, I might just remove the photograph from its frame and hide the frame behind a row of books. Surely a detective would — I scanned the photographs, moved several aside.

Where was it? I had to be looking right at it. Come now, Oliver. Four men, straw hats, striped shirts, bow ties, a barber pole. It had to be here. A blanket of dread settled over me. Look again, Oliver.

I needn't have troubled. The photograph was gone.

Chapter Forty-seven

"You are clever girls, you and Elinor," old Adolphus said, his pince-nez catching the light. The fumes of his thin dark cigar merged with those from his brandy-drenched coffee.

I ignored the rather obvious note of condescension. "Yes, we are." Having helped myself to scrambled eggs and broiled tomatoes and toast from the hot plates on the sideboard, I chose to sit at the opposite end of the Sheraton dining table from my host. I continued ingenuously. Oh yes, I can do that. "But I'd rather you said we are fine poets." I lavished my toast with butter.

He contemplated me as a panther, his prey. "Perhaps I shall someday. But in the meantime, you fritter away your talents on other, superfluous things."

I put down my fork. The audacity. "Superfluous things?"

"There are matters that should well be left in the hands of professionals."

"Oh, I see." My anger boiled over. I knew exactly what he meant. "Well, whatever you and your musical chum, Lester Nolan, caught poor Fordy Vaude up in has gone and killed him." But he had outsmarted me, and now I'd let him know I'd seen the photograph.

Adolphus was not at all the eccentric old gentleman Fordy had thought him. I had no doubt in my mind that he'd already known Fordy was dead when we'd arrived the night before.

"Can Oliver come out and play in the snow?"

Our duel thus averted, both Adolphus and I shifted attention to the doorway, where Dave Wolfe, wise eyed and ruddy cheeked, stood elbow on the door frame, one leg crossed over the other. How much of our conversation had he overheard?

Mary Adolphus appeared, slipping easily under Dave's arm. "Oh, William, Mr. Wolfe has arrived to collect Miss Brown — Olivia — and I invited him to breakfast with us."

Dave's lips were ice on my cheek. "How is Bunny?" I asked.

"Dislocated shoulder. Paul will drive him and the car back later if the roads are cleared. We'll take the train."

"If it's running," Adolphus said with a cold smile. "Do sit down, Mr. Wolfe. Our man, Jacob, will telephone the railroad and see that you're on the next train."

"What did the old coot say about Fordy that got you riled up?" Dave asked after we'd settled in our seats and the train rolled out of New Haven.

"So you heard. . . ." We were smoking, huddled in our coats as the empty car was neither well heated nor well lit.

The train from Boston, though a mere two hours behind schedule, slowly made its way toward New York, and I was happy for it. Snow caked the windows, filtering through the glare of bright, hard sunlight.

Dave said, "Some of it."

"I felt he and his friend Lester Nolan had used Fordy badly, somehow involved him in some devious activity that made him a target." I shook my head with frustration. "I don't know what I'm saying."

He took my hand. "Don't stop. I'm following you. That flashy cop Nolan is connected to Adolphus?"

"I'm not sure, but I think so. Adolphus denies he had anything to do with sending Adelle-Adeline to Fordy as a nanny, not to mention a spy."

"She didn't seem sharp enough to be a spy." Dave's eyes flitted round the car. Satisfied, he pulled a bottle of gin from inside his coat, unscrewed the cap, and offered me first swallow.

"You are a very dear man," I said.

"Fordy was a good chap, a swell friend."

"You didn't know him at Yale?"

"I'm a Harvard man. Met him in the Village when Jack and I came down, then again in France. You could always count on Fordy to bail you out."

"Of what?"

"You know. Debts. We all owed him money."

We passed the bottle back and forth. I tucked my feet up under me. "How was he able to do that?"

"That financial business of his did all right."

"He never talked about it. Did you ever see his office?"

"No. I think he was ashamed of how he earned his money."

"Yes. Fordy'd wanted so to be thought of as an artist." Aided by the dim light, I was drifting, half-asleep. "I'm cold."

Dave patted his lap. "Come over here with that fur and we'll keep each other warm."

"I would never decline an inviting suggestion from such an attractive man," I said. He slipped his hands inside my coat and gathered me into his lap. His lips were sweet with gin.

It was early evening when I returned to my house on snow-bedecked Bedford Street, parting from Dave somewhat reluctantly. I had much on my mind that needed appraisal by Harry, so with some hasty kisses on my doorstep, I sent him on his way.

I was a little tight and fumbled the key in the lock. Harry's door popped open.

"Sherlock requests da pleasure of yer company, Olwer," Ding Dong said, giving me a little bow.

"How nice, Mr. Ding Dong. I'm just going to tell Mattie I'm home and I'll come right back. Ask Sherlock if he can hold his horses."

"Get on with it!" Harry shouted.

"So I'll say good evenin' to youse, Olwer." He leaned back into Harry's flat. "O revor, Sherlock."

Mattie came down the stairs and took my little valise. "You were snowed in?"

"Yes. But I had a very successful reading and was wined and dined and hosted royally."

"And you're feverish and overtired and

ought to be in bed." She missed very little.

"Right as always." I hung my coat on the hall stand. "Tell you what. I'll change my clothes and have a cup of tea with you, then I have the most curious things to tell Harry."

"Tell you what," Mattie said grinning. "I'll serve us all tea and cakes downstairs so I can get to hear these curious things."

And wouldn't you know, it was my own dear Mattie who put one of the pieces of the puzzle together.

"Who was that brought you home?" Harry said, filling the room with cigar smoke. The swelling on his face had gone down, his bruises yellowed. He grimaced when Mattie handed him a cup of tea.

"Train. Car's in New Haven."

"Didn't ask you that."

"Why are you fussing? It was Dave Wolfe. We left Bunny in New Haven in the infirmary. He dislocated his shoulder moving furniture in his office, so he was in a lot of pain."

Harry's eyes glinted. He stopped puffing. "Dislocated his shoulder, did he? Moving furniture, says he? Now that's an interesting piece of evidence. You been holding out, Oliver?"

"Bunny? Oh, no, Harry. Bunny would

never have killed Fordy." But I was speechless. Bunny? Could he have? Did he owe Fordy money, too?

"Give us the rest," he said.

"Why, Harry, dear, how do you know I have more to tell?"

He went to the bathroom and brought back a bottle of beer, settled himself back at his desk. "Come across, Oliver."

"Okay," I said. "Adolphus is a pompous old guy, even a bit scary, if you ask me, and he's not innocent in this. I think he did refer Adeline to Fordy. And when I was able to do some snooping, I found a side table in his library full of framed photographs, one of which was of four young men in barbershop quartet outfits. I recognized two of them. One was Adolphus, and the other was your friend Lester Nolan."

The bottle smacked the top of Harry's desk. "I knew it!"

"I didn't recognize the other two men, but I do remember Fordy telling me that old Adolphus was into barbershop quartets."

"Barbershop quartets?" Mattie jumped up and did a little clog and skip. "Barbershop quartets?"

"Yes." I looked at Harry, and we exchanged shrugs. "Why?"

Mattie giggled. "It's a terrible thing to laugh about anything tragic, but it's as clear as the noses on your faces, you two."

Harry growled.

"All right," Mattie said. "What is the name of the poor girl who was murdered?"

"Adeline," I said, mystified.

Mattie was gleeful. "And what is the name of your client?"

"Daisy," Harry said. We looked at each other. "Bloody hell. '*Sweet Adeline.*' "

" '*Daisy, Daisy,*' " I sang, " '*give us your answer true . . .*' "

Chapter Forty-eight

Mattie packed me off to bed, fed me honey and brandy-dosed hot milk, and buried me under mounds of blankets. Burning with fever, I felt a singular clarity of mind.

Kate was in danger.

I croaked my fears to Mattie. "Tell Harry."

There was more, there was much more. On the tip of my tongue, in fact. But I could not make words of what was in my head — O, woe to the poet — and it all slipped away as I sank, not without a struggle, into a bottomless sleep.

A red-and-white-striped serpent wrapped itself round my arm and tugged. The cloud I floated on tipped, and the verse I'd put together flawlessly slid off in a jumble of letters, gone, free.

The rude serpent hissed in my ear, "Surface, Oliver." Another tug.

"Go away."

"Nothing doing."

I opened one eye. "Lost the couplet. See

what you've done."

Harry packed pillows behind me. He smelled of cigarettes and shaving soap. "Mattie, coffee for sleeping beauty here." His ponytail grazed my cheek like a shade.

There was nothing for it. I elbowed myself into a sitting position, cocked my head at him. "A body can't even retire in peace here. I'm hungry. What time is it?"

"Time?" He lit a cigarette from his and handed it to me. "Hell, Oliver, it's Sunday night. You've been out for over a day and we have things to do."

Mattie set a tray of coffee, toast, and a poached egg on my lap. "I've run you a bath, Olivia. She was feverish, Harry. She doesn't sleep, hardly eats, throws herself into strange situations, with your encouragement, I might add —"

"Go on," Harry said. "She's a whole lot tougher than you and I." He plucked up a slice of my toast, spread it generously with butter and a huge dollop of marmalade, and ate it in two big bites.

"If you two are finished talking about me as if I weren't here, I'd like you to tell me that Kate is all right."

"Can't do it, Oliver. According to Red Farrell, she got into a black town car in the early evening yesterday. He chased it for a few blocks, but it got away from him. I went over to have a look around. Her door was open and the place was a mess."

The implications of what Harry'd just told me made me shudder. I gripped his hand. "They're going to kill her, too."

"We don't know that," he said with little heart. "I stopped by the precinct and told Brophy."

"Who is 'they'?" Mattie asked.

"Nolan and Adolphus," I suggested.

"Nah." Harry contemplated me with bloodshot eyes. "They sent Adeline into it to find out what was going on. She must have figured it out, or at the very least gotten close. Kate's the only key left now to what they want to know."

I finished the egg and dawdled over the toast. Something was niggling at me. "Harry, was Adeline's tongue slit?"

He frowned. "The coroner didn't mention it, did he? Either they didn't spot it or it wasn't. Or maybe the cops are holding it back. I'll get Hook on the telephone and ask."

"Slit tongue?" Mattie cried, aghast. "What kind of people are they?"

"Murderers," Harry said.

"It's this hoodlum Lupo's signature," I added. "He murders for hire."

"Among many other things. This could be some big bunko scheme of his that Adeline interrupted."

I smoothed back my hair. "That Fordy was involved in."

"Something that kept the moolah coming. Fordy must've gotten in over his head, maybe wanted to get out. He became a threat."

"White slavery? Rum running? Extortion?"

Mattie, her eyes wide, clapped her hands over her mouth.

"Anything," Harry agreed.

The doorbell rang, splintering our train of thought.

"And what about the barbershop girls?" Mattie asked, reluctant to leave us.

"Right." I slipped my arms into my dressing gown, tied it round my waist, and swung my feet to the floor. "The quartet. If Adeline and Daisy are really sisters, whose children are they? Certainly not Adolphus's."

"And not Nolan's," Harry said. "His wife died years ago. No children. I'll hazard a guess that the name of one of the other two singers is Zimmerman."

The doorbell rang again.

"Don't say anything interesting until I

get back," Mattie said, leaving with the tray.

"Beat it, Harry, call Deputy Hook and let me get dressed."

What I did was have a nice soak while I gave some thought to the horrific events of the last two weeks. By the time they returned, I was dressed and bursting with ideas.

"It's not about bootlegging, Harry. The hoodlums just kill each other in the bootlegging business, don't they?"

Harry nodded. "It's about territory."

"Did you reach Hook?" I noticed the envelope clasped tightly in Mattie's hand.

"Left word with the missus."

"What's that you have there, Mattie?"

"Oh." She looked down at her hand. "All this horror made me forget." She gave Harry a telegram. "For you, Harry. The boy rang our bell by mistake."

Slicing it open with his forefinger, Harry unfolded it, read, folded it, and put it in his pocket. "I'll be on my way."

"Where? You're not going to share your news?"

"Curiosity killed the cat." He tweaked my nose and sauntered off.

I called after him, "If it has something to do with the case, you should share with your partner."

"I do have a private life," he responded.

Following, I stood at the top of the stairs and threw my words down after him. "When his lady friend calls . . ."

The door slammed.

"Are you having dinner with Gerry and Joan tonight?" I asked Mattie. She did so every Sunday.

"Do you want to come along?"

"No, but it's dear of you to ask. It's quiet, I'm rested, I'm going to work."

Our doorbell rang. She blushed, and my steadfast Mattie became flustered and fluttery. "That'll be Gerry, and I'm not even dressed."

I gave her a hug. "Go get ready and I'll entertain Gerry." I was an entirely new girl, replenished, full of energy, but what was I to do with it?

"So, Gerry, how's it going with the Vaude case?" I leaned over so he could light my cigarette.

He fixed me with his wise blue eyes. "Which one?"

"You think they're connected?"

"Okay, Olivia. Let's make an even swap. What do you have for me?"

I grinned at him. "Since you put it that way, Gerry dear, I know these so-called

Black Hand hoodlums — one Lupo the Wolf — leave their victims with a sliced tongue. Which means Fordy Vaude crossed paths with this Lupo."

"It's possible."

"You're not keeping up your end of the bargain, sir. Do you have any real suspects? And is there any news about Kate Vaude?"

He shook his head at me. "Nothing solid."

Plainly I was going to have to pull it out of him piece by piece. I tried another tack. "The elements in the nanny murder sound very similar to poor Fordy's. Did Adeline Zimmerman have her tongue slit also?"

Gerry turned serious. "Olivia, I don't know that you should be getting involved in all this."

I patted his hand. "I am already involved. I am even a suspect."

"You are not a suspect," he said firmly. "But you could become a victim."

"Why all these serious faces?" Mattie held her coat out to Gerry.

"Okay," I said. "Just tell me about Adeline and I'll leave it there. Was her tongue slit? If it was, it makes the murder less personal. I mean, unlikely that one of us did it, and I'd be glad of that."

Gerry helped Mattie with her coat, took

her arm, paused at the door, and looked back at me. "You have to know?"

"Yes. Tell me, was it or wasn't it?"

"It was."

Chapter Forty-nine

I sat at my typewriter, praying for a diversion, for I had not a verse in my head. My thoughts were of the Vaude children, of the aftermath. Their father left them twice, the second time forever. What were they to think? And now Kate's disappearance, which looked ominous. Of course, I had known neither father nor mother, and I had managed, with the loving care of others.

Pushing back my chair, I wrapped my shawl round my shoulders and peered down at the snow-festooned street. Subtle white light and gray shadow, snow-reflected streets, a man walking a dog carefully on the icy sidewalk. It was very still.

Across the way I caught the flare of a match. Someone was watching my house. I went downstairs, threw on my coat and hat, picked up Great-Aunt Evangeline's broken umbrella, then went down the stairs again. The light in my vestibule had gone out. I could have been in a closet were it not for the street lamp shining bleakly through the etched glass in my door. The shade of a man suddenly appeared on the other side of the glass. My hand tightened on the umbrella. Hesitating for only a moment, I thrust open the door to the street.

"Oliver!" Dave stood on my doorstep, his hand extended. "Where're you off to?"

Across the street I saw the dot of a cigarette beside the dark stoop. I put my fingers to my lips and pulled Dave inside. "Someone's watching my house."

He was startled. "Are you sure?" I heard something in his voice. Was it concern? Or something more?

"Look across the way, near the stoop. Someone's there. I can see his cigarette."

Dave hunched down and, heads together, we looked for the pinpoint of light, but all we saw were the shadows. Nothing whatever moved. We were close against each other, breathing each other's breaths, turning almost imperceptibly until lips soft as silk, arms entwined.

"You are so beautiful," he whispered.

The door opened. We froze, compromised.

"And a fine evenin' to youse, Olwer." Red Farrell squinted at me in the half-light. Slowly he shifted his peculiar eyes to Dave.

I said, "Dave Wolfe, Red Farrell."

Red stared at Dave. "Ain't we met before?"

"I would remember," Dave said with the utmost seriousness.

I pressed my lips tight to hold my laughter.

Red gave me a quizzical look and chewed the stump of his cigar. "Youse lost yer light here, Olwer." He elbowed Dave. "Gimme a lift, buddy."

A coughing spell came over me as Dave cupped his hand and gave Red his lift.

"Aha! Someone's copped yer bulb." Red came down, and Dave stepped back and dusted off his hands.

"Who would do that?" I asked.

Red flashed his ferocious grin at me. "Dere's all kinds. Don't youse worry none, Olwer. I'll just hang out here till Sherlock gets back."

I didn't ask Red how he knew Harry wasn't here, having come to the conclusion that it had been Red Farrell who was watching my house.

"Let's get some air," Dave said. Maybe he'd come to the same conclusion.

"Thank you kindly for your trouble, Mr. Farrell," I said.

Out on the sidewalk, a polished jet of

ice, Dave tucked my arm in his and we walked apace. The snow cover was lush, the soft silence enveloping.

First came an odd rumble, and then Dave said, "Da company youse keeps, Olwer. Youse outa watch yerself."

I looked up at him and, pressure released, we both howled, stopped, did again. Our laughter pressed close, imprisoned by the cover of snow. Then the magnitude of events hit me, and I turned into his arm and hid my face. He stood still and stroked my back until my sobs subsided.

Finally I said, "You heard about Kate?"

"Kate? What about Kate?"

"She's disappeared, kidnapped, dead, maybe." Choking up, I thought of the soft roundness of Kate's arm, the scent of peaches.

He gripped my shoulders. "When?"

"Don't know. Harry said."

"I went by to see her after we got back yesterday. She was okay, all things considered."

I dried my freezing tears with his handkerchief, and we started walking again. He was staring off into the distance. "Dave, what was going on there in Croton? You lived across the street."

"I don't know. I was in and out all the

time. Kate needed me. Fordy was never home."

"Where was he?"

"Traveling on business."

"What business?"

"Well, you know, Oliver. His family's."

"Of course, but didn't he ever bring anything home with him?"

"Not that I saw. You think this has something to do with his family business?"

I shrugged, not wanting to give away too much. "It's a mystery to me. And it's making my head ache."

"Bunny's home," Dave said. He tucked my hand back into the crook of his arm, and we walked toward Bank Street, where Bunny had his flat. "We'll just drop in on him. He always has the best hooch."

Bunny had the most well-appointed flat; he'd taken it over from Elinor Wylie and moved in his big mahogany desk and hung his Whistler print. We found him very much himself again, wearing a smoking jacket and more than a little tight.

Bunny's socially prominent family consisted of professionals, doctors and lawyers. They'd sent him to prep school and Princeton, expecting, no doubt, more of him than assistant editor status at *Vanity Fair*. But their disappointment was our

341

gain. He was an astute editor and a fine intellectual companion, and a good friend. He greeted us with a kind of fevered delight.

"Booth martinis?" he said thickly, swaying to a mystical beat. "Finished a batch. Making another."

Dave went off to the wc while I leaned against the icebox and watched Bunny stir and divide, unsteadily, the lovely liquid into three cut crystal glasses.

"What is this with you and Dave?" A demonic look came into his eyes as he poured the drinks.

"Bunny," I said softly, "Kate's gone missing."

"Missing?" He stared at me blankly. "Missing? Would you take that tray down for me, Oliver? Still having some trouble reaching." He removed a small envelope from his pocket and emptied a bit of powder into one of the martinis, explaining, "Dope for the pain."

I took down the tray and, while he set the glasses on it, told him what I knew. "It's a nightmare. Like *The Fall of the House of Usher.*"

"Remember which drink I put the powder in, Oliver. It's pretty powerful," he told me, mighty pleased with himself about something. "Or better still, don't." He tucked the envelope into his pocket.

I frowned at him. "What are you up to?"

He smiled sweetly at me, but his eyes gave him away. "I recall Fordy was in some trouble at Yale. Pornographic paintings." He arranged napkins on the tray with the cocktail shaker.

"You're right," Dave said. He came up behind me and kissed the nape of my neck. "I'd forgotten about that."

"Fordy was thrown out of Yale for painting and selling pornography," Bunny said, flicking a supercilious eye at Dave. "I wonder —" He stopped, and we all looked at each other.

"But is it worth killing over?" I asked. "And is it worth sending an experienced agent like Adeline Zimmerman undercover to investigate the commerce of pornography?" Dave and I went into the living room and flopped down on the sofa.

Following us a few seconds later, Bunny quipped, "Maybe she was working for Comstock," referring to the late, notorious Anthony Comstock, who'd founded the New York Society for the Suppression of Vice. He put the tray down, and before we could reach for our drinks, he shuffled them round like the carney hustlers with the pea under the walnut shell. He gave me a sodden leer.

"What's going on?" Dave said.

"Bunny's put his knockout powder into one of the drinks, and now he's shuffled them so God only knows which one it is."

A quick shade of irritation stained Dave's face.

"Nonsense," Bunny said. "We all know that Oliver has an overactive imagination." He took up a glass and challenged, "Are you afraid?"

Dave shrugged. He handed me a glass and picked up the last one. We raised our glasses to each other.

Bunny said, "Okay, whoever stays awake gets Oliver."

"Wait a minute," I said. "I am my own girl. No one gets me."

Before long, the room was filled with thick smoke and we'd finished off the second batch of martinis. Dave performed another startlingly good imitation of Red Farrell, and we all laughed. It was diversion, no doubt about it. Bunny talked about Dostoyevsky, then rose carefully and left the room.

Dave and I fell over on the sofa, giving each other boozy kisses. But my limbs were growing heavy, and my lashes kept grazing my cheeks. It became clear to me that it was I who had imbibed the sedative.

"None of that now," Bunny said, returning. He dropped a sheaf of paper on the floor with a thump and ordered Dave to read the first chapter of Dave's own novel. We peeled away from each other. Dave sank to his knees and reached for his manuscript but, clownishly, kept sinking. He turned his eyes to me, ambushed, and pitched over on his face.

I dropped down beside him, shook him. He responded with a snore.

Chortling, Bunny said, "Well, I guess we know who got my drink."

"You are a bad boy, Bunny," I said sternly. "You did that on purpose." I stroked Dave's hair, put my cheek against his, sat up. "What should we do with him?"

"Let him sleep it off right there. He looks comfortable." He patted the sofa. "Come sit with me."

Oh, well, I thought, what was there to do? And Bunny had plenty of gin. We polished off the rest of the martinis talking about Stephen Benét's work and Elinor's and their marriage. Bunny fell asleep with his head in my lap.

I sat for a while, amid the snores of my

would-be lovers, thinking about my frantic life. What was I doing? How long could I keep it up? My brain was muddled. I may even have dozed.

It was late when I slipped out of Bunny's flat. Bank Street was deserted. Tipsy, placing my steps with care on the icy street, I headed for home. I don't know when I became aware of the automobile, a black sedan. It pulled up beside me, its door open.

"Geddin," I was told in no uncertain terms.

I had nowhere to run.

Chapter Fifty

"How's dat a nice goil like youse walks on da street by herself in da middle of da night?" Monk Eastman tapped his driver, a brutish-looking man in a black suit and bowler hat. "Da Blue Boid, Shmeul."

Are you relieved? I can only tell you that it took a while for my own being to register that I was not in mortal danger. Indeed, my heart threatened to shake itself loose from its cage, and even the bizarrely benign presence of Monk Eastman, the ginger cat in his lap, couldn't stop the engine of my emotions.

I croaked, "Are you kidnapping me?"

He patted my hand. "We was drivin' by and seen youse on da street, ain't dat right, Shmeul? So I sez, We can't have Miss Olivia walkin' da street like a common —" Leaning forward, he gave Shmeul a flick on the back of the neck as if it had been Shmeul who almost said *whore*. "So I sez, Let's give her a ride home."

Shmeul nodded, or at least his hat did.

It was so ludicrous, because there I was

blubbering for the second time that evening. I was collecting handkerchiefs.

"Now I see youse up close, and youse look like youse could blow away in da wind, so I'm tinkin' youse should eat a decent meal, get some meat on yer bones," my Lochinvar said.

"What is the Blue Bird?"

"It's a joint on Fourteenth Street. Dey know me dere. Youse t'ought youse was bein' kidnapped? Y'hear dat, Shmeul?"

I settled back. "Two men with guns tried to kidnap me and my friend Mattie the other day, when I was in a building on Beaver Street."

"I know about dat," Monk said. "Dey wouldna got away wit it, not wit me around. Lupo knows yer under my protection, but I ain't takin' no chances, which is why we're lookin' out for youse."

The fear, the booze, the relief, all combined were like the sedative I'd not drunk at Bunny's. There were questions I wanted to ask. I barely managed, "What does this Lupo want of me?"

"He tinks yer buttin' into his business."

"I'm trying to find out why a couple of nice people were murdered, why a man who doesn't have a business has plenty of money, why . . . I think Lupo's . . ." I lost my train of thought, shook myself awake. "Responsible . . ."

"Yeah. Lupo's got an investment here he's protectin'. And it ain't bootleggin'. I'm lookin' into it. Youse keep writin' yer pomes and leave Lupo to me."

I bit my lip to stay awake. It was near to impossible. Maybe Bunny had sloshed his sedative into each of the drinks. "Mr. Eastman, please," I managed to say, "will you tell me when you find out?"

Instead of answering my question, he asked, "Which one is dat wit da beard?"

Beard? I wasn't thinking clearly. "Oh, you mean Dave. He's a writer." So he'd followed us to Bunny's and waited. "Why do you ask?"

I admit I don't remember what he answered, if he answered me at all. Surely he said something about eating good healthy food, but I remember nothing else until Harry said, "Bloody hell!" and I opened my eyes and found myself in Harry's arms.

"I guess I lost out on a dinner," I said as Harry kicked his door shut and dropped me unceremoniously on the dreaded couch.

"What the hell are you getting yourself into, Oliver? You know who that was who carried you in?"

"Monk Eastman?" I offered meekly. Wide awake now, I motioned for a cigarette.

"Might as well have been. It was Shmeul, his driver, his bodyguard. Served time for murder." He gave me a light in disgust and hovered over me.

"Oh, back off, Harry. I am not having an affair with Monk Eastman. He happened to see me walking home from Bunny's and gave me a ride. Bunny put his painkiller powder into one of the drinks, then shuffled them. Dave passed out. I left."

Harry stared at me through slitted eyes, still ringed with color. He was not forgiving me that easily. I smiled at him sweetly.

Sitting down at his desk, he said, "Someone unscrewed the bulb from the light."

"I know. Red Farrell was standing across the street, watching the house. He must have thought Dave was breaking in because he was here in two shakes. I appreciate your wanting to protect me, Harry, but really."

"I didn't ask Red to keep an eye on you, Oliver. You're a big girl, and independent, as you've informed me often enough. You

can take care of yourself." He lit a cigarette and put his feet up on his desk.

"Thank you," I said, though I believe he
was being sarcastic. "Monk said Lupo
won't bother me again and that he's
looking into Lupo's business on my
account."

"On your account? Sure. He's some
kidder all right. He doesn't do anything
unless it's on his account. Lupo's got
something lucrative going that Monk
doesn't know about. A little gang war is
just what we need."

"But he's been pardoned."

"Yeah, but that doesn't mean he's gone
straight."

"Harry, you have no faith in the intrinsic
goodness of people."

"You've got that right."

We stared each other down as we
smoked. "Did you have a good time this
evening?" I asked finally.

"I had an informative evening with a
knowledgeable fellow that cost us a case of
gin."

"What are you talking about, Harry?"

"Fordy made five trips to Italy this
year. Each trip lasted one month to six
weeks."

"He's an artist," I said with little faith.

"Maybe he was studying in Florence and Rome."

"He was in Rome, yes, but he didn't stay there. It was always the same pattern. He checked into his hotel, spent the night, checked out in the morning, and disappeared. A month or so later, his name would turn up on the steamship passenger lists and he'd be on his way home."

Chapter Fifty-one

"I was absolutely wrong," Bunny admitted as we sat in the Brevoort over gin-filled tea-cups two evenings later. He was not talking about his behavior with the sedative, for he refused to think he'd done wrong, but rather *Heartbreak House*, the play by Bernard Shaw we'd seen this night. "When I read it I thought it a dreary piece similar to *Misalliance*."

"Not at all," I told him. "It was thoroughly absorbing, though I kept hearing intimations of *The Cherry Orchard*."

He nodded. "You are right, of course. Shaw's perfected the country-house conversation he was working at in *Misalliance*."

Bunny often took me to plays, concerts, and the opera. In fact, he was my favorite companion on these outings because our discussions afterward were incredibly stimulating.

To their credit, Larry Langner and the Theatre Guild in their third season were responsible for mounting the American production of *Heartbreak House,* which had opened the month before at the Garrick to wonderful reviews.

Our conversation peaked, and now we stared into our teacups amid the late evening bustle, avoiding any mention of what had to be foremost in our thoughts.

A waiter came by and replaced our laden ashtray with a clean one. Bunny said, "How is the book coming? I'm eager to read it."

I squeezed his hand. Bunny's a very fine editor and always generous with his time, his criticism constructive and insightful. "I must lock myself in my room and finish it. The events of the last weeks . . . have depressed my spirit."

An odd idea had presented itself in the middle of my words, caused me to pause for a moment. Fordy was another one of the obsessively analyzed, always talking about his analysis. He'd mentioned it and his doctor when we'd had dinner together. What did the doctor know?

"A depressed spirit? Not you, Oliver." Bunny brought my hand to his lips. "Never you."

As a barrier to the rest of what he seemed well on the way to uttering, I asked him about Dave's novel.

He turned back to his drink, making no effort to conceal his disappointment. "Quite good, though more visceral than cerebral. Fathers and sons, something I do understand, but not in terms of the immigrant generation and their American progeny, which is his milieu."

"The Wolfe family saga?"

"Probably, though as long as I've known him, he's never talked about them."

"How long have you known him?"

"Met him in Paris with Jack. They'd been at Harvard together and had run into each other at a bistro. Dave was driving an ambulance then, heading back to the front. He planned to come home after the War and go to medical school."

"He changed his mind."

"We'd all changed by the time the War ended. Nothing would ever be the same again for any of us." His face took on the bleakest of expressions. "I was sure I'd die before Jack. He was the most vividly alive man I've ever known."

Now that we were both dispirited, it was time to call it a night.

I awoke in the hazy hours of dawn when the milk wagon stopped in front of my house and the clank of the bottles sounded through the Village streets. In the sepia shade of my room, Jack Reed leaned over my typewriter to read the fragment of a poem I'd abandoned.

"Jack," I breathed, suffused with an impossible yearning.

When he half turned to me I saw the outline of my typewriter through him. "We would have been such lovers as the world has never seen," he said with a gentle, rueful Irish smile as the vision faded away.

I knew nothing else until Mattie's soft knock woke me from as sound a sleep as I'll ever have. But with awakening came a deep sense of loss. Is it possible to be in love with a shadow?

"There's a fine gentleman here to see you," Mattie said, setting a tray on my bedside table and pouring my tea.

Some odd hesitation in her voice, and her reserve, alarmed me. "What fine gentleman? Not Thomas?" The only fine gentleman I know, besides my publisher, is Thomas Jenner, my attorney.

"Not Thomas," she said, and handed me a card.

The card read "Dr. William Henry Adolphus."

Chapter Fifty-two

"Damn." Distracted, I curled his card round my finger. The card came to life. Flipping into the air, it landed on my typewriter. "It's that dreadful man, Fordy's Yale professor," I told Mattie.

"I thought I recognized the name." Mattie pulled back the draperies and began fussing with my coverlet. "Shall I tell him you're indisposed?"

I felt indisposed. The late morning sunlight hurt my eyes, and my head throbbed. "No, I'm intrigued." I got out of bed and tried to think a straight thought. "Fix him a cup of tea, then close him into the parlor and get Harry."

After Mattie left, I sat on the side of my bed, sipping tea. Adolphus had told me to stay out of this affair, yet here he was calling on me. It was not to repeat his warning. He, in fact, wanted something of me.

I splashed my face with cold water, combed my hair, and put on a fresh blouse and my old brown skirt, which Mattie had taken an iron to and therefore greatly improved its appearance. Opening my door, I listened for Harry's voice. Not yet. I left my door ajar and went to my type-writer.

A door opened below, and another, then Harry's voice. I came down the stairs, stepping into the kitchen to plant a kiss on Mattie's concerned brow.

"Don't worry so," I told her.

When I, very much the gracious lady, opened the doors to the parlor, Harry was stoking the fire, and Adolphus, huge and broad as a Buddha, dwarfed my sofa, a look of supreme displeasure on his face. He got to his feet and I offered him my hand, which he bowed over.

"Dr. Adolphus has expressed an unwillingness to talk to me," Harry told me with singular formality. "Anything you have need to convey to Miss Brown, you may to me as well." Harry raised a languorous eyebrow at me and passed me a cigarette. "Isn't that so, Miss Brown."

"Oh, indeed, Mr. Melville." I settled myself in the welcoming depths of Great-Aunt Evangeline's shabby chair. "I do admit to some surprise to receive a visit from you, Professor, as the last time we met you told me in no uncertain terms that

I was not to meddle in the Vaude-Zimmerman affair."

"That is so, Miss Brown, but something has come up that requires my attention and your cooperation."

I rarely submit to my Irish temper, but I was about to now. As I opened my mouth to say my piece, Harry stepped in with, "What do you mean by cooperation, Professor?"

Folding my arms, I waited, silenced, but only for the moment.

The old man looked uncomfortable. He removed his pince-nez, rubbed the bridge of his nose between thumb and forefinger, restored the pince-nez. "You are in possession of a book of poetry, Miss Brown, that —"

"I have many books of poetry, Professor," I said.

"I am speaking of a certain collection of the works of John Donne," Adolphus said.

"John Donne?" Harry and I exchanged glances.

"Yes. I understand that Miss Zimmerman owned such a book, that when you arrived for the weekend, you were given her room, and you may have, when you left, inadvertently, of course, taken the book of poems with you."

"How odd," I said. "There was so much confusion even before we found Adeline dead. We packed in a hurry, and when I unpacked my valise here, I did find a book of John Donne's poems."

"I would thank you if you'll return it to me."

"Why you?" Harry asked.

"Because I am Adeline Zimmerman's godfather, and her possessions have a deep personal meaning for me." His voice broke, and I would have felt sorry for him had I not known there was more to it than his anguish.

"Well," said I, graciously, "I am sorry for your loss. Of course you may have it. If you and Mr. Melville will excuse me, I'll see if I can find it."

"By all means," Harry said, as cordial as I've ever seen him.

I took my steps two at a time. What was there about Adeline's Donne that we had missed, and how would I be able to tell her Donne from mine?

It happened to be easier than I thought. I opened the books a few pages at a time, comparing. About halfway I came upon some barely visible pencil jottings in the margins of one, and more here and there as I turned the pages. They appeared to be in some kind of shorthand. I closed Adeline's Donne and slipped it under my pillow. The book I brought to Professor Adolphus was the one that belonged to me.

"Thank you for your kindness," the professor said, making haste to leave. He took his cape from the hall rack and his walking stick from the stand.

"Just one last thing," Harry said.

"Yes?" Adolphus adjusted his broad-brimmed hat.

"How did you know about the Donne?"

Oh, Harry. I'd been so astounded by Adolphus's visit and the request, I hadn't thought to ask.

Adolphus paused, hand on the doorknob. Mattie came from the kitchen, and we three stood waiting for him to speak.

"Kate Vaude," he said.

"Kate? But Kate's gone missing, no one's seen her. She might be dead."

"Be assured, Miss Brown, she is not dead. She is under my protection."

"Your protection, Professor?" I said. "Just what is your protection, exactly?"

"The same protection offered to Adeline Zimmerman?" Harry asked, looking my visitor square in the eye. "Three cheers for the Secret Service."

I was nonplussed. "The Secret Service?"

Adolphus's color became florid. "We take care of our own, Mr. Melville."

Chapter Fifty-three

Thus spoke Adolphus.

Uttering no other word, he descended the stairs with the agility and speed of a much younger man. And if queried, I would have readily admitted that this news had left Mattie and me quite speechless.

Finally, Harry's imprecation delivered us, and we all burst into speech at once.

"Secret Service!" came from Mattie. She made for the kitchen, and we followed her.

"Adeline was Secret Service," I said, taking three glasses from the cupboard. "How did you know?"

Harry poured a couple of fingers of gin in each glass. "I have some friends in high places," he said, mighty pleased. "That's what Nolan's been so cagey about."

"He's Secret Service, too?" Mattie said. "I don't think Gerry will be surprised. He thought Nolan was working for the government and that Addie had been as well."

"You kept the right book?" Harry asked.

"Of course." I ran upstairs and returned with Adeline's Donne. "About halfway through she began jotting notes in the margins." I handed the book to Harry. "I can't make it out."

Harry stared at the jottings, flipped through the pages. "It's in code."

"Whoever killed her caught her spying," I said.

"More than that," Harry said. "She got on to something and didn't have a chance to pass on her information."

"So, it's what we thought: Adolphus and Nolan know why she was there. They don't know what she found. Maybe it's in the book."

"Should you have kept it from the Secret Service?" Mattie asked in a small voice.

"There's an honest girl, don't you think, Harry?" I said. "Definitely our moral barometer."

"Absolutely, Oliver."

Mattie flushed. "Oh, go on, you two."

"Of course," Harry said, "there's no way of knowing whether Adolphus told us the truth."

"And we don't know for sure that Kate is safe."

"We can ask Gerry to look into it, can't we?" Mattie said.

"We can." Harry grinned at her. "Why don't you invite him to dinner while I see what I can make of Adeline's notes. And Oliver —"

"Oliver," said I, "is going to make an appointment to see an analyst."

"A psychoanalyst?" Both Harry and Mattie looked at me, aghast.

"Someone highly recommended by Fordy Vaude," I said.

Dr. Greeve. An unfortunate name, don't you think? Especially for a doctor. I asked the operator to connect me to the number listed in the telephone directory, and after four rings a woman with a sibilant Viennese accent answered.

"Dr. Greeve's office. Who is calling, please?"

"My name is Olivia Brown. I wonder if the doctor might find some time to see me today."

"The doctor has full appointments this day, Miss Brown." I heard muffled voices coming through the hand the woman must have put over the mouthpiece.

A man's voice said, "This is Dr. Greeve. Would this be Miss Olivia Brown the poet with whom I have the honor of speaking?" He spoke clear, precise American, with no accent whatever.

"Yes."

"I will make the time for you, my dear." This surprising response was quickly followed by, "Perhaps three o'clock?" It was as if he'd been awaiting my call.

The good doctor's address proved to be a broad-stepped brownstone house on Tenth Street between Fifth and Sixth Avenues. On the oak door was an assertive, crimson-bowed Christmas wreath. I stopped at the foot of the snow-packed steps to give space to the man who was just leaving, and who should it be but Whit Sawyer.

"Oliver," he said, catching me in his arms. "So you've taken my advice at last."

I wriggled my way out of his embrace. "Advice?"

"You're here to see Dr. G., aren't you?"

"This is my first time —"

"Not another word. I can see you've had an epiphany. I guarantee you will feel such freedom, as if all the bad blood is flowing out and in its place, creative fluids."

"I'm sure," said I. For the life of me, I do not understand how any grown-up man or woman can devote so much time to being analyzed. "Are you seeing Dr. Greeve?"

"Have been for a year now. This was Fordy's time, you know, poor chap. Dr. G. understands the creative spirit."

"I'm looking forward to meeting him." I

blew Whit a kiss.

At the top of the stairs I twisted the bell handle marked discreetly SIDNEY GREEVE, M.D. and waited, shifting back and forth from one foot to the other to keep warm. It was ten minutes to three.

When there was no response, I tried the door and found it open. I stepped into a small foyer containing a hat stand. Two faded Oriental rugs overlapped each other on the floor. I hung my coat on the hat stand beside a man's gray tweed overcoat and hat.

The foyer gave way to a waiting room holding a small sofa and two upholstered chairs and another faded Oriental rug. The light coming from a brass table lamp with a multicolored leaded shade was dim and unassuming. On the walls were paintings of pastoral scenes.

I was about to sit when a door opened and a balding man of average height and weight beckoned to me. He would have been decidedly nondescript but for the deep creases across his forehead and thick pouches under his eyes. I had never seen him before, yet he looked familiar.

"It is very good to meet you finally in person," he said, indicating a chair that was positioned in front of a desk. The room was otherwise decorated with tall glass-enclosed bookcases and the mythical analyst's couch.

"In person? Have we spoken other than today?" The chair had an exceptionally tall seat, leaving my feet dangling off the floor. I felt the child being taken to task.

"Well, I've heard so much about you from —" He stopped and beamed at me. "I'm honored that you've chosen me as your analyst."

"From your other patients, you mean? Fordy and Whit. But alas, Dr. Greeve, I'm afraid I've not come to see you as a patient."

"You've been ill," he said abruptly, ignoring what I'd just said.

"Fordy's dead, as you must know. Murdered. Because of something he was involved with, something that took him to Italy for months at a time, something lucrative."

"You burn yourself out with too much drink, with free love —" I accepted his wrath, for I had come on false pretenses. It was laced with indignation.

"I'm asking you, Doctor, to reveal to the police what it was that Fordy confided in you. By doing so, you will prevent any more deaths."

He lit a cigar and watched me as a cat would a mouse. "It's your confusion as to your gender, my dear . . . Oliver."

I would not play the mouse for him. "No confusion at all," I said. "I love all my friends. I love my life."

"You will not live to enjoy it," he said darkly.

I got up and whirled round. "I'm enjoying it now, Doctor, and it's lovely, lovely. And I think the police will be informed that Fordy was confiding in you."

The air was piercingly cold, and the sunlight had faded to gray. But Dr. Greeve's animosity did not fade. I could feel his fury even as, unmindful of the snow and ice, I walked swiftly to Fifth Avenue and downtown toward Washington Square. I hardly took notice of the Christmas tree vendors who called out their wares to me.

Slowing my steps, I searched my mind for where I'd seen Dr. Greeve, for I was certain I had seen him before. I was surrounded by music; with the Arch looming above me, I passed under and found my agitation soothed by caroling voices.

Adolphus, Nolan, Zimmerman. Dr. Sidney Greeve was the fourth man in the photograph of the barbershop quartet I'd seen in Professor Adolphus's home.

Chapter Fifty-four

I was seething. The grayness overhead threatened to smother me. I took none of my usual joy from the music and the stands of Christmas trees that now appeared on street corners. Dr. Greeve's last admonition — *You will not live* — had shaken my resolve. I felt the intensity of the cold and, with it, the urgent need of warmth and distraction, both human and liquid.

As always, Romany Marie's Gypsy Tea Room would provide. Marie was in her usual spot, leaning on her counter over her anarchist newspaper, her folded arms all but hidden by her heavy breasts. I would long associate Romany Marie's with a dear friend whose death I still felt deep in my soul. We'd been here together that day, and Marie had read Rae's palm. How much she had seen, I will always wonder.

Marie looked up when I came through the door, unfolded herself, and astonished me with her warm embrace. Unexpected tears filled my eyes.

Mashed as I was in the pillow of Marie's

breasts, I didn't see Celia, but her voice, honed steel and unmistakable, issued from somewhere behind Marie.

"I never lie. Only mediocre sentimental persons lie."

As I eased myself from Marie's grasp, she released me. She was not partial to contentiousness, although there was plenty of that among us, especially when we'd swilled more than our share.

Celia was on her feet, standing over a table, her thick hair bound by a multicolored silk scarf, her anger palpable. It filled the convivial room, setting off waves of curiosity more than unease. Her seated companion raised his arms as if in self-defense. Dave Wolfe.

"None of that," Marie pronounced at once. "You arrre disturrrbing my guests."

A ripple of laughter greeted Marie's words, for we were given to debating everything, a few of us more assertive than others. Still, there was something almost sinister in Celia's anger, until she focused on me. Her pause was absorbing.

After a moment she said, "Oliver, come right over and tell Dave what a bad boy he is. Coffee, Marie." She was still angry.

Dave turned, an abashed smile, rose, and pulled over another chair. "Now

371

Oliver will think I'm a rat."

"And so she should when she hears —"

"I'm all ears," I said, propping my coat on the back of the chair.

"Go on," Celia commanded, stabbing her cigarette into the ashtray. "Show her."

A grave darkness spread from Dave's cheekbones to his forehead. His hands clenched. I wanted to touch their fine dark fur, make them open to me. His eyes met mine, lit fire under my skin.

"Go on," Celia said again, but without her previous composure. She'd caught on there was something happening between Dave and me.

"Coffee," Marie said, breaking the spell. She set three cups in the center of the table, harrumphed pointedly, and left us to each other.

I reached for a cup. "Well, my dears, what have I interrupted?" Were we living in the previous century, I would have played the coquette with my fan. Marie's coffee was strong, Turkish. The better to sharpen the mind, I say.

"Celia's been going through Fordy's things," Dave said at once. "And Kate's as well."

Celia flushed, furious he'd gotten ahead of her. "As have you."

"Looking for something in particular?" I opened my case and offered cigarettes. Dave struck one match for Celia and me, extinguished it, struck a second for himself. No comment necessary about tempting further bad luck with three on a match. We filled our space with smoke. The drama began to ease.

"Letters," Celia said, "and photographs." She gestured at Dave with her cigarette. "Which our friend here has appropriated."

"I offered to return them," Dave said. "A fair exchange."

I looked from one to the other. They were speaking on a different plane. Letters from whom to whom? I wondered. Love letters? I asked, "A fair exchange for what?"

"But I don't have what you're looking for," Celia told Dave.

I pressed again. "What are you looking for, Dave?"

"I asked Fordy to read a collection of my short stories, six of them, before I showed them anywhere. He was a very good editor. They were my only copies."

"They must be with his things, then," I said. No one had ever mentioned before that Fordy was a good editor.

"I've looked, and they're not. And they're not at Kate's place, either."

Celia took a sip of her coffee. "He thinks I have them."

"When Fordy went off with you, he had a valise."

"We never truly went off together. As far as I know, he took his valise with him to his flat, and it should be there."

But wait, hadn't we had our picnic on a valise in Champ's flat? Could that have been Fordy's? Celia's gaze fell on me, suppressing any potential comment. I placed my hand over Dave's . . . at last. "Oh, do give Celia her letters and photographs, there's a good fellow. Perhaps the police have your stories. Have you asked?"

"No." With great reluctance, Dave took a banded collection of letters and photographs from his bookbag on the floor. He pulled one photograph from the batch and handed the rest across the table to Celia. "I'm keeping this one, to remind me of you." He waved it at her with a good-natured grin as I craned my neck to catch a glimpse.

"Nothing doing," Celia said. She snatched it from him and slipped it into her pocket.

"There now," I said. "All is well."

But all wasn't well. Neither Dave nor Celia seemed inclined to leave, and I had a sense that this wasn't about the letters and photographs at all.

I was going to be late for rehearsal, and while I wanted to sit there and wait them out, I couldn't, though I dallied briefly, hopefully, my hand on Celia's shoulder. To no avail.

She rose, took my face in her hands, and kissed me fully on the lips, aware of Dave's compressed reaction. "Begone," she said, sending me off with a tender pat on the derriere.

Chapter Fifty-five

The theatre was cold, exceedingly damp, with a faint smell of mildew mixing with the ingrained stable odors that still persisted long after the last horse had gone. It seemed weeks since our last rehearsal but was really only days.

Nothing had changed. Jig stood in the middle of the stage, waving his arms. "We are a community!" he roared, throwing back his head of thick white hair. "We must stick together. We must not let our plays go uptown where it is all commerce and notoriety."

"What's going on?" I whispered to Edward Hall, slipping my arm about his waist.

"The usual." His kiss held none of the old passion, and I felt a trace of regret. He had found someone else to love.

Jig's frustration was not surprising, for he was the supreme idealist, and money never entered into his thoughts if he could help it. Most of us actors, though amateurs, would have liked the uptown opportunity, where we could make fifty dollars a week and have our little slice of fame.

"Our existence inspires the best plays written in this country," Jig declaimed, twisting his forelock. "We give them a chance for life. We give our audience truth and beauty."

I applauded. Though Jig was sentimental and oftentimes overbearing, there would be no Provincetown Players without him.

He turned his brilliant smile on me. "Oh, there you are, Oliver. We ought to get started."

Harry's door was wide open when I came home, so I stuck my head in.

No concession to Christmas here. The room was a thick fog of smoke. Harry's feet were on his desk, and he held the telephone earpiece to his ear. "Yeah," he said. He waved me in. "Anything else?"

I took a cigarette from his case and added to the haze.

"Well, I owe you one," Harry said. He hung up the phone and looked at me.

"Dr. Greeve turns out to be the fourth man in the barbershop quartet photo, if we consider Zimmerman the third. He's also Whit's psychoanalyst, by the way. He thought I was going to be his star patient and was decidedly unfriendly when I asked about Fordy. He's probably here spying on us all. Who knows if he's even a psychoanalyst?"

"I'll bet he is. It's a perfect cover. They tell him everything."

I moved his feet to the side and sat on the corner of the desk. "Fordy didn't tell him everything."

"How do you know?"

"Intuition."

"Sure."

"Any luck with Adeline's code?"

"Not yet." He pointed to the telephone. "I'm getting a little help from a chap I know."

"A cryptologist?"

"He did a little of that." He stood up and put out his cigarette. "What are you looking at?"

Harry wore a clean white shirt and pressed trousers. He looked very nice. "You dressed for supper."

"It's not as if I don't know how."

He locked his door, and as we climbed up the stairs, I told him about how I'd found Dave and Celia arguing at Romany Marie's.

"Curious."

"Very."

We had cocktails in the parlor, all of us.

Gerry had brought us a Christmas tree and fixed it in its pot, and Mattie had dressed the room with evergreens and holly berries. Harry made a perfect martini. My mood lightened.

Gerry said, "I understand you two have some information for me."

"That Mattie," I said, "she can just about talk your ear off."

"I wouldn't say that." Gerry put his arm round Mattie, and she blushed like a schoolgirl. "You want to know if Nolan is Secret Service, if the Secret Service is involved in the Vaude murder case."

"Yes," I said.

"I reckoned from the beginning, when we were told to cooperate, that he was government, just didn't know which bureau. I know now that Addie Zimmerman joined the Secret Service when she left the Pinkertons. Nolan brought her in. Her father was Secret Service. He disappeared in Sicily maybe eight months ago."

"What's this case about, then?" Harry said.

"A whole lot of silver certificates in ten- and twenty-dollar denominations."

"Twenty-dollar bills. That seems so innocuous," I said.

"Not if they're counterfeit."

Chapter Fifty-six

"So now at least we know what Fordy was living on," I told Harry later. I'd left Harry's door ajar so that I could listen for Dave, who was escorting me to Bunny's Yuletide party. Harry'd been invited, but he had "other plans."

"His partner, or employer, must have been afraid he would rat on them." Harry slipped on his jacket and fussed with his cuffs, an un-Harry-like gesture. He was wearing a tie and looked very nice.

"So they killed him. Now they'll have to find someone else to bring the money in."

"It may be too late. Too public now. Lupo's not stupid."

The thought was chilling. "You think Lupo, because of his calling card?"

Harry nodded, took a clothes brush to his suit.

"You've missed some places," I said. "Here, let me. I'll do your back." He handed me the brush. Some glint in his eye made me laugh. I brushed my way across Harry's broad shoulders until Harry relieved me of the brush.

"Stick to your poems, Oliver."

I raised my fingers to my forehead and sighed. "So Adeline was killed because she found out Fordy was working for Lupo, and Fordy was killed because he was going to tell. Then why did Lupo try to kidnap me and Mattie?"

Harry pondered that. "And if it wasn't Lupo, it could be someone who wants everyone to think it was."

I thought, Monk, but didn't say it because hearing me say Monk's name made Harry nuts. "What if Lupo thinks I know something about the money?"

"Sez who? Monk Eastman? He could be up to his flea-bitten ears in this."

"A Jewish gangster working out of Sicily, Harry? Even I know that's implausible."

"All right, so he wants to muscle in on it."

"I hope you're talking about me, Harry." Dave stood in the doorway, dark and brooding, as befits a writer. A cigarette idled in his hand.

We'd each been so intense in our convictions, and the odd vein of passion that ran beneath, we hadn't been aware of Dave's arrival. How long, I wondered, had he stood there listening to us? I slid a glance toward Harry. He was cooling down.

"Dave," I said. "Talking about you?"

"Muscling in, Oliver. Sorry, Harry, old man, but that's exactly what I'm doing."

"There's nothing between Oliver and me, Dave," Harry said. "In fact, I'll thank the two of you to skedaddle. I'm late for my engagement."

"Truly, Harry and I have never been lovers," I assured Dave when we were out on the street. "He has an uptown lady he's been seeing for years."

"He's in love with you, Oliver, just as we all are."

Tucking my hand into the crook of his arm, I contemplated his remark as we walked. It was ridiculous. Harry was Harry. No more, no less. I changed the subject. "Are you still in Fordy's studio?" I would have liked to get another look at the place. The thought of making love with Dave was tempting, but not where a friend of ours had been murdered.

"For another week. The rent's paid till the end of the month. I've found a room on Thompson Street, about a block from the park." We stepped aside to let a couple pass us; the fellow was balancing a Christmas tree on his shoulder with one arm while holding his girl close to him with the other.

"Merry Christmas," they called.

I smiled at the pretty picture they made and almost missed Dave's, "Say, do you mind if we go by Fordy's place? I've been in the library all day, so I haven't been home. He's got a load of booze just sitting there, and I wanted to bring a couple of bottles to Bunny."

It was more than fine with me. We changed our direction and headed toward Washington Square South. I hadn't even had to make up an excuse. "What's going to happen to Fordy's things, the paintings?"

"I guess Kate will take them."

I stopped. "You've heard from her?"

"No, but there was a notice from a storage company slipped under the door this morning saying they were coming to pack everything up on the day after Christmas."

The red-brick house had a spray of Christmas greens on the door. Inside, it practically trembled with conviviality. Of course, we rarely need a reason for a party, but Christmas in the Village was acknowledged by one and all as a time of unfettered merriment.

As we climbed the stairs, a piercing

whistle sounded from below. We both peered over the landing. The whistle did not come again, but if it had, we probably wouldn't have heard it, for all the laughter and music erupting from flats along the way. Doors stood open, revelers invited us in, but we declined.

Near Fordy's door, I asked, "And you and Celia?"

Dave clasped my face between his palms. My chin pressed against the rough wool of his coat. "There's no Celia and me, only you and me."

His voice had a hypnotic timbre that found an echo deep inside me. My knees became jelly as his kisses teased my mouth until they found my lips. I confess I would have been totally captive of desire were it not for a most familiar acrid smell tickling my nostrils.

When Dave paused, my hand in his, to unlock the door, I cast a quick look about. Nothing untoward, but the smell became potent.

Eyebrows raised, Dave turned. "The door's open —"

He had hardly spoken when a steam-roller barreled into him, slamming him against the opposite wall. And I finished in a graceless, speechless heap on the floor.

The steamroller gave me a quick hand up, closing one of his weird blue pin-dot eyes in what I presumed to be a wink, and with the agile sinuosity of a primate, flipped over the stairwell and was gone.

Chapter Fifty-seven

Dave, once he'd recovered his wind, with hardly a glance at me, rushed into the flat. Our violent encounter with Red Farrell was enough to dampen any desire. I followed. The evidence of a break-in was everywhere, papers, drawings, letters, books tumbled from their cases. A suitcase lay open, clothing strewn about.

So, the Dusters were also searching for something. And was it the same mysterious object everyone else sought?

Exasperated, I asked, "What *is* everyone looking for?"

Dave kicked the suitcase. He shuffled through some papers, picked up a sheet, a receipt of some sort, let it drop. "Did you get a look at him?"

"He was pretty quick on his feet, went right over the railing like a chimp. All I caught was the awful cigar. What was there to take of any value, anyway?"

He sat down, averting his eyes.

"Dave?"

"Money. It's gone now."

"Money? Fordy's money?" I knew it was worthless. Did Dave?

Dismayed, he gestured at the emptied bookshelves. "I found dozens of packages of twenty-dollar bills stuffed behind some books. I was keeping it for Kate. Now what'll I tell her?"

"If it's gone, it's gone. I shouldn't tell her anything, as she'll never know the difference."

We arrived at Bunny's not long afterward, presenting him with two bottles of gin we'd found undisturbed in Fordy's liquor cabinet. Dave, much subdued, hardly said a word on the way.

Would he, I wondered, have given the money to Kate? He didn't appear to know it was counterfeit. And I couldn't ask without revealing that I knew. Did Kate know, and was that why she was in the care of the Secret Service? And just how involved was Dave with Fordy and Kate? After all, he'd lived across the street. And we writers are well aware of our surroundings.

The faint melody of "Avalon" on the Victrola was only distant underscoring for the din. We were great talkers, all of us.

Drink in hand, I stood tiptoe under the

mistletoe and looked for Celia.

"There you are, Oliver," Bunny said, planting a wet gin kiss on my lips. He was listing, rudderless. "It's not a party till you get here. Where've you been?" He could barely form the words.

"Dave wanted to stop at Fordy's. . . ." Bunny's face colored furiously. I touched my still-cold cheek to his. "It's not what you're thinking. There'd been a break-in."

Edward Hall cornered us, his girl in tow. Her brown eyes wore a startled expression, as if blinded by light. We all exchanged passionless Christmas kisses. I looked for Celia.

Holding up my empty glass, I said, "I need a refill."

"I'll do it," Bunny said.

"No, let me," said Edward. His girl looked crushed.

"Never you mind, I'm a big girl now. I can get my own." I didn't wait to mollify the crestfallen faces, for I'd seen Celia. She stood out above the others, vivid in a tunic of wine velvet, her long legs in trousers. Her laughter teased me. I stopped to fill my glass.

Surrounded by admirers, Celia glowed with excitement. "Berlin," she said.

"Berlin," someone repeated.

"The most exciting place to be," said someone else.

"When do you leave?" I asked.

"Anon," she said.

A deep gray shroud obscured the sky, making the lamplight yellow fuzz. My unsteady footfalls echoed on the wet cement, where patches of melting snow remained. The deep cold had retreated to the wings, awaiting its next cue.

"The night is young," someone called down to me.

"My Muse doth call," I responded, slowing my steps, gazing upward.

" 'Tis a siren's song."

"You slander my poor Muse," I said, diverted.

"Alas, your words do tell it true: I'd hoped to linger longer here with you."

And before I could reply, from across the way, at least two floors up, came another voice. "And therefore, blackguard, sometime hold your tongue, because you would sure dull her with your song."

The butchered couplet from one of Shakespeare's sonnets made me laugh. "I bid ye both good night and a sweet morrow."

At once I was pelted with every lyrical

form of good-night wishes and from all directions.

I rolled a sheet of paper into my typewriter. It was very late, and I was beyond tipsy.

My heart sits pretty on my sleeve
Bewitched by your caress.
Love must be nurtured like the lamb
With you its shepherdess.

Though freely give I love away,
It will cost you dear,
Should you tamper with my heart
And play me cavalier.

It should have been a sonnet for all the inspiration I'd collected on my way home, but my Muse had spoken.

Mattie had turned down the bedclothes, but I had no desire to sleep. I lit a cigarette. How quiet the street was at this hour. I parted the draperies.

A man, head bowed, stood in front of my house. He lifted his head as if he knew I was there at the window. Carl Danenberg. His whole being was an appeal. Hurrying, I grabbed my shawl and ran down the stairs to the street.

The only person I saw was Goo Goo Knox. His wilted derby lay on the street. He picked it up, dusted it off, and planted it back on his head.

"Good evenin', Olwer," he said.

"Good evening, Mr. Knox. Was there a gentleman here a minute or so ago?"

He shaded his eyes, looked up and down the street, and shrugged. "Not dat I seen."

Chapter Fifty-eight

"Come on in, Oliver," Harry responded to my knock.

The room was a smoky den, and Harry, a gray shade, feet on desk, glass to lips.

"Happy Christmas, Miss Brown," Nolan said, looming up in front of me. He was every bit the opposite of his words. Sinister, is what I'd say. A villain for the moving pictures.

"I think, Mr. Nolan, you've come in sheep's clothing." I'm sure I saw Harry's lips curve. "May I have a cigarette, Harry? And a drop or two of the blessed elixir?" I opened the box of cigarettes and fitted one into my holder.

"I'm sure I don't understand your meaning, Miss Brown," Nolan said, pacing.

Harry pulled a glass from his desk drawer and poured a splash of gin. Nolan stopped to offer me a light, but Harry'd already done me the courtesy.

"Oh, go on, Mr. Nolan, I suppose you've come to talk to us about counterfeit money." I raised my glass to him and took a hearty swallow. The gin made me bold. I dropped down on Harry's dangerous sofa and stretched out, wiggling my bare toes.

"For the past two years the Secret Service has been trying to trace the source of counterfeit silver certificates, five-, ten-, and twenty-dollar notes."

"Tell her what you told me about Adeline Zimmerman," Harry said.

"She was Secret Service." Nolan's voice was gruff, and he paused, as if to subdue some kind of emotion. "We knew Fordham Vaude made frequent trips to Rome. We sent her to Rome to keep track of him, but he gave her the slip once. Another time, she followed him to Naples, where she lost him again. We believe he went on to Sicily."

I sat straight up. "Sicily?"

"He was an artist. We are of the opinion he had everything to do with the counterfeiting process itself, and the delivery of the notes might have been through another source."

"Y'hear that, Harry? Mr. Nolan's saying Fordy was a counterfeiter."

"I heard."

"What do you want of us, Mr. Nolan?"

"I was just getting to that when you

arrived, Miss Brown."

"I'm all ears, Nolan," Harry said in the most uninterested of tones.

"We replaced Addie with another agent in Sicily and brought her back here."

"And you and Professor Adolphus sent her to Fordy and Kate as a nanny."

"Yes. We knew that Vaude didn't have the connections to do all this on his own. He had someone pulling his strings."

"Adeline's job was to find this person?"

"Yes. She was a trained agent," Nolan said curtly.

"What about your agent in Sicily?" Harry dropped his air of boredom.

"He followed Vaude to a farmhouse in the hills and was able to send us a portion of a wireless."

"A portion, you say?"

"He's never been heard from since." Nolan stopped pacing and stared at us in frustration. "You see what I mean here? You have no idea what you've been meddling in."

"Spill the beans, Nolan," Harry said.

"That agent who disappeared was Adeline and Daisy's father, wasn't he?" I caught Harry's raised eyebrow. I loved surprising him.

Nolan frowned. "Yes. We were able to

prevail upon the Italian authorities to raid the farm where we believed the counterfeit notes were being printed."

"You found the source, then," I said.

"We found the source all right. A little stone house full of paper, bottles of green and black ink, the press, photographic equipment, pieces of zinc and lithographic stones, and some empty crates. We didn't find what we wanted most."

"Fordy was an artist," I mused. "He knew how to make prints and etchings . . . and engravings."

Harry swung his feet from his desk and sat forward. "Elementary, my dear Watson," he said. "This is all about the plates."

Chapter Fifty-nine

The heavy gray mantle tenting the city lifted slightly this night, the eve of Christmas, and a dry, steady snow began to fall.

Mattie and I dressed the plump spruce with the hand-carved and -painted wooden ornaments and the colored electric balls we'd found in our attic. In the kitchen, Gerry donned an apron and made a rum-potent eggnog, while Mattie fixed a light supper.

Harry, in Great-Aunt Evangeline's chair, smoking his cigar, speculated that the Dusters were also after the counterfeit plates.

"Fordy took them." Hugging my knees, I sat on the floor in front of the fire and smoked, listening to the cheerful hum coming from the kitchen. "Maybe he was trying to get out, and the plates were his insurance policy. What do you think, Harry?"

"Dangerously naive, I'd say. Look where it got him. Lupo's no one to fool with."

I inhaled the bouquet of the eggnog,

savored the rum. "How heavy would these plates be? Could Fordy have carried them back in his luggage?"

"He wouldn't have chanced it. If I were he, I would have shipped them."

"He wouldn't have been foolish enough to ship them to himself, or Kate, would he?"

"I doubt it."

"So . . . they're either sitting somewhere waiting to be claimed, or —"

"One of our friends has them."

What a thought. "Well, Harry, unless your phlegmatic cryptologist comes through with Adeline's code, we'll have to join the search for the plates ourselves."

Harry gave me a dubious look. "Why don't you stick your pretty nose back into your poems and leave the detecting to me."

I was offended, pretty nose and all. "Very well, Harry. If that's the way you feel." I shook my finger at him. "But one fine day you're going to need me and you'll have to beg on your knees for me to come back and help you." I changed the subject. "So, what do you make of Carl Danenberg standing outside the house last night?"

"He's discovered his life has no meaning without you and wants to get back in your high esteem."

I blew a grand smoke ring at him. "He might just be interested in what everyone else is." And here we were talking about the plates again.

"Maybe." His eyelids drooped.

"If you fall asleep, I'll be very cross."

He opened his eyes and grinned at me. "You can't blame a fella for trying."

We bundled up and trudged our way through the snow to midnight mass — not Harry, of course, but Mattie, Gerry, and I. The darkened streets were crowded with people on their way to the various churches. Just before midnight a hush fell over the city, then church bells began to toll. Unexpected tears welled in my eyes.

Although I was not Catholic, I have always gone to midnight mass with Mattie. I truly loved the organ music, the sweet voices of the choir, the brilliance of the candles, the joy of the service.

Christmas Day passed without event, except that Joan Brophy, a spunky lady not unlike my own Mattie, joined us. Dinner was a heady affair of turkey, chestnut stuffing and sauces of cranberries and oranges, and pies and plum pudding.

After dinner, I played the piano and we

all sang Christmas carols. Harry and Gerry smoked the Christmas cigars Mattie and I had given them. We all drank port, another unattributed gift from who else but my admirer on Chrystie Street.

Harry left us in the early evening, and the Brophys, mother and son, and Mattie went off to a concert at the Academy of Music. I'd begged off, having had too much of everything. Very shortly, my house settled into a comforting silence. Fully clothed, I lay on my bed and thought about Adeline Zimmerman. A Pinkerton. The Secret Service. A girl like me. But not like me. How courageous she was to have undertaken such a life.

I must have slept, and deeply, for I woke surrounded by sound, very likely long after the ringing of my doorbell had begun. My feet were unsteady as I peered down at the street. I could see nothing unusual, not even one of the Dusters. The doorbell sounded again.

My clock in the kitchen told me it was barely half-past nine. I went downstairs. I could see no shadow through the etched glass. When I opened the door to the vestibule, there was no one there, and no light issued from under Harry's door.

I opened the door to the street. It was a

new world, white and swollen with indeterminate, unrecognizable humps and lumps. Dave, a package under his arm, turned at the squeal of the door. The light of the street lamp bouncing off the snow gave him a haunting Heathcliff appearance.

"I thought you'd gone out," he said.

"I fell asleep. Is that your novel?"

"It is."

"Well, don't just stand there," I said, "come in and have a Christmas toddy."

"Don't tell me you're alone tonight."

"Well, Mattie's gone off to a concert with her swain, so I guess I'm alone."

"This is good stuff," Dave said. He held the bottle of port as if it were a precious thing, which it was, and filled our glasses. He'd set his snowy overshoes in the kitchen. Now his feet were as bare as mine.

"I have a generous admirer."

He smiled at me, set his glass on the table, and pulled me down on his lap. "You have many admirers, some rich, some poor."

"The rich ones ply me with vino —"

"And the poor ones?"

"They give me their novels to read."

"You are a sweet thing," he murmured, lips in the hollow of my throat.

My fingers fumbled on the buttons of his shirt. I felt him move beneath me and wondered, Are Jews better lovers?

He gathered me up in his arms and stood. "I could fall for you."

"Oh, do," I whispered. "Do."

We were at the foot of the stairs when we heard the door open and close.

"Olivia?"

Dave slowly set me on my feet.

"Mattie?" I said. "Dave Wolfe's come to have a Christmas drink with us."

"Don't let me interrupt," Mattie said. She was very gay and practically floated up the stairs.

"I have to get going," Dave said. "I just wanted to give you my novel."

He buckled on his overshoes, leaning against the door frame. I walked downstairs with him. "You could stay," I said. "Mattie's not a prude."

"I'll be back when you've finished reading."

"I shall sit right down tonight, then."

The ardor of his kiss left me breathless.

I watched him until I could no longer see him. Passion deferred breeds passion extreme.

No sooner was Dave out of sight than a black sedan rolled down Bedford Street from the opposite direction, its tires crunching in the snow. It came to a sliding stop in front of my house.

For a moment or two, nothing happened. Then the driver, a squat figure in black, opened the door, stepped out, and came toward me as if he'd expected me to be standing there.

I'd ridden in that car. The driver was Shmeul, Monk Eastman's man. He tipped his hat to me. "Miss Brown, da boss sends his compliments. He got youse da goods."

Chapter Sixty

I translated "got youse the goods" to mean Monk Eastman knew who the murderer was, and it was a fair bet he also knew what everyone was looking for.

The rest of the message, however, left me in limbo. Shmeul was to come back for me at two, at which time Monk would tell me what I wanted to know.

Hubris overcame caution, I must admit. Wouldn't I dearly love to solve the case myself. "So there, Harry," I said aloud to his door.

I ran up the stairs full of the excitement of the moment, then stopped. Should I tell Mattie? No. She might insist on coming with me, and that wouldn't do. There was no danger. I truly felt that Monk would never harm me and would, in fact, if it came to that, protect me.

Mattie was brushing her hair when I came to her room. "The concert was lovely," she said.

"Dave left his novel for me to read," I said.

"These romantic-looking Italian boys." She was referring obliquely to someone who'd come swiftly into my life and left it just as swiftly.

"Dave's not Italian, he's Jewish," I said mildly, turning down the bedclothes for her.

"Oh, isn't that odd. What made me think he was Italian?" She set her brush down, and I braided her hair.

"His dark hair and eyes." Tongue-in-cheek, I added, "In truth, he's just old black Irish."

We both laughed at that. I had only to tuck her in, which I did, and kissed her forehead. "After I read his novel, I may go and meet that romantic-looking black Irishman."

"Be careful," she said. I waited until she drifted off, kissed her forehead again, and closed the door behind me.

I didn't like being untruthful with Mattie, but I knew she'd never sanction my meeting Monk Eastman alone.

It was almost midnight. My concentration was not on my writing. Dave's manuscript was in the parlor where we'd left it. I took it up to my room and untied the cord, then folded back the brown paper. *The Legatee*. By David Wolfe.

I closed my eyes and felt his lips on my throat. Setting aside the manuscript, I turned to my typewriter.

Passion deferred breeds passion extreme.

I stared at the words, my fingers dull on the keys. Nothing came to me. "Muse," I said "where are you?"

Gone to Berlin with Celia, did my Muse respond.

"O fickle Muse," I said.

I returned to Dave's novel. It described in tragic, almost Greek terms the battle for dominance between a successful, powerful father and an artistic son. My instinct told me it would not have an uncomplicated conclusion. Bunny was right. It was good and I was eager to tell him so, but it couldn't be tonight.

Time crept up on me. I put down the novel and plucked Jack Reed's galoshes from my closet floor. They might not be very stylish on a girl, but they would keep my feet dry. I straightened my desk, re-arranged the space. Sorting through letters to be answered, I found one I hadn't opened. Pale blue envelope. Nice hand. No return address.

I took the letter and Reed's galoshes down to the kitchen and brewed myself a cup of tea. Then I sat at the kitchen table and opened the envelope.

The mirror behind the bar was murky, my image blurred. It was the way I was beginning to feel. Blurred. The mirror gave me an indistinct reflection of the Blue Bird Café and its patrons and the girl in the long, glittery black dress who leaned against the piano, singing "Baby, Won't You Please Come Home."

No one I knew came here.

Shmeul had been waiting for me at two o'clock, hunched over the wheel, his hat pulled practically to his nose. And without Monk.

"Where's Monk?" I said.

"The Blue Boid." A man who doesn't make idle conversation.

Shmeul drove to Fourteenth Street. Near Fourth Avenue, he turned down an unlit alley and waited. A narrow shaft of light came from a side door. Someone beckoned to us.

The Blue Bird Café was just another saloon, the ambience a blend of sour booze and smoke, the room lit only by candles stuck in bottles on each table and the gamboling flicker of cigarettes and cigars. Faces appeared disembodied, pale and spectral.

Shmeul brought me to the corner seat at

the bar. "Wait here," he said, tilting his head abruptly in an obvious signal to the barkeep that he was to take care of me.

So I shook off my overshoes and listened to the sad songs of unrequited love and sipped the gin in the chipped teacup and thought about the photograph. Celia, seated on the beach in Provincetown, her magnificent hair grazing the sand, legs crossed and stretched in front of her, unencumbered by anything as mundane as clothing. Her face impudent to the camera. *"N'oubliez pas,"* she'd written on the back. Don't forget.

Someone sat down next to me, jostling my arm, jostling my reverie. "Excuse me," he said. He stayed within my space, demanding my attention.

I could scarcely see him at first, but the voice was familiar and his features settled into a shape I knew. "Why, Mr. Danenberg," I said, "you've been following me again."

The bartender set a cup in front of him. The deep gold of Scotch. "I want to apologize," he said. "I behaved badly, disrespectfully, when I only have the most respect for you."

"It was the heat of the moment. I do not hold a grudge." I lifted my cigarette holder

407

to my lips and tried to see his eyes. His manner was without guile, but I had seen different. Was I in danger with all these people here? No, this was Monk's place. I'd felt all along, since I arrived, that I was being watched over.

"I know you're trying to find Adelle's killer, and I thank you for that."

"You still love her in spite of everything?"

"Yes. And you may think I'm mad, but I know she loved me."

I saw he wanted to believe this, and who was I to say it wasn't true? "That may well be."

"She was doing her job, you see."

"Yes."

"And when it was done, she would have come back to me."

Could he have murdered her, feeling as he did? "Do you know who the other man was?"

"Mr. Vaude," he said with a finality that didn't bear dispute.

"But Mr. Vaude is dead."

"Yes," he said. "He was a traitor. That's why Adelle was watching him."

"A traitor? Why do you determine that?"

"He was bringing counterfeit money into the country."

"Is that worse than bootlegging?"

He stared at me, shocked. "How can you ask? Prohibition is a bad law, and it will be repealed."

"And you and your family will lose your livelihood."

"That's all right. We will be happy to go back to selling books."

I gave his hand a pat. "So you followed me here to offer your apology."

"No." He stood and peered out into the café. "I'm as surprised to see you here as you are to see me. The Blue Bird is where accounts get settled."

Chapter Sixty-one

After Carl Danenberg took his leave, the bartender set another gin in front of me and lit my cigarette. "Have you seen Shmeul?" I asked.

He shrugged and gave the counter a quick wipe, emptied my ashtray. I have little patience for waiting, and something told me that Monk Eastman would not be here this night. And if that was true, why hadn't Shmeul come to take me home? I decided to give Monk until the gin was gone and then I would see myself home.

It was sometime after four when I pushed away my empty glass and pulled on my overshoes. What had Carl said? *The Blue Bird is where accounts get settled.* Shivering, I left the bar, choosing not to go back the way I'd come in, as it was a dark and perhaps dangerous alley. Weaving through the thinning crowd, I looked for the front entrance. The plate-glass front window had been painted over black, and no light came from the double doors leading to the street.

My hand was on the latch when I had the oddest sensation, as if an arm had slipped round my waist and held me ever so gently. I could feel the heat of him, smell his sweat, the mixture of tobacco. I was dreaming. In the darkness I sensed the breadth of his shoulders, his sensuality.

"Wait," he whispered. I was more than willing.

Bang! The explosion came from the other side of the door. Then: *Bang! Bang! Bang! Bang!* Four more, one after the other.

I stiffened. "What was that? It sounded like shots." I reached for the door again, and now there was no arm to stop me. In fact, others had heard it also. People stirred, rose, hesitating, waiting out the danger.

The heat was with me again. I spun round and stared into the darkness. His face shimmered. His eyes were huge. There was sweat on his brow. My breasts felt the fleeting pressure of his touch. I leaned toward him. "Reed," I murmured, scarcely breathing.

"Now," he said.

The door opened with a suddenness, pitching me forward. I cried out, and my cry came back at me. Not a soul on the

411

street. Then I saw him. Near the entrance to the subway a man lay on his back in the snow. His groan cut into my fugue. I knelt beside him, putting my hands on his wounds to stop the gushing blood. The snow was crimson.

"Get help!" I screamed. "Call the police!"

He groped for my hand, and I gave it to him. His lips moved, chewing. "Lupo's boy." The voice was very faint, but the strength in his hand was fierce. Blood spewed from his mouth, then he was quiet.

I wouldn't have to wait any longer for Monk Eastman.

Chapter Sixty-two

A siren shrieked, stopped, shrieked again. Was joined by others, a symphony in terror.

I couldn't move, couldn't lift my head. My hands were sticky with Monk's blood, my clothes drenched. Gunsmoke poisoned the air.

Someone grabbed me roughly under the arms, dragged me back into the alley. My scream was tardy, drowned out by the sirens. He put his icy hand over my mouth. His trembling found a perfect match with mine.

I was a small package with sharp elbows. My elbows met solid flesh.

He grunted. "I'm not going to hurt you. I had to get you out of there. Okay?"

When I nodded he removed his hand, but not the scent of gunpowder. We were both panting.

I tried to make sense of it. Monk dead. I'd liked him, even trusted him. I leaned against the brick wall of the alley. "I don't understand why you killed him. What is he to you?"

"Killed who? I didn't kill anyone. I don't even know who was killed."

"You killed Monk Eastman."

"Monk Eastman? No kidding?" He sounded awed. "How could you think I'm a killer, Oliver?"

"Then why are you here?"

He held my hand tight in his. "I came back and saw you get into that black sedan. I followed you. It doesn't matter. We have to get out of here."

"But if we tell the police what happened . . ."

"They'll think you did it." He pulled me along after him. "You have his blood all over you."

Benumbed, I couldn't collect my thoughts. The police wouldn't think I did it, would they? I'd been fond of Monk. Fond of a gangster, Oliver?

The back door of the Blue Bird stood open, emitting a feeble beam of light. It suddenly became clear to me that the place had emptied as soon as the gunshots sounded. As if everyone there had conspired in Monk's murder.

A ramshackle truck was parked where the alley opened into a small lot, and beside it, Monk's sedan. I saw Shmeul sitting at the wheel, head bowed. How could he sleep? I broke free and knocked on the window, but Shmeul didn't look up. I opened the door.

Shmeul came tumbling out, the dead weight of his body glancing off me. I staggered and sat down hard on the ground. Shmeul looked up at me with one eye. The other was a hideous hole. "Oh God, no!" I gagged and threw up all the gin I'd drunk.

"Miss Brown, is that you?" The silhouette of a man appeared in the open doorway of the Blue Bird.

I heard a swift rustle behind me, then sound exploded in my ears, my nostrils filled with gunpowder, my eyes burned. Now I was dreaming. I rose, drifting forward in a soundless world. Carl Danenberg tottered to his knees, clinging to the doorjamb, then slumped face forward in the snow.

"What are you doing?" My scream was muffled to my ears.

Dave Wolfe lowered his gun to his side. "I'm sorry, Oliver."

"You have such talent. It's all in your book." I was standing outside myself, listening to the pleading in my distant voice. Was it for my life or his?

"If you read my book, you know a man can't escape his heritage." Dave's voice resounded with bitterness. He made the sign of the cross and raised his gun.

My brain sent me rapid signals. Monk's last words . . . *Lupo's boy.* As in a faint, I dropped to the ground and rolled under Monk's sedan.

Out of nowhere came the unmistakable sound of the crank. The run-down truck sputtered, broke into a loud rumble. Tires ground into the snow.

"Wha —" Dave's yell was cut off by an unpleasant thump.

When I peered out from my protective cover, I saw a gun on the ground an arm's length away. And not far from Shmeul, Dave lay crumpled and unmoving. I reached out to grab the gun, but someone caught my arm, dragged me out from under the car and, like a bundle of old clothes, threw me into the back of the truck.

"Jeeze, Ol'wer, youse nuttin' but trouble." Ding Dong jumped up after me and slammed his palm on the cab. "Get goin'."

Red Farrell stepped on the accelerator, and the truck shot down the alley, paused, then rolled out slowly and moved off with a screech of tires. I looked down at my hands and started to cry. "Monk's dead."

Ding Dong patted my shoulder awkwardly. "Yeah."

Chapter Sixty-three

"Bloody hell! Where're you hurt? Why didn't you take her to St. Vincent's?"

Ding Dong grinned his crooked grin. "Take it easy, Sherlock. Olwer ain't hoit. Monk Eastman got bumped off in front of the Blue Boid. It's his blood." Ding Dong cocked his head at Red Farrell, and they left.

"Let's have a look at you," Harry said brusquely, but it was enough to make the tears start again.

"Dave did it, Harry. Can you imagine all this time living among us, and he's . . . a killer, Lupo's son, Lupo is his name, not Wolfe, but it's the same, isn't it?" I was shaking all over, couldn't keep myself or my teeth from chattering. "He killed Monk, and I saw him with my own eyes kill Carl Danenberg tonight and would have me —"

Harry didn't seem at all surprised. He handed me a glass of gin. I drank it all at once. "Where are your shoes?" he asked.

I looked down at my bare feet. Caked with blood. Jack Reed's overshoes. "Lost,"

I murmured. All feeling stopped.

Bang, Bang! I heard the shots and knew Lupo was coming for me, tried to run, but was trapped. I hit the floor with a thud and woke, sweating, my heart shuddering in my breast.

Where was I? I looked down at my hands, my feet. No blood. So it had been a horrible dream. But Dave . . . I got to my knees and was tripped up by the shirt tails.

I was in Harry's flat. I'd fallen out of Harry's bed, and under Harry's shirt I was naked. I must have been very drunk because I remembered nothing.

Where were my clothes? In fact, where was Harry?

I climbed back into his bed and pulled the rumpled bedclothes over my head. Well, now you've done it, I thought.

A key turned in the lock. I uncovered my eyes.

"Good morning," Harry said cheerfully. He brought a cold gust of air with him, some newspapers, and a bundle, which he dropped on the bed.

I pushed aside the newspapers. "Look, Harry, I'm sorry —" There was a streak of blood on the inside of my wrist. I stared at it.

"Guess I missed a spot," Harry said. He lit a cigarette for me and a cigar for himself.

"It wasn't a dream, then. Monk and Dave and everything."

He sat on the bed and showed me the newspapers. The headlines screamed in bold type about gangland shootings, but I knew better.

"It's my fault," I said.

"Your fault Monk got killed?"

I nodded. "He was trying to find out what Lupo had to do with all this."

"Are you nuts, Oliver? Monk Eastman had more enemies than you can shake a stick at. And believe me, he wasn't doing anything for you, not if it didn't put gelt in his pocket."

"You're a hard man, Harry. Where are my clothes?"

"You were a mess, and you wouldn't let me wake Mattie."

I couldn't look at him. "You cleaned me up?"

"Well, I couldn't in all conscience leave you like that. I cleaned you up and got rid of everything. There're fresh clothes in the bundle."

"Then we didn't . . ."

I could see he thought my presumption

was hilarious, and he was having trouble holding himself in check. "Hate to disappoint you."

"I'll do my best to get over it," I said, reaching for the bundle.

On the eve of the New Year we made a party, Mattie and I, and everyone came. Well, everyone except Harry, who was, as always, late. I'd even had a telegram from Stephen Lowell saying that he might be in town. We opened the Champagne, which had appeared on my doorstep the day of Monk's death. Again, without attribution. But it would be the last of his largesse.

A week had passed since Dave's revelation, and we were still obsessed with it, which was understandable. He'd been one of us.

"You've seen Kate?" I asked Paulo.

"She's taken the twins and gone off to Paris," Paulo said. "Everyone's there now."

"Not everyone," I said.

"That girl, Adelle, or Adeline," Paulo said. "She was a nice kid."

"What about Fordy?" I said.

Paulo responded, "Fordy made his own bed. He had Kate and the twins. He wasn't alone in this world."

I thought, You are wrong, Paulo, we're

all alone in this world.

"Where's Daisy?" Paulo asked. Bunny'd arrived alone.

Bunny shrugged. "Gone."

We take care of our own, Adolphus had said.

"Dave couldn't escape his destiny, who he was," Bunny said. "It has all the elements of a Greek tragedy."

"I think if you want to escape that destiny, you might try moving a little farther than Greenwich Village," I said. "Four people are dead because of his destiny."

"Be that as it may," Bunny told me, "I'm going to see his book gets published."

It was true we believed in art for art's sake.

Stopping to give Gerry Brophy a kiss on the cheek, I asked the big question: "Have the plates turned up?"

"No, but the Secret Service arrested Lupo for importing counterfeit bills from Sicily. He'll go up for a long time."

I went off to the kitchen, looking for Mattie. Champ was at the window, gazing down at our moonlit yard where our erotic birdbath had once stood. "Champ?"

She had a vivid blue scarf banding her white hair. "My dear," she said. "Celia left something with me for you."

I raised a dubious brow. I'd not forgiven her.

Smiling, she said, "Are you not the least bit curious? Well, it'll keep. You'll have it come spring when my work on *The Lovers* is finished."

Which is how the missing counterfeit plates came to be part of the base of the new birdbath in our garden, the sculpture of the two women voluptuously entwined, the one Champ called *The Lovers.*

Remember the packing crate in Champ's flat? I'd set the sack of apples on it.

When I wandered back to my parlor, Harry was there, pouring himself a drink. I tapped him on the shoulder. "I suppose your phlegmatic cryptologist has never come up with any answers and will never return my John Donne."

"Actually, he came up with the answer the night Monk got shot, and I was able to get a message to Brophy. As far as the Donne is concerned, I don't know, Oliver, why don't you ask him yourself?" Harry put his hands on my shoulders and turned me around.

A tall, utterly lovely man smiled down at me and filled my empty glass. "You must be Olivia Brown," he said. He had hazel eyes and long sooty lashes. "I'm Kendall

Cooper. I've heard so much about you."

And wouldn't you know, Stephen Lowell chose that very moment to make his appearance.

A poet should have a simpler life.

Afterword

The character of Monk Eastman is based on the real Monk Eastman, a Jewish gangster of the period. Although much of what I've written about him in *Murder Me Now* is true, including his bravery on the battlefield and his pardon by New York's governor Alfred E. Smith, his love of animals, especially cats, and his demise, his association with Olivia Brown is pure fiction.

The Black Hand, the precursor of the Mafia, was very active at this time, thanks to the many Italian immigrants they could terrify into submission, and to Prohibition. Ignazio Lupo, known as Lupo the Wolf, was thought to be the boss of the Black Hand. He was a pivotal figure in the conspiracy I've fictionalized, but the actual events took place ten years earlier and in upstate New York. Lupo was apprehended by the Secret Service and ended his days in a federal penitentiary.

The Hudson Dusters, the Irish street gang, were also real people. Their "territory" was Greenwich Village. I've used their actual names, though perhaps they are drawn somewhat more mellow than the originals, as I've made them my Baker Street Irregulars.

In the twenties, many of the Village bohemians, particularly as they married — yes — and had children, began to spread from the small flats and restricted space of the Village. Some did form an enclave in the hospitable Village of Croton, particularly along Mt. Airy Road.

I gave Edmund "Bunny" Wilson a role in *Murder Me Now* that is entirely fiction. He was one of the Village bohemians, a close friend of Edna Millay's, and an editor at *Vanity Fair.* He became a celebrated writer of fiction, essays, and criticism and for a time was married to the writer Mary McCarthy.

Romany Marie's Gypsy Tea Room, and the speakeasies Polly's, Luke O'Connor's Columbia Gardens (the Working Girls' Home), Chumley's, and the Hell Hole all existed in the Greenwich Village of 1920. Only Chumley's remains.

As for the brilliant, irrepressible John "Jack" Reed, the appeal of his larger-than-life personality crossed genders. I think every woman of the day was a little in love with him. I would have been.

For the flavor of the time, I am indebted to the Barbara and Arthur Gelb biography of Eugene O'Neill; to Luc Sante's *Low Life*; to Allen Churchill's *The Improper Bohemians*; to Jeff Kisseloff's *You Must Remember This*; to memoirs by Susan Glaspell, Floyd Dell, Lawrence Langner, and Max Eastman, and, especially, to the wonderful letters of Edna St. Vincent Millay.

The employees of Thorndike Press hope you have enjoyed this Large Print book. All our Large Print titles are designed for easy reading, and all our books are made to last. Other Thorndike Press Large Print books are available at your library, through selected bookstores, or directly from the publisher.

For more information about titles, please call:

(800) 223-1244
(800) 223-6121

To share your comments, please write:

Publisher
Thorndike Press
P.O. Box 159
Thorndike, Maine 04986